CW01499912

THE
LAST
AMATEUR

AND
OTHER STORIES

Ian Plenderleith

Published by Halcyon Publishing

First published 2025

Cover design and interior graphics: Doug Cheeseman
Layout: Rob MacDonald
Edited by Adam Bushby & Rob MacDonald

Printed & bound by:
Ashford Colour Ltd
Unit 220, Fareham Reach
Fareham Road
Gosport
Hampshire
PO13 0FW

In ever-loving memory of my uncle,
John Dickson (1939-1978)

About the author

Ian Plenderleith has been playing, watching, coaching, refereeing and writing about football for quite a while. His other books include *For Whom The Ball Rolls*, *Rock n Roll Soccer*, *The Quiet Fan*, *Reffing Hell*, and *The Football League Review*.

Contents

Bullet and his Redhead Warrior

It had never occurred to any us of that Bullet might one day get a girlfriend. He was single, and probably always would be. No one had ever asked him about it, because Bullet — real name Billy — was a man of very few words and very hard stares. He had no hair at all, and an oval skull with a slight point, so that was why we called him 'Bullet'. Never to his face, though. Once when he thought Bullet was in the bog, Andy had asked, "Is it nae Bullet's round?" Bullet was right behind him, though, and said, "What did you just call me?" That was one of the longest sentences we'd ever heard him say. Andy got away with most things by dint of his smile and verbose Scottish manner, so managed to convince Bullet that he had actually said the word 'Billy', but his Scottish accent had made it sound like Bully. Bullet gave Andy the dark eye for the rest of the night, and then for a couple of weeks after.

Bullet was always there on Sundays, and we had no idea where he lived or what he did during the day. He was never away on holiday. You'd hardly call him an intimate. We weren't a gang, just a bunch of mates who'd been going to the same pub for 15 years. Some of us had been to school together, like me and Tanner, and some of us had worked together at some point, like Andy and Scratch, and now all of us played on the same Sunday league team. Except for Bullet. We'd asked him once, "You want to play on Sunday, Billy? We're a couple of men short." He just shook his head, with no further explanation. Nothing like, "I don't have any boots", or "Sorry, I'm shite at football". Not that this would have mattered, in fact he'd have fit right in. But all we got was a single shake of the head, and we never asked again.

No one could really say when he'd become part of the group. Somehow, he'd just always been there. We thought he might have been a workmate of Mark the Liar, who'd moved down south, but we asked Mark once when he came back home for Christmas, and he said that Bullet had had nothing to do with him, and that to be honest, Bullet kind of unnerved him. And it was true, sometimes you might say something, and you'd see Bullet giving you this concentrated stare, like he wanted to kill you for expressing the view that United would be better off playing Rashford as an out and out striker, or that if the Scottish people wanted to leave the United Kingdom then you could hardly blame them. You weren't exactly sure what it was you'd said that might have pissed him off, you just knew that he'd been stirred, and then you might even start backtracking on what you'd just said.

On the other hand, Bullet was our security. No one ever bothered us. He'd have kicked the shit out of anyone who so much as squinted at our table. Although it was very much our local, and we represented the pub's name every Sunday, albeit without a great deal of class. The shirts that Norman the landlord had bought us seven years ago had been damaged by time, sporting attrition and poor laundry etiquette, but they still proudly bore the name The Foaming Quart, and we still got a free meal every Sunday for our troubles.

After that, we stayed and spent our money until midnight. There had been a couple of times, though, when things had ended badly on the pitch, and so occasionally a beer-inspired rabble from somewhere like The Dirty Duke would show up later in the evening to sort things out. And when they came in, Bullet would stand up and they would turn around and fuck right back off.

Were those the nights that Bullet lived for, though they had only happened four or five times over the last ten years? I don't know, perhaps only once or twice, now that I think about it. It's irrelevant — the rare face-offs had become legendary yarns that had spun their own sequels, true or not. We loudly celebrated Bullet on those five or maybe just two or three nights, and we bought him enough drinks to kill him outright. We sang songs that glorified him, and the rest of the pub would join in. And the whole time he just sat staring at the door — still vigilant, in case the group decided to return — while refusing to acknowledge our bibulous choral tribute. He would drink everything we put in front of him, but seemed to walk out the pub as sober as the minute he'd walked in. He didn't smoke and didn't eat so much as a bag of pork scratchings. He apparently survived on lager alone.

Sometimes we sang songs for him anyway. Andy would shout at some late hour, "Whit aboot a fuckin' song for yon Billy?" And off we'd go. At this, Bullet would sit back and look almost thoughtful. Sometimes, I worried a bit that he thought we were taking the piss, and that he'd suddenly go nuts. Maybe he loved it. It was impossible to tell, because without any word from his tongue, you had to go by expression. And I reckon when we were singing "Billy, You Are A Hero", he was veering close to something you might classify as actual pleasure.

I'm struggling for much else to tell you about Bullet from that time. Usually on Sunday evenings, the wives would come and join us if we could get babysitters, and at first they tried to coax something out of him, but you know that women aren't going to waste their time for long on someone who doesn't talk. "What's Billy's story?" Faye, my wife, asked me on the way home one Sunday night. "Nobody knows," I replied. She wasn't happy with that answer, and we ended up having a row. She thought I was involved in something shady with Bullet and that I was trying to cover it up. It just wasn't possible, in her eyes, that I had been drinking with someone that long and yet knew nothing about him at all.

Then something happened that we'd never thought possible. Bullet got a mobile phone.

There'd been several stages in the development of mobile phone use among our group. At first, it was scorned. We made it a rule that no one could have his phone out at the table. That was in the days when people only used them to make calls. If your phone went off, you'd be jeered at and made to take it outside, no matter what the weather. If you weren't quick enough, it would be grabbed off you and someone would answer on your behalf, and that was never a good thing, especially if your wife was calling and she was told that you were out back with your tongue down Janet's throat (Janet was Norman the landlord's wife, but was more loyal to the clientele than she was to Norman).

Tanner had nearly lost his job because of that. He'd been on call, and was supposed to be available at immediate notice, and his phone rang in his coat pocket while he was at the bar. Andy answered it and yelled, "He's nae available right noo because he's oot on the drink", and we all roared (except for Bullet, who never laughed or smiled at anything). Tanner, who was a site manager at some new property development down at the docks, wasn't supposed to drink while he was on duty, even on a Sunday. Andy ended up going to Tanner's office the next day and apologising to his boss and lying with great conviction that his team-mate had been drinking orange juice the whole night.

Soon every twat had a smartphone and we were using them all the time, and you knew to keep it on vibrate because if it rang then you'd be subject to songs, chants and more noise than you could talk over until you'd taken it outside. Bullet was the only one who went without, but that wasn't strange given that the rest of his life was invisible. It seemed normal, in fact, that he had no phone. He never complained about other peoples' phones, or gave you one of his terrible stares if you were sat there sending a text message or checking your emails. If someone was showing a funny video or something, he'd certainly look, just as he always listened to everything that was being said around him. You no more expected him to have a phone in his pocket, though, than you expected him to announce that he wouldn't be there for the next six Sundays because he was fulfilling one of his life ambitions by joining a field trip to the Dry Tortugas.

So we were sitting there one Sunday evening, and it was a bit of a lame night. We'd lost 5-0 and Andy had had a row with Scratch over one of the goals. A really stupid row, as you'd expect given that it was about a goal in a game of pub football where we'd been three goals behind already. They'd apologised and made up, but you could tell that it was still bothering Andy that Scratch had yelled at him. Every time Scratch went to the bar or the bog, Andy would say something general like, "You'd think we'd all know by now that it's just a fuckin' game, eh?" And we'd tell him to get over it, that it wasn't a big deal, and that at least Scratch had said sorry for losing his rag and promised to pay his tab all night, so what more was there to be done. "Aye, ah ken," Andy would say, but he was sullen, which wasn't like him at all, and Scratch wasn't talking a lot either. Tanner and I were remembering the time we'd used to work together at the dog track as teenagers, carrying messages for the bookies, so we were off in our own little world of nostalgia, and of course Bullet was just sitting there. The wives had yet to turn up, and I was on the point of calling Faye and telling her not to bother to come down, that I'd probably be back early tonight and maybe we could watch a film.

Then Bullet shifted in his seat, which was almost an event in itself, and we all suddenly looked at him, as though sensing that something monumental was about to occur. He fished into his pocket, awkwardly grappled around for a few seconds, and out came this phone together with a grey-tinted handkerchief and a bunch of cash which fell on the floor beneath the table. You'd think that would be the first thing you'd pick up, because it was a lot of money, but Bullet was focused on pressing the right button to answer the call. We all exchanged glances and waited to hear what was sure to be an enlightening conversation, which went something like this:

"Yeah, Foaming Quart. Yeah. In the corner. To the left as you come in. Yeah. Yeah. [quieter] Me too. [Long pause]. I can't. Too many people around. Yeah. See you."

Only now did Bullet recover the cash he'd allowed to fall beneath the table — I suppose he could be sure that no one in the Foaming Quart would have dared to make a grab for it. Then he sat back up in his usual position and sipped from his pint, ignoring the fact that we were all staring at him. Finally, Tanner cleared his throat.

"So, Billy. I didn't know you had a phone." This was unusual. Apart from asking him if he wanted another lager, which was a stupid question because he always did, no one ever, ever put a query towards Bullet, or even a statement like this one.

"Yep," said Bullet. He was looking straight ahead, right past us and at the television, which was showing silent German football.

Tanner looked at the rest of us, hoping that someone else might follow up. Andy obliged with, "Ah didnae think that was your kind o' thing, Billy. Phones an' all that. What kind is it?"

Bullet took another gulp of his pint, then looked at Andy and said, "It's from a new company called None of Your Fucking Business."

We all laughed, although no one was sure if Bullet was trying to be funny. And then in what seemed like a matter of seconds, there was a stocky, pale girl with spikey red hair in black jeans, a black turtleneck pullover and shiny Doc Martens easing her way past Andy and Scratch and squeezing in beside Bullet, and without a word of introduction started pushing her tongue straight down his throat. Bullet responded with a fervour that rendered his possession of a mobile phone quite the non-event.

"Jesus fucking Christ on a solid gold cross," muttered Tanner, but not loud enough for Bullet to hear. Scratch stood up and said it was time to get another round in, though he didn't ask the girl what she wanted as she had her back to him. I went to the bog. Andy and Tanner turned around and suddenly feigned an interest in Borussia Mönchengladbach against Werder Bremen.

I took my time. Janet was out back smoking a cigarette, so after taking a piss I went outside to chat, and updated her on Bullet's love life.

"Good for him," she said.

"About time, I suppose," I said.

She took a long drag on her cigarette and surveyed me. She was about ten years older than me, but she had something about her. A strong disposition. The authority of the bar. Black stockings and shapely calves. Everyone knew that Norman was only in charge by name.

"What about you, Archie?" she said.

"What about me?"

"Keeping Faye happy?"

"I hope so."

"You'd better do more than hope, boy." And then she stubbed her cigarette out on the ground and brushed past me on her way back inside. I felt annoyed with myself for being outside with Janet, and for the fact that when she touched me I'd felt the kind of thing that five pints of beer can make you feel, knowing that I shouldn't have been out back with Janet at all.

Inside, things had settled down. Bullet and the redhead had stopped snogging, and now she was just sitting there, smiling across the table at Tanner and Andy, who'd turned their backs on the German football again, but didn't look like they'd any idea what to say. Scratch was still at the bar. Bullet had resumed staring at the table-top, though now his face was smeared with red lipstick. Normally there would have been a few more of us, but because of the bad result and the row, a lot of people had cleared off early after a couple of pints, so the pub in general was a lot quieter than usual. I thought about picking up my coat and making my excuses, but right at that moment Scratch came back with the next round, so there was no escape. Then I looked across at the bar, and Janet was staring at me in this contemplative way that unnerved me. When she saw me looking at her, she gave me a little smile, then busied herself with picking up some empties. I thought about asking Andy for a cigarette — even though I'd given up a year ago because I was slowing down on the football pitch — so I'd have an excuse to go out back again. Something in my groin was bothering me. Faye had refused to have sex with me since our second son was born three years before. She still wasn't ready yet, she said. And now even Bullet was getting some action.

"What are these ones called?" asked the girl, gesturing at me and Scratch.

"This one's Archie," said Tanner. "The one with the drinks is Scratch."

"Scratch?" said the girl, laughing, and ignoring me. She wasn't exactly posh, or well-mannered, but she was well-spoken, I suppose, though you had the impression she was trying a little bit not to be. "Really? You're really called Scratch? How did you get a name like that?"

"You want a drink, luv?" Scratch asked her, politely ignoring the question as he put the pints down.

"I'm not called 'luv'," she said amiably. "I go by my warrior name, which is Valoronia." She took a pen out of her handbag, then leaned forward and wrote it out for us on a beer mat, then held it up in front of our eyes. We all read the word VALORONIA again and again. "It's easier to learn new names once you've seen them written down, isn't it?"

"Drink?" said Scratch again. "Otherwise I'm just going to sit down and some other fucker'll have to get you one."

"Or maybe I can get it myself," she said, but in a sort of American accent, and then she burst into laughter. "Your faces!" she said, and then just as Scratch was making to sit down she said, "Pint of bitter, please." And off he went back to the bar.

She'd either already been drinking, or was some kind of nutter, or possibly both. I could feel Andy next to me trying not to laugh, and I knew that if I looked him in the eye, that would be it, we'd lose it. Tanner was just looking bemused while surveying the new arrival. He wasn't the kind of bloke to sit there saying nothing. Sure enough, he was carefully weighing where to take the conversation next, so after another minute or two of us all sitting there in various states of helplessness, sipping our pints while Bullet's new girl smiled at us, Tanner said, "So, Valoronia, which tribe do you fight for?"

She was ready for him. "Oh come on, you know how it is. There are no tribes in Ganrovia, as such. I'm part of the Ganrovian clan, of course, but we all fight alone. I started out as a kitchen serf, like everyone, two years ago, and fought my way up through the Village Square Duels to qualify for the Junior Mountain Marathons. Then I had to get my Dagger Credential and enough points for a Pebble Pouch and my Canine Entourage. I finished my seven years ... " (at this point she knowingly made speech mark signs with her fingers) " ... in the Wild Wastes in three weeks! No one's ever managed that, according to some people on the Ganrovia chat forum, though I'm not so sure — I bet the Korean kids are faster. Anyway, ever since then I've been a Warrior, of course, and am currently about half way along the 44 Melancholy Rivers. What about you?"

"I'm a lover, not a warrior," said Tanner, and at this Andy and I relieved ourselves of laughter. Scratch came back with Valoronia's pint of bitter and asked what was so funny. Bullet was glaring at Tanner, but Tanner was a big central defender, and was about the only person I knew who didn't seem particularly bothered when Bullet gave him the look. Tanner was as gentle as a minnow, and hated any kind of violence, but people kept their distance from him, like he was an unknown quantity of danger. Valoronia, meanwhile, looked confused and slightly hurt at the laughter.

"Didn't you say these were players?" she asked Bullet, who went red (another first) and muttered something about a football team. Valoronia went red too. "Oh," she said, "I'm sorry." Then she hissed something in Bullet's ear that we couldn't hear, and he went redder still and actually whispered back to her for quite a long time. Finally, she turned back to us at the table, and although we'd half-started to talk about something else she commanded our attention in a second by saying, "Sally."

"What?" said Scratch.

"I'm called Sally," she said.

"Is that short for Saloronia?" Andy wanted to know. I kept a close eye on Bullet, who was going red again.

"No," she said, very quietly. "Just Sally. I shouldn't have told you my warrior name. It's supposed to be a secret among people who play."

"Don't worry," said Tanner. "We promise not to tell anyone." We all looked down simultaneously at the beer mat with the word VALORONIA on it in big letters. I knew exactly what was going through Andy's head. He wanted to pick it up and shout out to the pub that Billy had a girlfriend and that her name was Valoronia. That's V.A.L.O.R.O.N.I.A. I nudged him and said, "Don't." He whispered back, "Yer nay fuckin' fun, Archie." If it had been anyone else besides Bullet he would already have done it. Meanwhile, I actually felt sorry for the girl. She looked like she wanted to get up and walk straight back out of our pub and never be seen here again.

"So where did you two meet?" I asked, trying to be friendly, but also genuinely curious, like I'm sure the others were.

"Oh, well ... " she started, visibly brightening, but Bullet just put his hand up and said, "No." She stopped right there and looked at him.

"Why not, Billy?" she said.

"None of their fucking business," he said. Same company as made his phone.

"Come on, Billy," I said. "Just because you never say owt, doesn't mean that your girlfriend can't." I knew there was a risk that he'd glass the fuck out of my face within about two seconds, but in that moment I didn't care. Suddenly I was pissed off at him and his 10-year silence. Yet even though he instinctively sat up like he was shaping to have a go at me, the word 'girlfriend' seemed to calm him. It was an acknowledgment and a reminder that he was now, at least in our eyes, no longer single. Maybe that came with certain responsibilities, not to mention the status of having finally pulled a woman in his fourth decade (Bullet's age was a matter of debate when he wasn't around, but we reckoned he was at least 35. The lack of hair made it hard to tell).

"The game," he grunted, and Sally/Valoronia elaborated.

"There was a Ganrovia convention in Newcastle last month. Players from all over the world. That's where we met. But there's a code of secrecy about the game. You're not supposed to tell non-players about it." She looked worried again. "I've really messed up."

Now we were all starting to feel bad for her. "Look," said Andy, "Let's just pretend that we never heard the first part of the conversation. Honestly, we've all said daft things we regret when we're down at the pub." He picked up the beer mat and tore it into tiny pieces. "All forgotten already," he said, like he was talking to a five-year-old, and Sally smiled nervously and thanked him.

"Still feel like a bit of a tit, though," she said, and took another drink from her pint. It was all getting too embarrassing, so I stood up again.

"Another piss already?" said Tanner, and I muttered something about needing some fresh air. Sally had thrown an already crap evening completely out of kilter.

I stood outside in the back car park and waited. A few minutes later Janet came out with her cigarettes.

"You again, eh?" she said quietly, and I didn't respond. She offered me a tab and I took it. We both stood smoking in silence for a while.

"What's she like?" Janet asked eventually, and for a second I'd no idea who she was talking about. I'd been thinking of something else entirely.

"Who?"

"The Duchess of fucking Cambridge," she said. "Wake up, Archie — Billy's bird, of course."

"Bit weird. She's a gamer. That's how they met. In Newcastle."

"Lovely," she said, and then stubbed out her fag and stood right in front of me. I moved slightly into the shadows and out of the car park light, up against the frosted kitchen window. She followed me over and we started to kiss.

"What are you planning now, Archie Lovell?" she whispered after a warm 30 seconds or so.

"I've no clue," I said, and at that moment a car pulled in through the back gate. No one could see us in the shadows. Two doors opened, and we heard the voices of Faye and Tanner's wife, Gabrielle. They were talking about one of the women at the kindergarten.

"Fucking cow asked me if there were 'problems at home' because Danny clocked some kid on the bonce with a fire engine," Gabrielle spat, and Faye laughed.

"I'd give her a fucking problem right up the cunt," said Faye, and they passed us by as they went into the pub through the back door, so close that I could smell my wife's perfume. As soon as they were in, Janet kissed me again, even longer this time, and then placed her hand in my jeans pocket, right where she knew what she would find.

"Hard times," she said. "Your wife's a vixen and a vampire, but I like her, so that's all you'll get from me." Then she moved away and went back inside the pub to work. I watched my breath for a while in the cold night air, and wished that I hadn't succumbed to smoking a cigarette with a woman who wasn't my wife.

***

The following Sunday, Bullet and Sally came to watch us play, and they kept coming every Sunday after. They were the first and only fans we ever had. Some of the lads stopped their families from coming to watch because they didn't want to be seen swearing, fouling and fighting, and because we weren't worth watching anyway. Most of the wives and girlfriends, for obvious reasons, just weren't interested. Faye would struggle out of bed, drop the kids off at her mother's for the day, and then go home to sleep for a few more hours, somehow undisturbed at the thought of us being 3-0 down and a man short after 25 minutes.

Sally threw herself into supporting The Foaming Quart with a verve that was beyond necessary. Tanner thought she was trying to make up for her blunder on the first night we'd met. Andy said she was trying to turn Bullet into a sociable human being. Scratch just found her annoying. During the game she'd shout out encouragement almost non-stop whenever we had the ball, while cheerfully swearing at the opposition players and the referee. Bullet stood glowering next to her, unmoved by the events on the field, but looking fierce enough to stop anyone from having a pop back at her, or telling her to shut the fuck up. Occasionally, she would go quiet, but that was when she was incongruously sticking her tongue down Bullet's throat. After a while, I stopped even noticing her.

At half-time, she'd rush over with a bag of oranges cut into quarters and try to chivvy us up for the second half as she handed them out. "Their left back's useless," she'd say to me. "You can get past him any time, Archie, he's slow as a fucking mule." The other unnerving aspect of this was that everything she said about the game made sense. We'd always been a team without tactics, and utterly without leaders. That's the way we liked it. Even though Sally might point out that their keeper looked uncomfortable with crosses, so we might want to start playing the ball out wide and then put him under pressure, we didn't want to hear it. We wilfully ignored her advice. We played the way we played.

As if that wasn't enough, when we got down the pub she'd want to talk about the game at great length. We did that anyway, of course, but only by talking about how Scratch had taken out their cocky midfielder with an elbow to the face behind the referee's back. We weren't really interested in hearing how Andy would be better playing up front instead of midfield because, in Sally's words, "he never tracks back anyway". Again though, thanks to Bullet's ever-presence, no one told her to shove it, and maybe we did take a little bit of her advice on board, but without ever admitting it. At one point, we went three Sundays in a row undefeated, and Sally seemed the most delighted of all. Well, she was our biggest fan. Bullet's feelings on our loss-defying streak remained a secret.

After a couple of pints, though, her interest turned back to Bullet, and they'd tongue and schmooze and slurp like school kids.

We managed to ease ourselves away from our regular table and leave them to it. We didn't leave them on their own, exactly — we'd spread ourselves to neighbouring tables and stand around at the bar more than we used to. When the wives and girlfriends showed up, the distance increased. In pre-Sally days our team had occupied one specific corner of the pub, but now we tended to dominate the whole place. Norman and Janet grumbled that some of their regulars weren't turning up on a Sunday anymore because they thought it was a more like a private function. One night, after several pints, I tried to persuade Janet to come out back and talk about it with me. She just smiled and shook her head, which was a good thing.

The other women kept their distance from Sally. For a start, she was with Bullet, which already made her weird in their eyes. Second, she didn't talk or drink or dress like them, at all. Then there was the fact that, by the time the lasses showed up, Bullet and Sally were halfway to fucking, though they never once left the pub before us. They would always see it out until last orders, like the rest of us. The main reason, though, why they couldn't stand Sally was that she had opinions, and she wasn't afraid to express them. In that respect, she more than made up for Bullet's apparent vow of silence.

I rarely heard her talk directly to the other women, because I was usually off my head by late in the evening, maybe singing songs or watching the football highlights on the big screen, or sometimes even asleep in the corner of the pub if I'd had a busy week and too much ale to wash down Norman's grey roast beef in its watery gravy. It was Faye who'd complain bitterly about how Sally harangued them when she emerged from Bullet's pin hold to go to the bar or the bog.

"What kind of thing does she say?" I asked her. We were in bed, and it was late on the Sunday night, and Faye had been complaining in the car home.

"She just talks shit. Starts having a go, you know?"

"About what?"

"About politics and stuff. She just bulldozes into our circle and announces how she expects we'll all be voting Green in the council election next week. Like, making this assumption, but knowing full well that we don't agree with her at all."

"Who are you going to vote for?"

"None of your business, it's a secret ballot," said Faye, then laughed at the serious expression on my face. "Oh come on, you know I'll vote the same as always. Definitely not for the fucking Greens."

"What else does she say?"

"Some crap about animal experiments and the brand of make-up we wear. Like, oh, where do we buy our make-up? Out of nowhere, this leading fucking question. I mean, look at the state of her, Archie. Like we'd be taking beauty tips from someone who looks like a fucking student. What was it she kept going on about? Oh yeah, is our make-up ethically sourced?" Her impression of Sally's accent was good, and I laughed. I reached over and put my hand high up on her thigh.

"It was even worse last week. She was on about how many of us had driven down to the pub in our big cars when we could just as easily have walked or taken our bikes. I pointed out that Gabrielle and I had car-shared, so at least we'd halved our carbon footprint, but that didn't shut her up. It wasn't just the saving petrol, it was the good it would do our bodies. And there's her with an arse as wide as Wales, and you've got Gabrielle who could probably still get a job as an underwear model. Fucking cheek of it."

I laughed again, and moved my hand further inside her thigh. Faye removed it and said, "No, Archie, not like that."

"Still not ready?"

She sighed and turned away. I wanted to say something more, and actually moved my jaw muscles and opened my mouth, but couldn't even find one single word that would have been the right thing to say at that moment. I turned over too, so that we were back to back, and before long the alcohol overcame my angst and I fell into a sleep plagued by dreams of Janet and Sally snogging behind the bar. Then they stopped and Janet said, "Bet you'd like a round of this, Archie", and they both laughed until the glasses started shaking on the shelves.

On the Sunday after the election, Bullet and Sally didn't turn up for the game, and then they didn't come to the pub either. It was remarked upon in passing, but it wasn't like it was going to ruin our day. Then at about seven in the evening they did show up after all, but you could tell something was wrong the minute they came in. First, Bullet looked strangely calm and detached, while Sally looked like she was the one who wanted to kill the next person who stared at her pint. They came and sat at our table and put down their drinks. Sally was always smiling, and it was a bit irritating, but now she looked so glum you really missed her normal happy expression. I was about to ask her if everything was alright, when Tanner, oblivious to her mood, said, "You missed a cracking game today, Sal. A 3-3 draw, and Archie here got the equaliser right on the whistle — absolute belter from 25 yards."

I was about to add some more detail to this unusual scoring event, even though I'd been on about it for most of the afternoon, but Sally cut me off.

"Never mind that shit," she spat. "Who did you fuckers all vote for on Thursday?"

There was a general silence, marked with a little murmuring. It wouldn't surprise me if some of the lads didn't even know what she was talking about — a couple of the younger players who were still in their late teens and spent most of their lives with their earphones plugged in and their eyes staring at a mini-screen. Most of us would have known the result, though. The Tories had taken the previously hung council, despite a bullish Labour campaign where they'd been loudly predicting that the result was going the other way. I suppose they had to, really, but it didn't half make them look like dicks when they lost all the seats they'd won the last time around. The Greens, meanwhile, had been wiped out, while a new party called Think Britain had won its only two seats in the county.

"Tanner?" asked Sally accusingly.

"None of your fucking business, as someone once said," Tanner replied, looking at Bullet. I thought Bullet would go nuts, but something even stranger happened. I saw the thinnest edge of a smile flirt with his usually malevolent mouth.

"Seriously?" said Sally. "That's the best you can do? You don't even have the conviction to put your gob where your ballot paper is? Your schools and hospitals are getting shut down or privatised, the bus routes are being slashed while fares double, there are more jobless, more homeless, more hungry people than ever before, right in front of our fucking eyes, right out there on the street in front of this very pub, and this fucking town votes the Tories back in? And then, when you've done it, you don't even have the fucking guts to admit it?"

Sally had stood up during this storming little monologue, and all the time Bullet was stroking her arse, like he had nothing else on his mind besides getting her kecks off. Now the pub was completely silent, until Tanner said moodily, "Okay then, Sal, I admit it — I voted Tory, like I always do. It's called democracy. They gave me a choice of parties, and that's the one I went for."

That wasn't going to satisfy Sally. She was crimson, but sober, unlike the rest of us. "Well, somehow that doesn't surprise me, Tanner. I mean, why would you give a fuck about other people, right? You're a manager, and you earn good money, and your wife does too with that crappy little shop of hers in Kingsley selling high-end cheese and wine to other fucking Tories. Main thing is, you both get richer, right? I understand, I really do."

Tanner just smiled and shrugged. "I'm successful," he said. "Have a revolution and hang me from the rafters." No one laughed, though.

"Don't tempt me," she answered, then pointed at Scratch. "And what about you?"

"Think Britain," he said, defiantly. Sunil, our goalkeeper, said, "Really?" Scratch didn't dare look him in the eye, but it was a great rag to throw to Sally.

"Yeah, nice team-mate you got there, Sunil. Doesn't surprise me any more than Tanner being a Tory. Think Britain appeals to morons — it's in their manifesto, pretty much. So why shouldn't Scratch, who's a moron, not vote for them? Fair dos."

Janet, of all people, started laughing at this from behind the bar. "You tell 'em, love!" she called out. Norman said nothing, but he didn't look happy. I decided to intervene and try to calm things down. "Look..." I said, but that was as far as I got.

"Forget it, Archie. Anyone want to bet how Archie voted?" She looked at me. "A round of 50 pints says that Archie didn't bother to fucking vote at all." I went red, and a lot of people started laughing, including Tanner and Andy. That would probably have been their guess as well. But all this inflamed Sally even more. "You think it's funny, you twats?" she shouted. "This is the worst case of all. Never mind the greedy fuckers that vote Tory and the racist fuckers who vote for Thick Britain. It's people like Archie who should know better that get right on my tits. And ... " Here she pointed at Bullet " ... one of his best mates here got made redundant last week after 17 years with the same company, and does Archie give a shit? No, because Archie wants to get hammered and talk about his big goal he scored against some other shite pub side. Am I right, Archie?"

"Yeah," I said flippantly, "you're right. Well done." At least we knew now where Bullet had worked all this time — at the Forster avionics plant in Trentside. A Chinese company had bought it two years ago, and last week they'd shut it down citing "international market trends".

"You know I'm fucking right, Archie, you know it," she said, pointing at me, and then she tipped the whole table over, drinks and all, and finally Norman said, "Hey, hang on," as close to an expression of passion he would ever emit, but Bullet and Sally were way ahead of him, marching off out the pub arm in arm before anyone could stop them or challenge them or further involve them in a political debate. And the worst thing was, I did know she was right. At the same time, I was perplexed that she somehow knew me, knew all of us in fact, well enough to tell who we'd voted for, or not.

I was home that night before Faye had even left the house, and was moody all week. The following Sunday we were playing The Dirty Duke, but Sunil didn't show up. In the changing room, Tanner blamed Scratch because he'd voted for Think Britain. Scratch didn't think it was his fault at all.

"I ain't got anything against Sunil, he's my mate," he protested.

"Then why the fuck did ye vote for Think Britain?" said Andy.

"I can fucking vote for who I want," said Scratch. "I don't have to tell you why."

"Alright then," said Tanner. "We'll vote on who plays in goal today because Sunil's not turned up. I vote for Scratch. All those in favour?"

The vote was unanimous, the only problem being that Scratch was shit in goal, and was in a terrible mood because we'd made him play there. At 4-0 down, when a Duke player gloated in his face about the goal he'd just scored by dribbling around him, Scratch responded by thumping him (it didn't help that the player was black), and the game degenerated into a mass shoving brawl. Eventually the ref sorted it out, sent Scratch off, and I ended up having to go in goal instead. Final score: 12-0.

Maybe the Duke players had got wind of something, but for the second week running there was no sign of Bullet and Sally, either at the game or in the pub. We were all sitting around feeling sorry for ourselves that evening, drinking heavily, when the door to the Foaming Quart burst open and the Duke lads stormed in to show us that winning by a dozen goals hadn't been enough, they wanted to finish the job off. Without Bullet, there was no deterrent. They wrecked the place, and they beat the shit out of us. Some, like Tanner, just ran out the back exit, and I haven't seen him since. Andy, Scratch and myself were among the ones who stayed and suffered for it, until the cops came and closed the pub down. It's been shut ever since — Norman and Janet moved to a boozer out in the West Country. The next Sunday, only five of us turned up to play, and that was the end of the team as well.

One thing did change, though. When Faye arrived at the pub on the night of the fight to find me bleeding and bruised, sitting on the back step right next to where I'd been kissed by Janet just a few weeks before, she couldn't have been more attentive. She drove me home and persuaded her Mum, who was babysitting, to take the kids back to her place for the night. Then she ordered me to lie on the sofa and began to tend to my bleedings.

I'm no fan of violence. I'd have scarpered out after Tanner if I thought I could have got away with it, though in retrospect I'm glad that I didn't. At least I can look Andy and Scratch in the eye if I bump into them on the street. But Faye was weird. She started licking my wounds. When I protested that she was hurting me, she started to groan. We ended up fucking like greased rabbits. It hurt like hell, but the more I complained that I was in pain, the more Faye was into it. This went on for several nights, until my wounds started healing, but then when we went to bed she'd just start hitting me. Playfully at first, then ferociously. And instead of telling her to stop because I don't like it, don't even understand it, I just let it happen because I seem incapable of doing anything else. I went for a drink with Andy one night and told him all about it, but he didn't seem to want to know the details. "She's obviously crackers," he said, "but at least yer gettin' some. I wouldnae complain too much."

I bumped into Sally one day too, shopping in Tesco. She was heavily pregnant, and smiled at me again as if nothing had changed. I congratulated her, sincerely. There was no sign of Bullet, though.

"What's Billy up to?" I asked. "Did he find another job?"

She continued to smile at me, in quite a strange manner, but without responding.

"Sally?"

"Yes?"

"What's Billy up to?'

"He's doing fine."

"Good, good. He working?"

"Yeah, kind of. He's in the army."

"He joined up?"

The smile was still in place, but I could see that she was about to cry. "He joined up the day after I found out I was pregnant," she said. The smile finally dropped. "I thought he'd be made up. But he just went quiet and wouldn't talk to me, and then he was gone. I didn't even find out until he wrote me a postcard."

"Hell, I'm sorry. Where is he now?"

"Middle East, somewhere. Probably Iraq or Afghanistan, I don't know, I haven't seen him since. He hasn't even written."

"I'm sorry," I said again. I'd no idea what else to say.

"I'll be seeing you," she said, and walked past me, but I could see her shoulders heaving as she went. Then she just pushed her trolley off to one side and started almost running towards the exit.

Later, there was an inquiry into Bullet's death. Officially, the Army said he'd shot himself while on sentry duty at four in the morning, off his head on three different kinds of drug. But a few months later some private who'd had his leg blown off by a roadside bomb and been discharged, told *The Guardian*, among many other things, that Bullet had been the victim of a late-night hazing ritual that went seriously wrong. The Army had covered it up. Sally went in all guns blazing to demand the truth.

If the Army had beaten Bullet, Sally wasn't going to have any more luck. I saw her picture in the paper, standing outside court, cradling Baby Billy and lambasting the establishment. It's been two years now, and they keep blocking her, but she's fighting on. A lover and a warrior, all in one.

I wish The Foaming Quart was still open and that I could take Bullet there for a pint. That I would have the courage to slap him around the head and say, "Hey, Billy, wake up, you stupid twat, you're going to be a dad!" Though, most likely, we'd both just sit there staring at our pints and saying nothing. Nothing at all.

Cold Balls

My agent, Jocky Hogg, phoned me up me up with some good news, I suppose. His call dragged me awake into a hangover I might otherwise have slept through, happily out of this world. It was work, though, and at least it didn't involve an after-dinner speech with me embellishing the same old yarns about how I'd stopped a world-class striker in his tracks with a tasty ankle tap unseen by the referee, and then insulted his mother and his sister too.

"What is it, Jocky? A supermarket?"

"They want you to make the draw for the semi-final."

"What semi-final?"

"How many semi-finals do you think there are right now? The Scottish Cup, ye pillock."

"Who wants me to do that?"

"The gentlemen at the Scottish Football Association."

"The gentlemen at the Scottish Football Association have hated me ever since the Yuletide of my Exposed Backside," I said. "They always have. Is everyone else unavailable on that particular day?"

"You know, Ewen, sometimes I actually use my connections in the game to get you work. I know you think I just take 25% of your income while scratching my arse, but mostly I do my job and I do it very well."

I said nothing.

"You're welcome," he added.

"What do I have to do?"

"Oh, it's very complicated. Turn up on time at STV this Sunday night sober enough to stick your hand in a bag and take out four balls. You don't even have to do any reading, you just hand the ball to Scottish football's esteemed leader Eddie Hillhouse."

"How much?"

"Five grand, and that's after I've taken my cut. Plus first-class rail ticket."

That woke me up good and proper. "Five grand? Bloody hell, Jocky. Don't you worry, I'll be there."

"Thought that might get yer attention."

"Aye, right enough. Thanks, pal!"

"It's amazing how the more cash I get them, the more my clients like me."

"Right now, Jocky, I don't just like you, I want to be in a relationship with you, going forward, with a view to marriage and several grandchildren."

When I thought about it afterwards, though, something didn't quite make sense. The generosity of the fee, mainly. Five grand for two minutes' work. And the fact that it was me they'd asked to do it. I'd played for Scotland twice, and in one of those games I'd been ordered off, screwing up our country's qualification chances for the following summer's European Championships. I'd played for Hearts, Aberdeen and Dundee United, but never for Celtic or Rangers. I'd won bugger all, except for Player of the Year when I moved down the leagues to Stenhousemuir. I was a journeyman, and the only reason anyone knew my name was because I held the Scottish domestic record for most yellow and red cards. Not just in a single season, but over the course of a career too. "It's a wonder he racked up so many, he was suspended that often," quipped my ex-boss at Hearts, Jimmy Linighan. Like Jimmy hadn't encouraged me to take out any player who looked like endangering our chances of a hard-earned away point at Dundee on a Tuesday night.

I'm also well known, of course, for one year dropping my trousers at the SFA Christmas dinner and mooning in front of our aforementioned President Eddie Hillhouse and his wife Angela as they sat at the top table. It made for the headline CHRISTMAS CRACK-ER, along with a blurry photo, across the front page of the following morning's *Scottish Daily Mirror*, followed by a three-month ban from all competitions. Worth it, though, for the number of free pints it got me over the following years.

Five grand, for pulling four balls out of a sack. What's the catch?

"Do you ever regret that your career came too early when you see the amounts that players earn today?" The stupidest questions are the ones you get asked most often. Of course I bloody do. I finished up with nothing. I tried to coach, but I couldn't. Couldn't discipline players for drinking when I'd done it my whole career. My teams were as filthy and uncultivated as I'd been for 15 years as a dirty pro, and about as successful. Fired by Forfar, sacked in Stranraer, dismissed in Dumbarton. Unemployable everywhere else. Then a second divorce took me for everything I owned. "You're a happy drunk, Ewen," said Allie when she handed me the lawyer's letter, "and that's all very well for you, but not for me and the weans. Although there are even some parts of you I like on a quiet Sunday afternoon."

"That's usually when I'm asleep," I said, and we both laughed. I wasn't so jolly when I saw the settlement she was asking for, but my fight had waned into sorry submission the day I hobbled off the park for the last time, away at Brechin City with a 3-0 defeat on the scoreboard. I signed off on the deal to save us all from any more pain.

Now I deliver the post, and what doesn't go on maintenance goes into the till at The Bollok and Dagger on a daily basis. I live back at home in Falkirk with my ma, sleeping in a single bed. Speakers' fees are a bonus, maybe three or four a year, but they're never more than a few hundred quid, and what Jocky Hogg doesn't take, I give up in rent. Most of which my ma then puts back into my wallet, and we both pretend that I don't notice. "You could do with cutting back on the drink," she says once a week, just like she used to say to my dad and her own dad too. He left instructions to have it etched on his gravestone, but she put the stop on that. After all, it was her phrase, not his.

I got the big treatment when I arrived at STV. Make-up, tea and cake, and they actually had a spanking new navy blue suit there ready for me, a perfect fit, with shirt and tie to match. As though they somehow knew the suit I'd turn up in would be threadbare, no longer quite able to accommodate my expansions, and 25 years out of date.

Jocky was there too, ensuring that "all goes to plan", as he put it. That made me even more on edge. What part of pulling four balls out of a sack couldn't go to plan? "You get to keep the suit," he whispered. "It's part of the deal. Just don't fuck it up." He then led me into a meeting room, and there was Eddie Hillhouse, greeting me like we were best pals going back to Argentina '78. It was the first time we'd been in the same room since that famous festive night when I'd shocked his poor missus with a view of where my sun comes shining through. Poor Angela was dead now, but it had been a few years. I decided it was best not to offer my condolences, especially as we were suddenly getting on so well.

"Mr. Hogg tells me that you're back in your native Falkirk now, Ewen," said Eddie Hillhouse, and tempting as it was to say,

"What the fuck's it got to do wi ye, ye auld cunt?" I smiled and agreed with both him and Jocky that yes, indeed, I was back in my native Falkirk, although no one added that I was back in my native Falkirk living with my ma, delivering the post and drinking myself to death.

"Not still involved in the game?"

"Not so much now." Not unless you count falling asleep in front of the TV watching Motherwell v Hibs on a Sunday afternoon.

"That's a shame," he said, offering me a cigar. Just kidding about that part, but it was that kind of atmosphere he was trying to create, and it was all making me even more suspicious. Did they think I was stupid? What did they want for their five grand? "We could use your experience at a higher level right now. I was talking with Mr Hogg just now about maybe getting you involved in the national team youth set-up."

"Ewen would love an opportunity like that, Mr. Hillhouse," Jocky assured him, which was news to me. And no doubt news to the Scottish FA youth set-up, which as I understood it right now featured lots of ambitious, up-and-coming young coaches with computers, UEFA licences, and fancy ideas from Europe, and very few fat and aging centre backs who could show a young lad how to kick the shit out of a skilful opponent and then claim to the ref that he hadnae bloody touched him.

"Aye, that would be very interesting, right enough," I said, playing along to see where these blathering frauds werc taking me. It didn't take long before they got down to the real business. Eddie Hillhouse took out a brown envelope and held it up.

"Now, Ewen, here's your flat fee for today," he said, like he was talking to a small child. "You'll get it after the programme, provided everything goes to plan." What did he think, that I was going to moon the nation at high tea-time on the Sabbath?

"I've been on TV before, Mr. Hillhouse," I thought it was worth pointing out. "I'm not a man of nerves, in general."

"Oh aye, of course, of course," he said dismissively. "Now, there's just a wee extra instruction I want you to take note of. When you put your hand in the bag, there will be two extra cold balls, and two quite warm balls."

The temptation to make an off-colour joke at this point was hard to resist, but I was too intrigued to be puerile. Yes, even me. Come on, out with it. What's the skulduggery?

"Now," Eddie went on, looking me in the eye. "It's very, very important that you listen carefully now and follow my instructions." Again, like he's talking to an eejit. "First take out one of the cold balls. Then take out the second cold ball. Then the warm balls third and fourth."

"Or the other way round," said Jocky, and Eddie Hillhouse shot him a look, like he was complicating things.

"I get it, right enough," I said. "It's a fix."

"Absolutely not," said Eddie. "Absolutely not. It's a mere matter of protocol, for the good of the game. I just need you to follow the instructions, Ewen. Can you do that?"

I looked at Eddie for a few seconds. Now I really wished that I had the cigar, so that I could blow smoke in his direction.

"There are four teams in the bag," I stated. "Kilmarnock, Ayr United, Rangers and Celtic."

"That's correct," said Eddie.

"And don't tell me. One of the cold balls is Celtic, and one of the warm balls is Rangers. Or the other way around."

"It's in the interests of football, Ewen," said Jocky. "Nobody wants Kilmarnock or Ayr in the final."

"Except for fans of Kilmarnock or Ayr," I said.

"Aye, but there really aren't that many of them," Jocky reasoned. "If we were taking a vote, it's Rangers v Celtic that people would want to see in the final. What we're doing here is more about democracy."

There was a moment's silence. I was about to disagree with Jocky's version of democracy when Eddie looked at his watch and snapped, "We're on in five minutes." He put the envelope in his pocket. "Five grand each," he said, standing up. "If you mess it up, there's not a penny." Mr. Nice Guy was back on suspension. "And," he finished off, pointing at me, "we'll be having that suit off your back." Then he left the room.

I looked at Jocky, who came as close as he could to blushing. "Five grand each, eh?" I said. "When did we become 50-50 partners?"

"It's a one-off deal," he said. "Don't be an arse, Ewen, let's just get this done."

"Only if I get my usual 75%."

"60-40," he said.

"Deal," I said, and we got up to leave the room, and I suddenly felt like a scheming, low-down skunk. I'd always liked away games at Killie, they'd put on a great spread after the match. I'd played with their current manager at Aberdeen, Billy Warnock. And now I was about to fuck him and the whole town over, just to tilt the odds in favour of the Old Firm, who had all the odds in their favour already.

Still, six grand was six grand, cash in hand. The suit was lovely too, I felt like a new man inside it as I walked down the corridor and into the studio, where I was introduced to the nation as former Scottish international Ewen Barr. What the hell, Rangers or Celtic would win it one way or another. Into the bag my hand went, and out came the first cold ball. I handed it to Eddie Hillhouse, who read out the number 2, and handed the ball to the presenter, Andy McClure.

"Number 2 is Rangers FC," said Andy McClure.

For a lovely, thrilling second or two I thought about turning to the camera and telling the nation that this was all a hoax. Instead, I opted for the simple task of picking out the second cold ball, and my hand went back into the bag. I fumbled around. I felt all three balls.

There was a problem here. None of them seemed to be cold. Eddie and Andy were standing there, Eddie looking like he would stick his hand in the bag himself if I didn't hurry up, Andy with the kind of stick-on smile that could be removed in a second and replaced with the grimace of a steel-spined assassin.

"The balls keep slipping out my hand," I quipped to the teatime audience, and Andy let out an unnatural staccato laugh. I felt all three again, but they were all as warm as the other. Well, we'd have to gamble. I picked one out, my heart thumping, and handed it to Eddie.

"Number 3," he almost growled.

"Number 3 is Celtic FC!" cried Andy McClure. It was hard to tell if his exclamation came from the excitement of an Old Firm game in the semi-final, or if he'd been in on the whole scam and was now surprised that we'd somehow managed to screw it up. Eddie Hillhouse had turned pale, and off stage I could see Jocky with his head in his hands.

"Well, there's one in the face to all those folks who claim the draw's always fixed," I smiled straight in to the camera, and Andy McClure let out a laugh of pure plastic, while Eddie threw me a look that would have felled an elephant.

The rest of the draw was something of an anti-climax, as semi-final draws often are once you've picked out the first two names. I could only hope that Eddie realised when I gave him the balls that neither of the other two were cold. As soon as we were off air, he marched off stage, and a few minutes later we all convened again in the same room where we'd planned the fix just a few minutes earlier.

"What the fuck happened?" Jocky screamed right in to my face, but Eddie held up his hand.

"It wasn't him," he said. "There was only one bloody cold ball in the bag. Someone else fucked up."

Right at that second, Andy McClure barged into the room, dragging a young lad behind him.

"Hello, everyone, allow me to introduce to you Lance, the world's most incompetent fucking intern."

"Hello, Lance," said Jocky. "Been having trouble with your mathematics? Couldn't count as far as two? Or were you feeling too weak today to carry two wee metal balls to the freezer in the staff kitchen?"

This poor lad looked terrified. He stood and looked at all four of us as though we were about to pass a death sentence.

"How?" was all that Eddie Hillhouse wanted to know.

Lance said nothing. So I took a guess.

"Killie fan?"

He looked at me, as though relieved that we had an explanation. As though I might be on his side.

"Aye," he said. "Since I was a wean."

Eddie looked at Andy McClure. "How did you not know this? Do you not talk about football in the STV sports department?"

"No one talks to me at all," said Lance. "They just shout orders."

"Jesus Christ," said Jocky, shaking his head.

"You've cost Scottish football a lot of money today," said Eddie Hillhouse, talking to Lance like he was the criminal, not the rest of us. Like Scotland wouldn't now win the World Cup after all. But Lance was gaining in confidence as he was beginning to understand what a rabble of roguey old bastards were gathered here before him.

"Sorry about that," he said, loosening himself from Andy McClure's grip and standing up straight. "But at least the integrity of the game's still intact, eh?"

At this point, we suddenly all realised that Lance here had us by the goolies, hot or cold. What was to stop him going straight out to the nearest journalist and shopping the lot of us?

"It's alright, son," I said. "I'm sure we can all agree that the draw was absolutely regular." I nodded at Eddie Hillhouse, who didn't seem to understand at first.

"Right, Eddie?" I said a little louder, touching my inside jacket pocket, and then he caught on, let out a strangled snort, but reached inside his own jacket and took out a brown envelope. I watched longingly as Eddie handed it to Lance, who hesitated for a second before accepting it, looking inside, and letting out a short whistle.

"Football, eh?" he said. "Bloody hell." He turned to me and said, "My old man said he saw you playing for Dundee United at Killie. Called you the worst player to pull on a Scotland shirt in the last hundred years." And then he walked out the room, and no doubt left the building for the final time.

The four of us stood there, Jocky swearing and shaking his head, Eddie staring at his hands placed before him on the desk. He was old now, in his late 70s. When would we bring fresh ideas into Scottish football?

"Well, I'll be wanting something for my trouble," I ventured. After all, I too could easily go and look for the nearest newspaper.

"You've got to be bloody kidding me," said Eddie.

I walked over to the desk. "No, Eddie, I'm not. I'm quite serious. It's not my fault there was only one cold bloody ball."

Eddie suddenly looked like he no longer cared. He reached into his pocket and took out a second envelope, no doubt the one allocated to Jocky. He handed me the packet, and Jocky said, "Hang on, wait a minute," but I was on my way out already, pushing past Andy McClure. Jocky finally caught up with me in the car park.

"Forty per cent," he said.

"Of nothing," I said. "I've got my five grand, that was the deal. Go and ask your friends inside for your cut."

"We're done Ewen, you fat bastard," he shouted as I walked off towards the station for my first-class train ride back to Falkirk. I would be having drinks ordered to my seat, no doubt about it.

"Yeah, yeah," I shouted back. "Good luck finding someone to replace Scotland's worst ever international on your client list."

Eddie Hillhouse has yet to get back to me about becoming part of the Scottish youth team set-up. My ma said to me last night, "You could do with cutting back on the drink." And Celtic won the Cup. They beat Kilmarnock 4-0. I fell asleep long before the end.

The Cinder
Park Refugees

It's been five years since I told everyone that I was finally done with football. No one believed me, because I'd quit too many times before, it was a running joke at the club. By then I was in my mid-60s, burnt out from years of volunteering with sparse gratitude in return. I'd happily coached numerous youth teams at TSV 62 down the years, but in the end, I was just filling in because no one else could be bothered, especially with the teenage boys. Some clueless dad would quit overnight because he'd fallen out with the players or had been handed a ban for threatening or even assaulting a referee, and then I'd get the call. And it was always me who got the call. They knew I was the only one in the club incapable of saying no.

"You know we wouldn't ask you if it wasn't an emergency, Frank." That was our President, Volker, on the line, always just after 10pm when your resistance was low. The late hour implied that this was a crisis, and you were the final chance of saving the day after everyone else had said no.

"Is there really no one else," I'd ask, like this question was suddenly going to trigger a list of new candidates in Volker's brain.

"I've been making calls all night," Volker would plead, without being more specific about who all those people might have been. "If no one steps up, then we have to take the team out the league, simple as that. And where do we get new players for the men's teams in a couple of years if we don't have the U17s now?"

And I would say it was another two nights a week training, and then a game at the weekend, on top of the U13s I was already coaching.

"You don't have to do much with them," Volker would reply, my consent now apparently a done thing. "Just be there and make sure they turn up for the games on time, just until the summer. We'd really, really appreciate it if you can fill in just for a few months."

And so I would try to take control of a squad of 15, about five of whom could play football a bit. Any given ten boys might turn up for training, usually split in to two cliques that would, at some point in the evening, start to argue with each other following a tackle on the wrong side of tasty. Occasionally, someone would push a team-mate over, and once or twice a fist was thrown. You couldn't throw anyone out the team, though, otherwise you'd never have got 11 players out on the field the following Saturday afternoon. When I stopped caring that we were 5-0 down and was already yearning for my armchair, a cold Pilsener and the Bundesliga highlights, then I knew it really was time to say "no" to Volker's next call.

To prove to the club, to my wife Ilse, and mainly to myself that I was serious about quitting, I adopted a rescue dog instead. Sadie was a sleek and very loveable black Labrador, who must have been abandoned by someone without a soul. On evenings and weekends, I'd sometimes walk her past the TSV ground and stand to watch from a distance for a few minutes if there was a game on. Someone might spot me and wave from afar, and then I'd enter the ground and stand with the club stalwarts, fending off jokes about how I looked ready to start coaching the U7s again. They'd offer me something to eat from the snack stand — I was entitled to a free sausage for life, they said. It was nice to get the acknowledgment every now and again. But there was only the very sporadic tug of regret that I was no longer involved. I'd just start getting caught up in the action and kid myself that I was missing the sport, and then some foul-mouthed, cack-footed toe-rag would scream in the referee's face that he was utterly wrong, and no one would say anything about it, not even the ref. I'd give Sadie the word, and we'd be on our way, happy to leave the wrought and raucous hubbub behind us. Level-10 football played out in front of a crowd of 35 — a game of profound importance, if you believed the noise.

On weekday afternoons, I'd take a tennis ball along for Sadie to chase across the old cinder pitch, which still belonged to the club, but was a couple of hundred yards away from the smart new complex with its plastic pitch, floodlit cages and a basketball court. The cinder pitch was where I'd trained lads for decades, but was no longer deemed good enough for the new breed of amateurs. True, it had always flooded after an hour of rain, and was hard as granite when it froze, or during the summer months if we had a long, dry spell. But it was a pitch, nonetheless, with a goal at either end. Now the corners were blighted with moss, and weeds poked up in random spots. Not even kids used it any more for a casual kickabout. They preferred to sneak into the club grounds and play on the smooth, reliable surface. To me that's just wrong. All young players should learn to factor in the unpredictable bounce.

One afternoon, it was around the turn of spring, I was walking through the park with Sadie an hour or two earlier than usual. Ilse and I had had a routine row about something not cleared up properly in the kitchen. Our arguments were always solved by one of us leaving the room or the flat. Then we'd avoid each other for several hours before talking again like normal people. The rows were never mentioned, they were just quietly submerged into the history of our 44-year marriage.

I'd been in a rush to leave the house, so had forgotten to bring a tennis ball for Sadie. I thought about going back, but didn't want to risk running into Ilse before either of us had had the chance to calm down. As it happened, the pitch was occupied anyway, for the first time in years. I could hear the animated calls of the players as we walked around the pond and towards the club, and to my surprise they sounded like grown men, not young boys. Sadie raised her ears and looked poised to join the action as we approached the pitch. She was conditioned to run on this stretch, and pressured the leash the closer we got to the bouncing ball.

Amid much local discussion, the city had built temporary housing for refugees in a corner of the park that — like the cinder pitch — had not been used for years, except as a horticultural dump for the park maintenance team. It turned out that the refuse could easily be disposed of elsewhere. There was a shortage of space for an influx of young men and families fleeing wars, oppression and economic deprivation in various parts of the world. In an impressive show of conviction and efficiency, the new structures appeared before a co-ordinated opposition could raise enough protests to stop them. It probably wasn't strictly legal, but it was necessary, and no one died. Although Ilse did ask out loud why they had to come to "our park, of all places". When I asked her if she felt there was no longer enough space in the park for her to take her annual walk there, she didn't deign to respond.

It was the refugees — men in their teens and their 20s — who were putting TSV's abandoned cinder pitch to good use at two o'clock in the afternoon. I calmed Sadie into a sitting position as we watched the raggle tag mixture of tongues and shirt colours play an intense and fast-moving game. It was impossible to tell who was on which team, but all the players seemed to know. They yelled in a mixture of French, Arabic, pidgin English and occasional German ("Scheisse!"), and sporadic disputes about fouls and the custody of throw-ins were dealt with in seconds. Near misses provoked sharp agony in the face and gestures of the culprit, and a curt collective groan of discontent from his team-mates. Goals, though, were greeted with nonchalance, like the players expected to score every time. Then someone would call out the score: "Seize à douze!" No one was really playing in goal, but whoever was standing in the six-yard box seemed to be allowed to throw themselves at the ball and use their hands.

The ball was a desperate item, coming apart at the seams, and with tatters of synthetic material flapping off the panels. It rolled out close to us a couple of times, but some of the players seemed wary of retrieving the ball with Sadie so near, and she was obviously interested in the ball herself. It certainly wouldn't have helped its state if she'd got her jaws around it. Seeing the hesitancy on the part of one young man — his pale blue shirt drunk on sweat, his eyes full of urgent questions — I walked to get the ball myself and lobbed it to him with my right foot, my hands being taken up with the dog. I nodded at him and smiled, but he remained apprehensive. I pulled Sadie away and we watched the game a little further back. We stayed for maybe an hour, and when we left they were still playing at the same pace, without having taken a single break.

I began to take Sadie down there every afternoon at two, when I would normally have been taking a nap after lunch. Before we reached the cinder pitch, I'd throw the tennis ball for her on a stretch of grass for half an hour to give her some proper exercise. Then we'd walk around to the park's east side to watch the refugees. There was a freedom to their play that was missing from the football I saw at the weekends over on the club's main pitch. Players dribbled, and no one yelled at them if they lost the ball.

Snazzy tricks would be celebrated for half a second by co-players, but then the game swiftly moved on. Mistakes caused pain only to those who had made them, and again for just a fraction of a moment. Move on, try again, fail again, try again. One slender young man playing on the left wing tried and failed a dozen times to knock the ball through the legs of the same defender. Not once was he reproached for serially losing the ball. When he finally succeeded, the defender merely grabbed his shirt and pulled him to the ground. Both men laughed, embraced, and the game continued with a free-kick. Though the game was not played in purely that kind of spirit. A couple of bad fouls lead to head-on-head square-ups, and it took collective intervention to separate the two parties before the game continued exactly as before. No sanctions, no ref necessary.

Meanwhile, the players were becoming used to our presence. During the course of that whole first week, we were the only living creatures who seemed to notice the impromptu match, and who stopped to watch. I caught on that the teams were the same every day, and that were 27 players in all — 14 on one side, 13 on the other. There was an approximate divide which I reckoned was along the lines of: Northern Africa and the Middle East versus Sub-Saharan Africa. The sides may also have been balanced on talent grounds, because the two teams were evenly matched, and there was rarely more than two or three goals difference in the score-line. One day, I stayed long enough to see the match come to an end, at exactly 3.55pm. The players upped and left for their accommodation, as though another group had been waiting on the touchline to take their place.

At the weekend, there was no sign of the players. On Sunday, I watched TSV's first XI lose 4-0 to a team that were almost bottom of the table. I mentioned to Volker that I'd seen several possible recruits playing on the cinder pitch on weekday afternoons. He looked at me, like I was taking the piss.

"From the accommodation in the park," I said, and he just said, "Oh, them." I asked him what he meant by that, and he muttered something about paperwork, and the club having enough players as it was.

On Monday morning, Ilse wanted to know why I'd been into town to buy a new football.

"Surely you're not starting up with that all over again," she said. "At your age."

"It's a gift," I said. "There are some young men playing on the club's cinder pitch every afternoon, and their ball's knackered."

"Ah, so that's why you've been staying out so long."

"Just watching. It's nothing organised, they just love to play. But they don't have a proper ball."

"You just told me that. It's okay, I wasn't planning on making you take it back to the shop."

I made for the park even earlier than usual, hoping to arrive at the cinder pitch just as they were starting to play. On my way down there, though, I started to feel awkward. I had not yet spoken a single word with any of the refugee players. How exactly was I going to explain that I, a passing stranger, wanted them to play with this spanking new ball, and that I wanted them to keep it? Not a mere replica, but an official match ball. But I was retired now, and really, had nothing else to spend it on.

Even though Sadie and I reached the pitch well before 2pm, the game had already started. The new ball was concealed in a carrier bag, and for a few moments I felt so uncomfortable about offering this unsolicited gift that I almost turned around and returned home. Or, back to the shop for a refund. Then right at that moment, the game ball ran out of play and directly to my feet. It was in even worse condition than the week before, completely out of shape and potentially dangerous to head due to the various flaws and flaps. A bearded young man stood before me, waiting for the ball's return.

I held up my hand and then, with my arm looped through Sadie's leash, knelt down to retrieve the new ball from my bag. It was fully pumped already, I'd got them to do that in the shop. I threw the ball to the young man, smiling self-consciously. He caught it and looked at it, like he was wondering how long it would take for the object to explode, and where should he throw it in the meantime.

"C'est pour vous! Der Ball ist für euch! The ball is yours!" The players were all staring at me, hands on their hips.

"Was wollen Sie von uns?" What do you want from us? It was the player with the light-blue t-shirt who'd been so wary of Sadie the first day we had watched. From all the calls, I now knew that he was called Mamadou.

"Nichts!" I exclaimed. "Nothing! Just play!"

The player with the ball bounced it a couple of times. Then he signalled to me to pass him the old ball. I shrugged and I did as he'd asked. I thought he was going to continue playing with it, but instead he turned to the players and held both balls up and seemed to ask which one they wanted to continue the game with. I pulled Sadie back a few yards, as I was becoming more central to the game than I wanted to be. There was a long discussion on the field, and now and then a player would point at me. Finally, Mamadou came over and said to me in slow but grammatically perfect German:

"Why are you giving us a football?"

"Because your old ball is dangerous. It could damage your head." I pointed to my forehead and made a wincing gesture, but Mamadou just laughed.

"Okay," he said. "We will try to play with your ball." He nodded at the bearded player to throw the new ball into play, and the game resumed. For the first few minutes, though, the players had real trouble getting accustomed to its weight and perfect rotundity. Indeed, when my ball sailed far beyond one of the goals, a player ran over to retrieve the old ball from close to where we were standing (and where Sadie had been struggling to get her teeth on it), and the game continued while another player ran to fetch the new ball. But no sooner was the old ball back in play than it was deemed a reject, and from now on my gift was the centre of their attentions. It wasn't long before they'd got used to its flight and, to my eyes, were playing much better for it.

After about an hour, it started to rain lightly and Sadie was beginning to whine, so I started making for home. No sooner had I begun to walk away from the field, though, than a player came running towards me with the ball in his hand. "Mister, your ball!" he shouted, and when I tried to make clear that the ball was now theirs, all 27 young men came to remonstrate with me. They could not accept this ball. Why was I giving it to them? And again the question: what do you want from us?

"I just want you to keep playing football," I said. They stared at me, so I added, "I am your fan."

One or two players started laughing at this. "He is our fan!" Translations quickly moved through the group, and there was more laughter. Until a huge player who always, always played in central defence of the Sub-Saharan African team said, "But which team do you like the best?"

"You are both very good," I said. "Both very even. I am a fan of both teams."

"You are the fan who always wins," said a short, wiry midfielder — Soufian, I knew his name from the shouts. He always wanted the ball, no matter where it was on the pitch and even if he was 70 yards away from it.

"Like a fan of Bayern Munich," said someone else, and when I responded with, "Bayern Munich — please, no!" there were several murmurs of disagreement, and one player pointed to his filthy shorts where you could just make out the Munich club's logo. "Very good team," he said. "The best!"

Eventually, I persuaded them that I did not want to take the ball home. They should look after it, though. They nodded, and then they waited. For a second, I felt like the trainer, and that I should give the command for them to return to the pitch. I wanted to do it. Then I remembered where we were, and so I smiled and said goodbye, and then turned for home with Sadie, and the players started to walk back to the pitch. Then Soufian turned and shouted, "Thank you, Mister... what is your name?"

"Frank," I called back.

"Thank you, Mister Frank. See you tomorrow!"

From now on, we were greeted with cheerful waves as we approached the pitch. I would applaud good play, shout encouragement, cheer all goals, and make disapproving noises if there was any bother. Jean-Paul, a serious young man with a sweet left foot, took to bowing in front of us whenever he got on the scoresheet. Other players developed their own gestures and dances for the one fan and his dog. A scrappy right-back called Bibou, I think, would slide-tackle his opponent and then turn and ask, "How did you like that, Mr Frank?" I would tell him that I'd liked it very much, unless I thought he'd crossed the line and would blow a fake whistle and show him a phantom card. It wasn't long before I'd worked out who would be in my theoretical 'Best Of' starting XI, and who would be on the bench. The nice thing about being a mere observer was knowing that I would never have to put any of the players through the disappointment of not being selected. Or who knew whether or not they would have been disappointed at all? Presumably, they had other things to worry about. Not that I ever found out. On the few occasions where I managed to chat to them on their way back to their accommodation, they were always in a hurry because they had German tuition classes that started at four on the dot. It wasn't the right time or place to start enquiring about where they'd come from and how they'd landed up in the corner of a park in a mid-sized central European city. The one time I tried to broach the subject with Mamadou, in a very general way, he just said, "I am focused on the future, Mr. Frank. We all are here. We have to be."

One day, about a month after I'd first started watching the refugees, another man came and stood next to me. He was in his 40s, short-haired but bearded, wearing jeans, a faded t-shirt advertising some beer or other, and a denim jacket that boasted several patches bigging up his loyalty to the city's main football club. I smiled and nodded to him and said hallo, but he wasn't in the mood for small-talk.

"Who the fuck are these people?" he wanted to know.

"Footballers," I said.

"Where the hell from?"

"All over the world."

The man snorted. "Or, more likely, from the north-west corner of the park, am I right?"

I said nothing, although later I wished that I had said something to put him down or at least challenge his naked hostility. He walked off in the direction of TSV and the next thing I knew, I saw him haranguing the groundsman, who'd just arrived for work and was unlocking his office in the clubhouse. Denim Man was gesturing in our direction, but the groundsman just shrugged. Presumably, he didn't give any more of a shit than anyone else that the cinder pitch was being used. There was no barrier to it, and no sign telling people to keep off. In fact, the players were helping to keep the weeds down.

Denim Man walked away, and I completely forgot about him. Around a week later, though, Sadie and I arrived at the pitch to find the refugee players sitting under a tree close to the pitch, in a distraught huddle. I walked up and asked them what was wrong. They pointed to Denim Man, standing in the middle of the pitch with his foot on a ball.

"What's he doing?" I asked.

"He says he has a permit from the city to play here," said Amadou. "He is allowed to use the pitch from two o'clock until four o'clock every afternoon."

I walked over to Denim Man. I was shaking as I crossed the unmarked sideline, dreading the confrontation and wondering what on earth I was going to say to him, and how he'd react. Even before I'd reached him, he called out, "Fuck off and stay out of it, gramps."

"What the hell are you playing at?"

Denim Man repeated my question, imitating me in the style of a moaning old bastard, then adding in a simpering voice, "Let the nice black boys play, then we can all live together in perfect harmony."

I took a deep breath. "I don't believe your permit is valid," I said.

"It absolutely is," he said. "But what the fuck's it got to do with you?"

"I'm coaching this team."

"Are you really?" Denim Man didn't believe my lie.

"Let me see the permit, or we will take to the pitch and play."

Denim Man gave me the permit, which looked genuine enough, but I started to wave it around in my right hand and shout, "You can't do this!" Sadie, of course, loves it when I wave things around in front of her nose, and she immediately snatched the permit out of my hand. "Hey!" roared Denim Man, making a grab for the document just as I let go of Sadie's leash. Sadie ran, and Denim Man — no athlete, despite having booked the entire pitch for himself — ran after her. The players were now on their feet, cheering on Sadie, who outran Denim Man with dancing and delight. I waved them back on to the field and their game resumed in an atmosphere of boyish glee. I waited until Sadie had properly soaked the document and destroyed it before I called her back to me and took it from her mouth. Denim Man walked towards us, but several of the players placed themselves between us.

"Ne touchez pas Monsieur Frank!"

Denim Man stopped and made gorilla noises and gestures. The players just laughed, waved at him dismissively, then turned around and got on with their game. Their adversary stormed off, but I felt uneasy for the rest of the afternoon, my hands shaking even as I praised Sadie for being such a good girl and fed her snacks from my coat pocket. I half expected him to come back with an angry mob, tooled up to the teeth.

The next morning, I called the city's Sports and Recreation Department, and was eventually put through to someone who dealt with pitch permits. I was told that the TSV cinder pitch had been booked every weekday afternoon between 2 and 4pm for the next six months.

"For what purpose?" I asked.

"A youth football development programme."

"There's no such thing. It's just one bloke who's trying to stop the others from playing on there. There's a group who plays there every afternoon, they've been there for months."

"They shouldn't have been playing there without a permit."

"For goodness sake, man, they're refugees with nothing to do all day because our government won't allow them to work. Do you think they know how to go about getting a fucking permit? This is just some arsehole who objects to the colour of their…"

The bureaucrat had hung up on me. And a week later, Denim Man was back with a motley crew of half a dozen pale mates, none of whom looked remotely like football players. They were mooching around in one of the goalmouths, kicking the ball to each other with the verve of reluctant school boys who'd rather have been in the library. Or playing hookie. Some of them were smoking. The goalkeeper defended his net with a cigarette in one hand and a beer in the other. The refugees watched in silence.

"Use the other half," I told them.

"He says he will call the police if we try to play."

"So? The police won't do anything."

"We can't risk that."

But some of the players had already started to make goals at either end of the touchline to make a half-field game. Denim Man ran over to tell us that he'd booked the entire field.

"You're only using one penalty area," I said.

"There's more of us coming."

"From your Youth Development Programme? Are they all in their 40s too and as shit as your mates here?"

"Gramps is getting a fucking mouth on him, isn't he?" But he didn't get too close to me. I wished that Sadie was the kind of dog that might instinctively growl at the Bad Guy, but she just stood wagging her tail, perhaps hoping he'd start to wave another permit around.

"Go play with your team," I said. "Maybe you'll get into the Aryan Over-40s League."

Denim Man showed me the finger and went back to his group and started to talk into his cell phone. After a few more minutes of slothful sport, some of his players sat down to rest. A couple drifted off, another went to the beer kiosk a couple of hundreds yards away and came back with more bottles. I nodded to Amadou that they should take over the whole pitch, and they did. Within 20 minutes, two police officers had arrived. Denim Man gestured at the game while talking heatedly to a young male and a young female cop, who looked dubiously at the pitch while not taking notes. I walked over and heard Denim Man refer to me as "an interfering old twat". The male cop then asked me what my connection was to the refugee players.

"I'm their trainer. I belong to TSV 62 — this is an initiative to integrate the refugee players into the club."

That untruth didn't seem to interest them. "He has a permit," the cop pointed out.

"For a Youth Development Programme, apparently," I said, and pointed to the renegades drinking beer behind the goal. There was spring sunshine to round off the happy picture. The cops were already in shirt sleeves. "This is just one shitty white man … "

"He has a permit," the cop interrupted. "There's nothing else we can do about it."

"This is absurd! These lads play here every day. They're great players, and they're not doing anyone any harm. What else are they supposed to do all day?"

"But they don't have a permit." He pointed at Sadie. "And dogs aren't allowed here either."

Denim Man let out a spiteful laugh at that, and I was about to lose it when I felt Amadou's arm on mine, pulling me back. "It's okay, Mr Frank, we will play on the grass today. The grass is good." He smiled at me. "Come on, the sun is out!"

"So, are we done here?" the female cop asked.

"Looks like it," I said. "Great job in enforcing the law, officers. Is that what you signed up for?"

"Can't bear to lose, can you Gramps?" goaded Denim Man, who was now enjoying himself. "Some coach you are." The two cops just turned and walked away. The refugee players were traipsing off towards the grass area, taking fallen tree branches with them to use as goals. Amadou continued to guide me away and to assure me that everything was going to be alright.

"This country is a disgrace," I spat.

"That's just how it works here, Mr. Frank. Don't fight it. We are here in peace. We can not get badly involved with people like that."

"Look at them!" I exclaimed, turning back towards Denim Man and his pathetic entourage. None of them were playing, but they'd left a ball on the penalty spot as a marker of their territory. "They're drinking beer at three in the afternoon, and they stop you from playing football!"

"That's because the world doesn't work like we want it to. You can either cry about it or get on with your life."

I didn't stay to watch them that day. I was too upset, and it just wasn't the same on the grass without proper goals, and peoples' dogs running on to the pitch, and toddlers followed by stressed mothers straying in to the action. Maybe, without a proper field, even one as knackered as the cinder pitch, I didn't feel like the trainer I wanted to be. Or some kind of guiding light. Or just a figure who was showing interest, not hostility. But was that for the good of my players, or just for my own conscience? Listen to me, they're not 'my players'. I just bought them a bloody ball, that's all. Maybe Denim Man's right. I should mind my own business.

The very next day, I was forced to take care of my own business anyway. I fell from a step-ladder while trying to kill a fly that had been annoying me all morning while I was reading the newspaper. Ilse found me when she came back from grocery shopping. "Oh, for goodness sake, what now?" A broken ankle, as it turned out, and a week in hospital, and then several weeks of rest at home, missing the perfect spring weather except when Ilse wheeled me outside to sit on the balcony. She had to walk Sadie too, but at least one good thing came out of it — she discovered that she actually loved the dog, and that daily exercise was a very good thing for her. "I can move again without pain!" she told me numerous times, as I sat there with my foot up, under strict medical orders not to risk further injury. "It's like I've got a whole new body!" Good for you, dear. She probably liked the time outside of the flat too, given that I was now at home all day. I cursed my own stupidity and vowed never to kill a fly again. And I probably wasn't even Sadie's favourite human anymore.

"There was a big hullabaloo outside that refugee centre of yours," Ilse announced one Saturday as she breezed in, having already raved about the beautiful weather, the blossoms and all the people out in the park.

"What kind of a hullabaloo? And it's not my refugee centre, what are you talking about?"

"Demonstrators, shouting that it needs to be closed down. And worse."

"Bloody hell. How many people were there?"

She came and sat down in the chair next to me. Sadie nuzzled her nose under my right hand, looking for affection.

"I didn't want to hang around there in case someone mistook me for one of the crowd. Kept my head down, as you do with these kind of people."

"I'd say you should do exactly the opposite."

"That's what you always say about anything I express an opinion on."

"Doesn't alter the act that I'm right. Did you pick up any useful details at all? Were there any cops there?"

"Five or six, looking bored, like this was nothing to do with them."

"Or that they'd rather be joining the demo."

"Don't talk like that, Frank. You're not a student now."

I sighed and the conversation just hung there until Ilse rose to her feet and announced that she was going to make coffee. She and Sadie had stopped off for cake. Did I want some?

It was only on the evening news that we got the full story. It was a demo organised by a "local group of concerned citizens", and it didn't surprise me at all to see Denim Man and some of his neanderthal chums at the forefront of the chanting. It's not safe for our kids to play in the park. Young mums have been threatened, teenage girls have been approached and propositioned. Blah fucking blah. But then the story took a different turn. Mamadou came out to talk to the reporters and explain that no one in the centre wanted any trouble, and that none of them had actually been in any trouble. He then turned, standing close to one of the police officers, invited the demonstrators to come inside the refugee centre for a cup of tea and to discuss any specific problems they had with any of the residents. That prompted Denim Man to start finger-pointing at Mamadou and ranting about who the park belonged to. Mamadou remained calm, smiled at the camera, and said he had done his best. It helped that he had obviously been diligent at his classes, because he now spoke an almost flawless German.

The spineless city council, though, bowed to the pressure and closed the place down. The residents were distributed to "other centres", probably the same places they'd come from in the first place. By the time I was fit to walk again, the place was deserted and boarded up. Two weeks later, it had been dismantled. Ilse and I were now walking Sadie together, and as we passed the place, I was very glad of her company. The cinder pitch, meanwhile, was once again unused. Thanks to the hot summer, the weeds had surged, making it almost unplayable. There was no sign of Denim Man and his Youth Development Programme. I no longer stopped at TSV 62, even when they waved at me. I somehow held them culpable for what had happened, and for showing no initiative to help the young players on their doorstep.

I contacted the City to try and find out where the refugees had been relocated to, but was told the information was confidential. "Why do you want to know?" came the reasonable question, and I'd no idea how to answer it. Why did I want to know?

Around a year later, though, Ilse and I had just come out of the cinema one evening when I heard a voice cry out, "Mr Frank!" We turned around to find Mamadou smiling at us, proudly clad in a policeman's uniform, patrolling through the city centre with another cop, who was already looking away with an expression of utter disinterest.

"My God, Mamadou — look at you!" I laughed, and introduced him to Ilse. Mamadou politely pronounced himself delighted to meet her. The other cop was standing sideways, like he was ready to move on already, and Mamadou should definitely be coming with him.

"How did you end up … " I gestured at the uniform. Mamadou patted the badge on his chest.

"They came for me!" he almost shouted. "They saw me on TV, and sent someone to talk to me. Said I would be a good mediator in disputes."

"Unlike me."

"Ha ha, yes, unlike you, Mr. Frank. You are too emotional, but that is no bad thing. Sometimes."

"And then they trained you up?"

"Yes!" He leaned forward and added, "Looks good for their diversity stats too," and we both laughed.

"You still playing football?"

"No time, Mr. Frank. I have to look after my family now. And I must be going, my colleague here and I have to patrol down by the river tonight. Always plenty to do there on a summer's evening."

"Yes, of course. But quickly, what happened to the others? Do you have any idea?"

"Oh, they went here and there," he answered, still smiling. "They are all fine, I'm sure." Then, before I could ask any more questions, he quickly added "Very good to see you again, Mr. Frank. And very nice to meet you too, Mrs. Frank." And finally he turned and re-joined his impatient colleague, who looked just the kind to report back that Officer Mamadou wasted too much time on patrol engaged in frivolous conversations with random members of the public.

"Well, what a thing," said Ilse. "So there you go, everything turned out well for them after all."

"For one person," I said.

"And his family. That's several more people than you knew about five minutes ago."

Ilse was right, as always, even as I fought the instinct to contradict her. Instead, I said we should be setting out for home. Sadie would be needing her walk.

The Throw-In

Thousands of fans are taking their mobile phones out of their pockets at the exact same moment. It can only be half-time, a quarter of an hour to be filled with quarter-baked analysis. I've got a text from Walker. "You've been on the telly, mate!!!!" Walker never uses one exclamation mark where four will do. One is just not enough to convey his excitement and surprise.

It's 0-0. Usually, I only hear from Walker when my team's losing. Today, his team is actually playing mine. For the sake of concealing my identity, let's call them City and United. Walker's for City, I'm for United. He's watching from his armchair, because he never actually goes to any games. This is a point of discussion on the few occasions we still meet, and a point on which I hold the moral upper hand. A very old point of discussion, as can happen between blokes of a certain age. We trawl through the ritual banter as a prelude to the rest of the evening. It's like when your mum wouldn't let you start your tea until you'd washed your hands and said grace. Get it out of the way before we order the first pints and start complaining about back ache and house prices. We know it's dull and irksome for the wives, who don't mind watching football, but hate to talk about it. Walker and I talk about it anyway, tapping the dreary barometer of normality.

It's no surprise that I've been on the telly. My season ticket is three rows back from the touchline. I always tell Jenny and the kids to look out for me, but they never see me. At least, that's what they say. I doubt they actually watch it, though they say that they will. Unless Jenny's being sarcastic, which she is, sometimes. I don't like it, and she knows it, which makes me think that sometimes she disguises it really, really well. My son Greg is eight and has no interest in football. Even I've now given up passing him a ball, indoors or outdoors, only to suffer the pain of watching it roll past him. He used to ignore it, now he looks at it with a combination of defiance and utter disdain.

Sally is five, and I have to admit she's my favourite. You shouldn't have favourite kids. It shouldn't feel like City v United when you're faced with your kids across the breakfast table. One chewing his toast and staring at his plate, sullen and detached and looking like he'd rather be somewhere else with a different family. The other perky and bright and funny and flicking Rice Krispies across the table into the goal you've made out of the salt and pepper pots and shouting, "Yeeeeeesssss!" Sally will always want to watch the game with me at home. She loves it. "Let's have popcorn!" Or pizza, or hot dogs. Though once the food's done, she tends to disappear. If I'm honest, the food's sometimes done before the build-up's over and she doesn't even wait for kick-off.

It's been a terrible game so far. United should be beating this City side, but we've created nothing, we just can't get going. Neither can City, it has to be said. It's been all blunder and thunder in the middle of the park. No one's been able to get hold of the game. Very frustrating. The fans have been taking it out on the team, which I know doesn't help much. Still, wages and all that. If you're getting 80 grand a week to control a football, then at least control the fucking thing.

Should I go to the bog? I don't really need to, but I'm always worried that I'll start to need a piss halfway through the second half. It used to be part of my half-time routine, back when a whole bunch of us (apart from Walker) used to go to the game together, and you'd been in the pub for three hours before kick-off. I'm the only one who still bothers. Some of them can't afford it anymore, some of them just can't be arsed with it taking up your whole day. I used to say they were being kept at home by their wives, but their wives eventually stopped finding this funny, if they ever did in the first place. Though I wasn't actually joking, I was pissed off at them for not wanting to come any more. "Missus keeping you locked up again, Frankie?" Ha ha, 15 years since you first made that crack, keep it up and you'll get a silver jubilee bants medal.

On the one hand, it's a relief not to have to join the crowd for the loos, despite 'the stadium facilities', as we now must call them, being much cleaner and spacier than they were back in the day when you usually got someone else's piss down your leg. Then you'd need to go again 20 minutes into the second half, but you'd hold it in until the end because you were scared of missing something. Now, though, I spend half-time just standing and staring at the pitch and waiting for the second half, or scrolling through my phone and sending messages. I text Frankie that it's been a lousy game so far, but I know he won't reply. He's probably at fucking Six Flags. Though to come think of it, that's probably cheaper and a lot more fun than the 45 minutes we've just watched here.

I also text Whacker that it's been a lousy game so far, but I know he won't reply either, he claims that he hasn't watched a game in years. I don't think he was ever interested to start with, he was just up for drinking and being a prat after six pints, and then he grew out of it.

So I text Jonesy that it's been a lousy game so far, but he's probably not even up yet. He lives in California. He sends me pictures of the spectacular fucking sundown at least once a week, but never mentions football. When there was an earthquake out there, I sent him a picture of a collapsed building and he didn't text me back for months.

Then I text Siffo that's been a lousy game so far, and Siffo texts back, "What game? It's Sunday, mate, give it a rest." Siffo quit when games stopped being scheduled for three o'clock on a Saturday afternoon. Well, he stopped going to United. Now he goes to the North-East Counties League or some bollocks. "Proper kick-off times." Yeah, but shite football.

Mind you, that's what I'm watching today.

I put my phone back in my pocket. Still ten minutes of half-time to endure. The stewards stare up at us, blank as fucking pigeons. Out on the pitch, they're giving out awards and merchandise to someone or other. Community this, community that. Like United really cares about that shit, Siffo would say. I look around me. I don't know any of these people, even though I see them every home game. Sometimes we share words about what's going on out there, usually when there's been a mistake by one of our lads, or the referee. Sometimes we high-five each other or hug after a goal, but who the fuck are we kidding? We're strangers. When there's no one playing football in front of us, it's like we're not allowed to communicate. Heads down, phones out, or we stare at the protest plane flying over the ground that's trailing a banner: GULF OWNERS OUT, GIVE US BACK OUR CLUB!

The phone vibrates in my pocket and I fish it back out. A response, at last. Except it's not a response, it's Walker again. "You're a star, mate! They keep showing you again and again!!!!" Followed by lots of emojis with tears of laughter coming from both eyes. I stare at the screen, because I feel like I should continue to ignore him, but I can see that he's already writing his next message.

"Blokes in the studio loving it!!!"

"They should put you out there, says Gaz Neville. You've put more energy into the first half than the rest of the players put together!!!!" LOL.

What the fuck are you on about? I text back.

"The throw-in!" he types.

What fucking throw-in? I text back.

"Exactly!" he writes. "A fucking throw-in!!!!"

I call home and it rings for ages, and no one picks up. I call Jenny's cell phone and it rings for ages, and I'm just about to give up when she picks it up and says, "Andy? You okay?"

"I'm fine."

"We're in the middle of a game. Can it wait?"

Hey, I'm in the middle of a game too. Obviously, a different game. No one at home's watching my game. City and United's game.

"I just got a text from Walker. He says they keep showing me on the TV. Can you turn it on?"

"Seriously?"

"Yes," I say, though not with any conviction.

"Don't you tape all the games anyway? You can watch it later." Clearly, she's not going to turn the telly on, not even to see her own husband on national TV.

"Never mind," I say and hang up. Jenny absolutely fucking hates it when I hang up in the middle of a conversation. She knows that I know how much she hates it, so there's going to be hell to pay later, but I'm pissed off. Not at her, really. I'm suddenly pissed off that the three of them are playing a game together. Pissed off at Greg, aged eight, who never wants to play games with me, his dad, aged 46.

"You're going viral, mate!!!!!" Walker again, of course, with a Twitter link. I click on the link, but it won't download because at half-time there's a drain on the network and I only have 3G. I stand there staring at my phone, watching the little circle going round and round as it fails to materialise into whatever it is that's making Walker's afternoon. Then I start getting more text messages, sending me the same link. "Wild game!" says one. "Love the passion!" says another. "Lino's ear just got burnt off!" quips a third. "YOU EFFING EFFER!" from Jonesy in California, who must have got up early after all. I try them all, but of course the links are all leading to the same place, so the download isn't happening. I need to get a better calling plan.

The thing is, I can't remember anything unusual happening in the first half. Whatever it is, it can't possibly be that hilarious. Just me jumping up or holding my head in my hands, or something. It wasn't like there was anything to get really worked up about, other than United's general uselessness.

Speaking of which, they're ready to start again. I turn my phone off completely, because it won't stop vibrating with incoming messages, and they're starting to make me feel uncomfortable. What if clients are watching and they recognise me? I'm in commercial real estate and I have a boss, Richard Merritt, who has no tolerance for people who mess around. His sense of humour is ground zero.

The second half is as catastrophic as the first. There are no goals until City take the lead in the 94th minute with a deflected shot. It's the goal this game deserved, if it was going to get a goal at all. Their fans are going nuts in the corner. There's a special kind of celebration for this kind of goal. There's an extra energy to the sound and the movement. It's like someone's poured acid into a pit of hyper-active vipers. I imagine all the text messages and GIFs from Walker that will be waiting for me when I turn my phone back on. If I ever turn my phone back on.

I can't face doing that any more than I can face going home and Jenny's showdown about me hanging up on her at half-time. And seeing Greg and knowing he doesn't give a fuck that United lost 1-0 and never will. And seeing Sally and having to act the happy, cheerful dad when inside of me it's Sunday afternoon and we lost, and tomorrow morning and the four mornings after that I have to go to work and meet my targets and be serious around Richard fucking Merritt all day fucking long.

Inevitably, I go to the pub.

I walk fast, driven by the desire to dip my sorrow in pints of cold yellow lager, and am one of the first to reach the bar of The Sailor's Pipe. It's a good mile from the stadium, but it's a proper football bar because it used to be the closest pub to the old ground. United fans only. As ever, Stan's behind the bar, as he has been for 30 years. He gives me a strange, knowing smile when I come in, but I avoid his eye and his conversation after I've put my order in. I'm preoccupied with the price of the beer, vaguely annoyed that a pint now costs more than admission used to at the old ground. Then there's the depressingly unchangeable result, now engraved in football history. And there's Jenny's waiting for me when I get home, reproaches at the ready. There is a solution to that at hand, however. I can drink all day so that by the time I get home I'm in no state to even have a row.

On telly, they've already moved on from the City-United debacle. Ours was the lunchtime kick-off, usurped by the next Big Game. Saturation Sunday. I watch it anyway as the bar fills up. Either of these teams will leapfrog United if they win today. The best result for us will be a goalless draw. So I'm standing in the pub on a Sunday afternoon, drinking alone and watching a game that I hope will end 0-0.

The pub starts to fill up with United fans aiming to neutralise their disappointment. I look up and down the bar and around at the tables, but I don't know anyone. I don't come in here that often now. Stan's the only person I could name. As it starts to get louder, I'm sure I hear him say, "At least Andy here had a good game." I think about all the messages waiting on my phone, but I resist taking a look, I'm busy watching Spurs v Everton, which is as shite as the game I just watched. By half-time (still 0-0), things have settled down, most of the fans are sitting at tables with their drinks, and I'm one of the few propping up the bar, staring at the game while barely taking it in. There's an ad break, and then there are highlights of City v United. Stan suddenly whacks up the volume so loud that the pub goes quiet and he shouts, gesturing at me, "Andy here's probably going to want to see this," and sure enough, just a few seconds later, there I am on the big screen and all the smaller screens hanging from the pub walls. The commentator is telling us with standard irony, " ... but in the 34th minute there was at least one fan who managed to inject the commitment this game was sorely lacking, when he sought to put the assistant referee right on a throw-in." And there it is, right in front of where I'm sitting after two players, United's Steve McBeal and City's Oleandro Alvarez, challenge for a ball that's deflected off McBeal and goes out of play. McBeal picks the ball up anyway, and Alvarez tries to wrestle it off him. Behind them, I'm jumping up and down, hell-bent on shouting and pointing out that it's our ball, not City's. The assistant referee points with his flag to indicate that it's indeed a City throw-in. No one else among the 20 or so spectators is reacting at all, it's just me. I'm first of all yelling at Alvarez, and now I'm thrusting my arm at the linesman and clearly shouting "You fucking fucker!" over and over again. A steward moves across in anticipation of me jumping over the barrier to take matters further, but there's no danger of that. My season ticket seat is my preacher's zone. From there, I have free rein to vent my views.

The pub is in uproar. This has rescued their afternoon. On TV, they're now showing a slow-motion replay of the ball clearly being deflected off Steve McBeal. Clearly a throw-in for City. One hundred per cent beyond any doubt. I'm arguing the case for something that hasn't happened, in front of millions of viewers around the world. A throw-in. I honestly look like I'm ready to physically attack either Oleandro Alvarez or the blameless assistant referee. I'm shown jumping up and down in slow motion, and the commentator now observes that I'm channelling all the frustration of United's fans this afternoon. The highlights finally move on and Stan turns the volume back down as they go straight to City's late winner. And complete strangers are coming up to me, laughing and offering to buy me a pint.

I make the most of the free drinks, because things will only go downhill from here. There will not be another group of people with this percentage of approval. Although even here some twat comes up to me and says, "You're exactly what's wrong with football today." Skinny bastard with no scarf, no United shirt, probably not even a United fan. I say to him, "I've got a mate who'd probably agree with you." He then grins and shows me a tweet from the official United account saying they will be launching an investigation into the fan's identity and looking to review his season ticket status. Lots of fans tweet that, after today's performance, they'd be willing to take the rap and give up their season ticket in my place. Though as far as I'm concerned, they can have the fucking thing. No refund necessary. Stick a tailor's dummy in my place. It'd make as much noise as most of the blokes sitting around me.

In truth, I can't remember the incident. I can't remember the throw-in. I can't remember screaming at Oleandro Alvarez or the assistant referee, now being touted as a 'victim' with an identity, Mr. Graham Peterson of Barrow-in-Furness. And I was stone cold sober. And this makes me think that my outburst was no isolated incident, it just happened to be the one caught on camera. That it's not unusual for me to be acting like this. No wonder no one wants to talk to me at half-time.

By late afternoon, the pub's emptying out and the next game's over. Spurs and Everton finished 0-0. Now it's Villa v Southampton, and not a soul is paying any attention except for me. There are no more free pints. I finally fish my phone out of my pocket and turn it back on. 419 text messages. I scrawl through for the important ones. Just the one from Jenny. 'What the hell is going on? The phone won't stop ringing. Come home.' Just the one from Richard Merritt. 'This is not the sort of image that is good for our business. We need to talk first thing tomorrow morning.' Seventy-three messages from Walker. I can see the last one, which says, 'You're awfully quiet today, mate. Or are you still yelling at that lino?'

I walk slowly towards home, about a mile and a half away. It's a mild early spring evening, the clocks have just changed, and thanks to the new traffic-calming bollards they've put up (against much local protest — including mine), there are actually some young lads out on the street kicking a ball about. I half expect them to recognise me and start pointing and laughing or to film me with their cell phones, but they're too preoccupied with their game to notice a drunk, middle-aged man shuffling by. I stop in Mawsley Park for half an hour and snooze on a bench. When I wake up, I look at my phone and see that Jenny's tried to call me half a dozen times, and sent messages in block capitals. "ARE YOU OKAY?!? COME HOME! Sally's worried about you." Only Sally, not Jenny or Greg. Unless she's channelling her worry via our daughter.

When I finally walk in, though, it doesn't look like anyone's worried at all. Jenny's sister Marcia is over, and they're both well into their second bottle of white wine. Marcia has never held me in very high regard, and the feeling's mutual. She's like a negative mirror of Jenny. She makes comments, often out of Jenny's earshot about my job, hinting that I'm faking it. That a lot of people only make money by chance, not through talent or intelligence. "People make their own luck," I shoot back, but then she plays the innocent, asking, "Blimey, Andy, what makes you think I was talking about you?" I don't even really know what she does, apart from go out with men you never meet more than once. Head of admin at the council, or something. I don't care.

The two of them are giggly, almost flirtatious.

"Here's the man!" says Marcia from the sofa. "Who'd have thought a balding bloke in his 40s who walks like a duck would be the highlight of a Premier League game?"

"Have we secured copyright?" Jenny wants to know. "You're already the star of a hundred thousand memes."

"What's a meme?"

They both laugh. Jenny looks at her sister and screams, "See, I told you he wouldn't know."

"Well, Andy, you don't need to know any more. You are one now. If you want to know what a meme is, just look in the mirror."

"Or online. Hashtag angryfan, if you're searching."

I sink into the sofa next to Marcia. Jenny's in the armchair opposite me, shaking her head with a knowing smile.

No matter what I've thought or said about Marcia in the past, all of a sudden I want her to hold me, or at least to put a comforting arm around my neck. And then I want Jenny to come over and tell me that everything's going to be fine.

"So tell us, Andy," says Marcia. "Was it a throw-in to United or City?" And both of them are hollering with laughter all over again. I manage to get back up.

"Where are the kids?"

"Greg's upstairs in his room. Sally's playing with her dolls out in the back garden."

"I thought she was worried about me."

"She was, until I showed her that you'd read my message and told her you were probably down the pub."

"Explaining to everyone why that linesman got it wrong," says Marcia.

I walk out the living room and out through the kitchen. Through the glass patio door, I see Sally sitting on the concrete with the doll's family all eating dinner at a plastic stool that's standing in as a dinner table. I slide open the patio door, but she doesn't look up, even when I say her name. She's talking to herself, doing all the voices.

I walk over and squat down next to her.

"How's the Whallydock family today?" I ask. The Whallydocks is her made-up name. I've no idea where she got it from.

"They're fine," she says. "Though Petula broke her arm playing rugby and had to go to hospital. Now she's back home and everyone's having dinner."

"Poor Petula," I say, but Sally says nothing, she's busy laying out the dinner things, tiny plastic forks and knives. I watch her meticulous preparations in silence. When she's done, she sighs, and contemplates the finished table. Finally, she looks up at me for the first time since I walked out to join her.

"Daddy," she wants to know. "Why were you so angry at that man on television?"

"I thought he'd made a wrong decision," I reply.

"Why?" It's her favourite question right now.

"No reason. It turns out that I made a mistake."

"Did you say sorry to him?"

"No," I say. "I didn't."

"Hmmm," she says, thinking, probably trying to dredge up some incident where I've made her apologise for something, and given her a lecture about it to boot. But then she's looking up with a big smile and waving at Greg's bedroom window. I turn around and see him standing there, just staring down at us. I wave too, but there's no reaction. Then he takes a step back out of view.

"Greg's weird," says Sally.

"Maybe," I say. "Hey, should we get takeout?"

"Yes! Pizza!" Sally shouts. "Is there a game on?"

"No," I say. "Just pizza tonight. The game's already finished."

The Winner

South Shields 2 Matlock Town 3
(FA Trophy 1969-70, First Round)

"There he is." June knows when to look out for Jason, round about 9.30am. Just as she's washing up the breakfast dishes, giving her a prime view through the kitchen window. Those three words are as predictable as his appearance at our garden gate. I don't mind, though. By the time you reach your 70s, you love the security of routine. The thought of sitting here in the morning with my newspaper and June not being there to say "There he is" tears at me a little, somewhere in one of those tender, vulnerable organs that keep me alive, second by second. Deteriorating a tiny bit more with each passing day, with every chugging heartbeat, with just one more glass of wine. What harm can it do now after the thousands that have gone before?

Jason always stands and looks at the house for a long time. He seems to be staring at the front door and the house name

79

(The Causeway), as though assuring himself he's found the right place. He doesn't look at June, who doesn't move from her position at the sink, looking out at Jason and the street. It was her choice to buy this place when we retired, because she liked being able to see what was going on in the street from the kitchen window. In every other place we thought about buying, the kitchen looked out over the back garden. "What am I going to look at from there?" she asked our frustrated estate agent, a red-faced young man who was way too pushy for our taste. "The bloody grass growing?"

Jason is one year older than me. He's stooped now, but he was always the smaller one, the nippy one. The Pocket Warrior, our manager Jack Croft used to call him. Hard in the tackle, but damned skilful too, a great little dribbler. We shored up the central midfield for Matlock Town for over a decade. I cleaned up in front of the back four and then got rid. Jason won the ball wherever he was, usually further upfield, and then he'd create something for the fans to admire. He could pass, he could cross, he could shoot. There was always talk about "interest" from Stockport, Bury and Crewe, and any other number of third and fourth division clubs. If you asked him about it, he'd just smile. "I'm happy here," he'd say, and then he'd wink at you, like there was something much bigger going on. But it never came to owt, and I never asked him why.

People would talk about our partnership. If they mentioned Jason Tetley, they'd mention Ty Adcock as well. Then they'd talk about Jason Tetley at great length, because who wants to talk about industry, fitness, hard work and reliability? Never mind that I was always there, covering for Jason and everyone else, even our own defenders. Never mind that I never missed training, never missed a game, never came down with illness and injury. Never mind that I won everything in the air and on the ground, mostly without tapping any ankles. Referees knew me well, and they knew I played hard, but that I nearly always got the ball. If I didn't, I'd say sorry and help the man back up on his feet. I didn't play to hurt people. I wanted the ball, not a piece of someone's leg.

Jason scored 20 goals a season, at least. I'd get maybe one or two. Some years, none at all. There was a running joke about my long-range efforts, and which part of the ground or the town they'd end up in. Sometimes you could hear a low "Nooooooo" coming from the crowd if I shaped up for a shot from outside the area. That was enough to make me pause, put my foot on the ball, and make a short pass instead, which might be greeted with ironic cheers. If I did happen to score, Jack Croft would say, "That's your quota for the season, Ty. Don't bloody shoot again." The changing room laughed, and I laughed too, although I knew he was serious.

Except for that day at South Shields.

Jason undoes the latch on the gate and walks slowly up to the front door. He stands and peers at the wooden Causeway sign, as though it contains text of historical interest. *This is the house where former Matlock Town FC central midfielder Ty Adcock lives. If anyone had been paying attention back then, he would hold the club record for most consecutive appearances in all competitions. A one-club player, not like those fly-by-night no-names you get today.* I don't actually know how he found us here, so many years after we'd stopped playing together. I knew he was still in town, that he still ran his business, and that he retired and passed it on to his twin sons. Tetleys Lumber. If I'd ever needed lumber, maybe I'd have gone by. But I never did. I'm not much better with my hands than I was with my feet.

You'd never see Jason down the club at home games, or at team reunions. He quit the game with a knackered knee at 31 and never came back. I played on for another decade until suddenly everyone was too damned fast. Jack Croft came round to the old house one summer. "You don't have to say owt, Jack," I told him. "I'm done." They did me a nice testimonial against Blackburn. Maybe I should have split the gate with Jason.

"Shall I let him in?" June asks, but she's already on her way to the hall. I listen as she opens up and I hear Jason say, "Sorry to disturb you, but is this where Ty Adcock lives?"

"Yes, it is," says June with a patience I've been in awe of for half a century. "Would you like to come in?"

"If it's no trouble," Jason says. "We used to play for Town together, you see. I've not seen him in donkeys years!"

"Well come on in, then," June says, as friendly as you like. "He's in the kitchen. Would you like a cup of tea or coffee?" Though June knows the answer to that already.

"Tetleys, like my name," says Jason, and breaks into a croaky laugh. As they come into the kitchen I stand up and say, "I don't believe it! Jason Tetley! How long's it been?" I'm not as sincere as June, but I've been watching her and learning. I give him a solid handshake. He smiles and looks me in the eye, then he sits down at the kitchen table and tells us how he ran a lumber business for 40 years, but passed it on to his sons. "You can't go on forever," he'll say. Then he looks at June and gives her an unwieldy wink. "As the actress said to the bishop." Then that laugh again, like the joke made any kind of sense. June turns away and busies herself with the teapot. Since Jason started coming around a few months ago, we've taken to randomly dropping that sentence in to conversations when it's just the two of us. Then we laugh, and then we feel guilty.

Once Jason's got his mug of tea, he'll ask me what I've been up to all these years. I tell him that I stayed at County Hall in town planning all my career before I took retirement the day after my 65th birthday. He just nods at that, as though he doesn't really know what I'm talking about. I ask him if he ever goes to watch Town at all, but I know he doesn't. "Sometimes," he says vaguely. "Can't really be bothered, though. Not with the way they play the game these days." He doesn't elaborate on that. Instead he turns to June and tells her again that we used to play together. He sits up in his chair and straightens out his stoop. His voice becomes a notch louder and is now boosted by the certainty of known facts.

"He'd win the ball, and then I'd do summat with it!" he tells her in delight. There's no denying the truth of that. "He was a good player, your man. Never saw a challenge he didn't like the look of." It never seems to occur to him that June came to all the home games and many of the away ones too. Through three pregnancies, shlepping the kids along too, although only my eldest, Jimmy, had any interest, and even he wasn't much good.

"Really?" says June. "Hard to imagine now, isn't it?"

"Well, he's still a big bastard, isn't he?" says Jason, then he laughs the laugh again. "Big and ugly! That's what the fans loved about him."

"Oh, I thought he was quite the handsome one," says June. "Still do!" And she gives a false laugh and pats Jason on the arm, and then she's had enough. She takes her cup of tea and the morning paper, and I watch with some envy as she leaves the room. "I'll be out back if you need me," she says, but Jason barely notices that she's gone. He's too busy tapping the table and saying, eyes suddenly wide like dinner plates, "Ty, do you remember that bloody game at South Shields?"

The first few times he brought it up, I'd say, "Bloody right I do!" Then I got tired of saying the same thing. Now I usually say, "South Shields? Which game was that then? There were so many."

"FA Trophy, first round," he says. "Season 1969-70. We'd already hammered Darwen in the qualifying round. 5-1. I bagged a brace. Remember? Anyway, we go up to South Shields and we just can't get into the game. They're 2-0 up and we don't even look like scoring, all afternoon. Filthy afternoon as well. Not my kind of game at all. Thick mud, black clouds, defenders kicking me up in the air, an airy-fairy ref who kept saying, 'Play on, gentleman' in this bloody sing-song accent. Until Harry Hart does a perfect imitation of him and gets ordered off. Do you remember?"

"That rings a bell," I might say. Or, "Harry Hart, he was the one that went on to be a comedian, wasn't he? Collapsed on stage with a stroke at the Derby Pavilion back in the '90s." That's too much extra detail for Jason, though. He just wants to get back to the match of the day.

"So there we are, down to ten men, losing 2-0 away from home, pissing down with rain, and not a sniff of a goal all afternoon. We couldn't have complained if the ref had blown up early and said, 'Contest over, gentleman.' We'd probably have been glad just to get under the hot shower and head south five minutes early. And then, you must remember what happened next, don't you?"

"My 35-yarder," I say, and even though it's the same story every day, I can't help but smile.

"That's right!" says Jason, and he lets out his throat-wrenching laugh again. "You, of all people! We all thought it was a fluke. That you just belted the ball out of frustration. And where did it end up? Billowing the back of the South Shields net! There was even applause from the home fans. You still got that back then for good play. Plus, they must have still thought they were safe. Five minutes left, and a goal up against a team that had done nowt since three o'clock."

"Do you remember how we all just turned around and went back to the halfway line?" I say. I feel slightly embarrassed that every single morning I get into the story almost as much as Jason.

"Ey, I reckon the most we celebrated was me tapping you on the hand," says Jason.

I don't remember that part, but I do remember what he said to me as South Shields lingered over the restart. "Got to happen once in a lifetime, eh?"

Some days I mention this, some days I don't. Today, I let it go.

"And then, it was like the whole team was possessed. All of a sudden, there's just one bloody goal in it. And we go all in. Throw it all up front. They could have killed us on the break, but they couldn't shift it up there. We were like a bunch of jack-rabbits, snapping and yapping, and it was like the mud and the rain had gone and we'd just discovered it was the first day of spring! And then … " He looks at me and smiles, making a gesture to me to take up the story, as though we're sitting on front of a room full of Matlock Town fans come for a history evening.

"And then," I say. "I score again." Jason laughs at this point like it's the funniest joke he's heard during his entire life.

"You!" he chokes. "Who could barely hit the target twice a season, scores a brace inside two minutes. Another lovely goal, if I remember right. Didn't quite have the Oof! factor of the first, but I remember getting the ball out wide on the right, playing a 1-2 with Donny Ruddock. Nice player, Donny. He just nudged it back to me, subtle as you like. He had the measure of the mud. Perfect weight, like a supermodel pass." He chuckles again. "And then I see you, of all people, standing in space just outside the D. And I'm thinking, 'Oh bloody hell, not Ty, he'll never put another one away', but then I thought, 'Oh, you never know.' I mean, you had just scored one of the greatest goals any of us had ever seen." He's leaning forward now, looking directly into my eyes, keen as a fan, really wanting me to believe that he was going through this whole thought process in the half second it took him to receive the pass from Donny Ruddock and then side-foot the ball to me just seven or eight yards square.

"And what do you go and do? You sweep it into the far bottom corner. First touch. Not to brag or owt, but I did place it to sit up nicely for you. Just right. About the only bloody thing I'd done right all afternoon. But you got it on the sweet spot, Ty. And I was thinking, 'That's gone right where it deserves to go. That's the right and natural end to that move. My 1-2 with Donny, my pass to you rolling through the puddle with just the right power, and your finish in one move. I can still see your leg, the follow through. And this time, we did celebrate a bit. We were thinking we'd have them back at our place on Tuesday night."

Jason Tetley sits back and takes a rest at this point, shaking his head, smiling like a quarter moon. He drinks some tea. Then he looks over his shoulder out of the kitchen door and says, "Does your missus not want to hear this?"

"She's heard it all before," I say.

"Worth hearing again," he replies. "Especially the bit that happens next, right?"

"Just a shame we didn't have cameras in non-league grounds back then," I say, diverting the subject.

"Who needs cameras when you've got memories?" Jason wants to know, as he does every day. "Besides, there was that photographer from their local paper who picked it up. A bit grainy, given the weather, but somehow that seemed right. That's how it was, eh?"

"It was," I agree. "A grainy day."

"The 90th minute. No injury time back in those days. No one fannied about wasting time and taking the ball down to the corner flag, adjusting their socks, rolling the ball backwards and forwards when they're about to take a free-kick. Wiping the bloody ball on your shirt before a throw-in. None of that shite. Who thought of all that? Who was the first person to try all that crap out, and then everyone else copied it, and no referee or anyone at the FA did a bloody thing about it?"

This is Jason's daily digression. It's not always about exactly this issue, but it will be along the lines of how much more honest football was back in the day, and how he can't understand why it ever needed to change. Like what the game needs more than anything are cold showers, cramped dressing rooms with no heat, bogs for pitches, and ten-pound notes stuffed inside your football boots. Referees who were gentlemen — schoolteachers and policemen who knew how to keep a game in check. Players without shin-guards.

That was Jason, through and through. He loved to play with his socks around his ankles.

"I think we'd had a half-chance off a corner, a header that went well over the bar. Remember, Ty, we're playing away from home with ten men and we're absolutely kings of that field, like there's been some kind of takeover. We should have been knackered, dead and buried, but thanks to your goals we were suddenly moving like Brazil. And there's Donny on the ball again, this time he's out on the right. Didn't he go on to play for Chesterfield? Or was it Doncaster? Or am I just confusing Donny with Donny?" A chuckle. "Anyway, he's toying with their left-back, like we have all the time in the world to be dicking about with it. Which we did. We could go home now with the draw and no one would have complained if Donny had just put his foot on the ball and waited for the final whistle. But he didn't, did he? He slides this cross into the middle and I see their keeper going for it. There were a few of us just lurking in hope around the penalty spot, and they've got a lot of bodies in there now too, trying to protect the draw. But I could see I had a chance, that if their keeper makes a mistake, there's going to be a free ball right in front of goal, just for a second. And so Donny puts in the cross, it's low and hard, and their keeper dives for it, and he does get it, but it squirts out from under his body and up into the air, still going at pace, but his body puts just enough of a stop on it to let me throw myself in there and head it into the back of the net at full stretch, sprawled in the glorious mud, and then I feel you all piling on top of me!"

I'm watching Jason and trying to fake a smile. We've been through both of my goals in great detail, so why not his?

Because he doesn't mention that I was standing there, about to finish off Donny's cross with a simple tap-in when he flung himself in the way and took all the glory almost literally off my right toe.

"Knowing you, you'd have put it over the top anyway," Jack Croft said to me on the coach. He thought I'd think that was funny.

After all, I'd played a massive part in a famous victory. We had two crates of brown ale to see us home, and we were in the last 16 of the FA Trophy. That could mean a good home gate if we got the right draw. "I mean, you'd scored two already, Ty, and that's you done now for a good five years." Ha ha ha, how we all laughed.

I'd never come close to scoring a hat-trick in my life, though. I'd definitely never come close to scoring a hat-trick in five minutes to turn a 2-0 defeat into a 3-2 win in a cup tie, away at South Shields on a filthy winter's afternoon. I never came close to scoring a hat-trick again. Not even a brace. After this improbable, glorious blip, my scoring record went on as before.

One thing I did know for sure. I was going to take June off Jason.

June and Jason. A nice-sounding name for a couple. Married already when Jason started to play for us in his early 20s, not having made the grade at Mansfield Town. No one could understand why. He was better than most of us put together. But he seemed cheerful enough at Matlock, dominating games, training two or three times a week. He'd skip training a lot, though. "I just want to play," he told me once. "Training bores the pants off me. Who wants to do bloody shuttle runs?"

And he liked to play on Saturday night too, in the club bar. Despite his size, he'd attract a crowd. He'd drink and talk and laugh a lot, and then he'd break into song. He'd always be in a circle of lads. And his wife, June, would always be with the players' wives or their cast of revolving girlfriends, standing to one side, some of them talking, some of them looking as bored as Jason did at training. June was in that group, like she'd rather be anywhere else on the planet. And one time when I caught her eye, she caught it back and held it so long that it was me who ended up looking away. When I looked back up at her again, she was smiling into her Martini.

June had short black hair, and she was almost the same height as Jason. She wasn't the girl to stand out, even in a crowd of Matlock

Town FC's players' wives and girlfriends. But she had something, I felt, and that something was what came across when I saw that smile. She knew. I knew. And a couple of Saturdays later, when Jason was being particularly loud and boisterous, I slipped a note into her hand as I picked up my jacket and left.

The note said, The Sycamore Inn.

I waited at the Sycamore Inn for two hours. It was just before nine when she walked in. She came up to me and said, "I've just put Jason to bed. What have you done with your girlfriend?"

"Finished with her a fortnight ago," I said. "About an hour after I saw your smile."

She laughed and said, "You bloody liar."

That was probably four months before the South Shields game. In the meantime, I hadn't wanted to admit that I was in love with June. It was too messy. We talked again and again about what to do. I told her that I felt guilty every time I took a pass off her husband. She told me that she felt guilty every time she watched a game and wanted me to play better than him.

"Not much chance of that, I'm afraid."

"Well, you're better than him at some things. At least you're never drunk."

Matlock's small, though, and we knew we couldn't get away with it for long. We were constantly breaking it off, then rushing to get back together again. Snogging in car parks like teenagers. Snatching lunch breaks in the woods. Hurrying when we wanted to be taking our time. Laughing about the close shaves we had, like when she grabbed me in the corridor at the club between the bar and the toilets, and then Jason came merrily whistling out of the men's, and when he saw me and June, now with our hands to ourselves, he shouted, "Hands off my missus, Ty!" And I said something laddish back to him, along the lines of how he was the one that scored all the goals, and June refused to come near me for three weeks.

"What did I say that was wrong?"

"You could have told him right there," she said.

"So could you," I said, though neither of us knew if that was what we wanted.

And then, Jason took the winner off me at South Shields. He was all over the headlines. That picture from the photographer behind the goal is still enlarged and framed in the bar at the club. It was on the front cover of the club's official history. The blurred ball coming off his head, Jason flying through the air. And there, right behind him, is me. Except in the shot you can only see my legs and my crotch.

I don't know if I decided on the coach home that I was going to make it serious with June, or if I made that decision standing right there, in the second that photograph was taken, watching this blizzard of pocket dynamite propelling himself towards a ball that was rightfully mine.

Maybe Jack Croft was right. Maybe I would have fucked it up. Missed it completely. Blazed it over the bar. Skewed it wide. But when the cross was coming over, and especially when it bounced up from under the keeper's body, I was already telling myself, 'This one's mine. I've got this. Today's my day, it was meant to be. My five minutes of fame in front of 450 spectators at South Shields in the second round of the FA Trophy.'

"What's changed?" June wanted to know.

"I have," I said. "I've woken up. You two aren't right together. He barely cares that you exist. I barely care about anything else." I didn't mention the missed hat-trick.

"How can I believe you?" she said, but she was looking into my eyes the way she had done that first time in the bar.

When she moved in a few weeks later, Jason walked into the changing room before a home game against Heaton Welfare and stood right in front of me. The place went quiet. We faced off, but it was odd. It wasn't like he wanted to hit me.

"Just so's you and everyone else here knows," he said. "We're still team-mates. But we're not mates."

I nodded, resisting the temptation to say, "We never were", and he turned around and found a spot on another bench to get changed. The murmurs gathered pace back into normal conversation, and it was never mentioned again. Jason stayed the life and soul of the after-match party, more so than before. He'd get drunk and tell everyone that I'd done him a favour. There was a string of girlfriends, but they all got tired of never being the centre of his attention, and Jason never settled down. June and I avoided the place at all costs, and the only time I socialised with the team was at the annual club dinner. We preferred to drive out of town for a meal at a country pub. Or we'd get on the train to Liverpool to see her parents and stay away for the night.

Then we played together for nearly a decade until he was forced to retire. Yin and yan. The slogger and the dancer. The work horse and the nimble foal. The water carrier and the poet. Of course he was the player that the fans came to see. But without my industry, he'd never have had the freedom of the field.

We sit in silence, our tea mugs long since drained. It's mid-morning by now. Every day, I think about telling Jason that I was standing right there on the edge of the six-yard box, ready to finish off Donny's cross. And every day I stop myself. What would be the point after all this time? He probably knew it anyway. Maybe this was why he came around here every day. Maybe he didn't have dementia at all, he just loved to go through that afternoon, time and again.

If that was the case, I could invite him just to put a note through the door every day saying, "Remember my winning goal at South Shields?"

"Well," I say, "it's been great to see you again after all this time, Jason." Then I stand up, and then he stands up. He looks suddenly disoriented, as though he doesn't know where he is, or who I am.

"I've got things to be getting on with," I lie, and he seems to understand, because his face clears and he says, "Oh, of course. I've kept you long enough, Ty." Then I walk him to the door.

"Come by any time," I say, and he walks down the path, no longer with the same speed he once had, but there's still a hint of the old feint and dance. He opens and closes the garden gate and I watch him walk down the street, back the way he came. Not once does he look back.

"Do you think he remembers?" June says. Today she's come to stand next to me as he makes his way back to wherever he's come from.

"That he stole my goal?"

June splutters. "No, you silly bastard. That he used to be married to me."

"That's so long ago that even I've forgotten," I say. She slaps me on the shoulder, and we go back inside.

As I clear up the tea things, she's still got Jason on her mind. "I know he says the same thing every day," she says, "but I like him much more now than I did half a century ago."

She's expecting a response to this, but I can't get anything over the top of my tongue. I'm too caught up in the thought that without Jason's diving header, there might have been no golden wedding anniversary last year. None of our wonderful three kids, and eight grandkids. In short, all the happiness in the world that anyone could possibly ask for.

Except that I never got to score a bloody hat-trick.

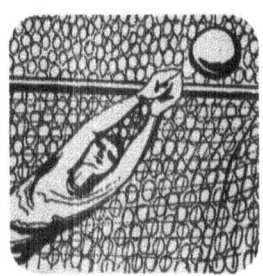

Fritz Cullen vs Chutzpah Fried Chicken

When we lured Fritz Cullen from the BBC, I was probably more excited than anyone else at Spark FM. Cullen, of course, was the cult commentator with the clipped, clever turn of phrase that he delivered off the top of his head at just the right moment. "A remarkable night under a glorious light!" That kind of thing. I can't remember any of them right at this second. They don't sound so good on their own, typed out on cold white paper. But I remember hunching over my hand-me-down portable plastic wireless as a kid, listening to his European Cup commentaries and feeling like the floodlights of Rome, Madrid and Munich were shining out of my tiny, tinny speaker. So far away across the elusive continental night, but so close to my callow, receptive ear.

And now, I was going to be his boss.

"I'm ready for a new challenge," Cullen announced to the public, and everyone knew that was bollocks. Just like when a player moves abroad. It's not the pasta, the opera and the Italian language that's the lure, it's that super-sized salary. We were an upstart commercial station backed by an American parent company, and were buying up rights and making our name in as many households as tired old Auntie. We aimed to exploit the BBC's complacency, and Fritz was our statement signing. You could tell they never believed he'd leave, because he'd been there for 30 years. Compared with his junior colleagues, he was earning very good money. With us, he could earn fantastic money. There's no way to say no when your salary's doubled for doing the exact same job.

There was a slight problem, however. For the first year of Cullen's contract, we only had rights to the League Cup and friendly internationals. Basically, he had the year off, aside from Tuesday nights that would start off in Peterborough and Shrewsbury and, even when they moved to Old Trafford and Stamford Bridge, no one was going to be overly thrilled. The League Cup seemed to survive only because no one had the guts to abolish it. England's sole inked-in friendly wasn't that exciting either — away to Lichtenstein, in order to prepare for meeting Luxembourg in their Euro qualification group. And Fritz wasn't the kind of commentator who'd try to talk up a lame game.

We'd handily outbid competitors for a tranche of Premier League and European games, but that contract didn't kick in until the following season. Fritz wanted to stay put at the Beeb for another year, but neither we nor they were keen on that plan. They were too indignant at his betrayal, while we needed to bed him in and get him accustomed to a different kind of organisation. He was no longer broadcasting to the public, he was commentating to customers. And although I wasn't in on the negotiations with Fritz and his agent, I always assumed that the terms of his task had been made very clear, and that he was fully on board with his new brief.

The problem started with his very first game, which he tried to get out of on the grounds that he wasn't yet ready to make the step across from the World Cup, where he'd just commentated on the final, to the first round of the League Cup three weeks later. Plymouth Argyle versus Bristol Rovers. "I've just come off my holiday," he reasoned. "I'm not prepared. Is there not a junior commentator who could step up?" I pointed out that we'd been running ad spots for the past fortnight trailing it as his debut. "At Plymouth," he said, with the voice of a man about to be hanged. I compared it to Pelé making his debut for the New York Cosmos in a friendly match on a bumpy baseball pitch. Perhaps that flattered him, and so he condescended to make the journey down to the south coast, even though — according to the terms of his fat new contract — he had no choice. This was a relief, while at the same time an outrage that he was even questioning it, given the salary he was pulling in return. He was earning more in a month than I got for a whole year, and that for just a couple of nights' work.

Still, I'd just turned 30 and was newly promoted to head of sports, so I remained in awe of his star power. And even if a hero of my childhood was already turning out to be a bit of a diva, I couldn't quibble on the night when he delivered a thoroughly professional first 45 minutes. He made Plymouth versus Bristol Rovers sound like it really mattered. Which, to fans of both teams, it really did. He'd done his homework on all the players. And listening from our London studio, a creeping sense of pride overcame me that we had delivered on our pre-season promises to up the game, to up our coverage, and spread the name of Spark FM.

There was just one sticking point. Fritz didn't mention the sponsors.

I didn't even notice until the half-hour mark and a text game through from Sarah Klein, the junior production assistant I'd sent down to Plymouth to be Cullen's gopher. "He's not doing Chutzpah!" For the second time, she wrote, the commentator had either forgotten or not bothered to make the pre-arranged announcement every quarter of an hour that "Plymouth Argyle versus Bristol Rovers is brought to you by Chutzpah Fried Chicken, five-star fast food in a batter that beggars belief!"

"Write him a note!" I texted.

"I did!"

"Did he read it?"

"He just shoved it to one side. Looked furious. I put it on top of his player notes."

I said I'd talk to him at half-time, but at half-time, Fritz Cullen wasn't picking up his phone. He did send me a curt message, though. "I don't talk during the interval. My voice needs recovery time as I prepare for the second half. Please respect my space."

"Please don't forget to mention the sponsors, as briefed," I texted him back. There was no further response. The message was tagged as 'unread'.

I called Sarah. "You need to mention it to him again."

"He won't even look at me! I'm just running around after him. If I try and talk to him, he holds up a hand and makes like he's listening to something else through his earpiece."

"Keep trying!" I almost shouted, then hung up. I was ignoring calls now too. Millie Shawaz from our commercial division. Trent Warren, head of marketing at Chutzpah Fried Chicken. Then a text from Millie. "What the fucking fuck is going on? Why no Chutzpah? They're fucking furious and they're calling me in the middle of dinner and yelling, and I have absolutely no idea what to tell them. Talk to them and DEAL WITH IT NOW!"

I called Trent at Chutzpah, and he was indeed a livid man. I said that my assistant was dealing with the situation now down at Home Park, and I assured him that we would be running the messages during the second half. There appeared to have been a misunderstanding with Fritz about his new role, but whatever happened in the second half, we would recompense Chutzpah in any way they wanted.

"Fucking right you will," said Trent. "I've got my boss going loopy on the line. We're like you, mate, we're expanding, we're hustling the market, and this was supposed to be our big fucking launch night. *Your product in the mouth of a legend.* Remember that's how you sold it to us?" Then he hung up.

Ignoring a call from Spark FM's president and MD, Sir Harry Vallance, I then called Sarah again. The second half was due to start in a couple of minutes. "Plymouth are back out already," she said. "But there's no sign of Fritz. He just got up and walked off."

"You have to tell him," I said.

"I fucking tried, Andy," she said, sounding like she was almost in tears, and even though I felt bad, I felt even worse about Sir fucking Harry trying to call me, so I said, "I knew I should have sent Jamie down", and then I hung up. And it wasn't even true, Sarah was way better than Jamie, who was a spoilt wanker forced upon us by Sir fucking Harry because Jamie was the entitled son of a privileged mate. And Jamie, who spent most of his life talking about some fucking band he was in with his "uni mates", had been pushing and pushing to go down to the Plymouth game, which was exactly why I'd sent Sarah instead.

True pro that he was, Fritz Cullen was ready at his mic just as we transferred from the studio back to the stadium, and he continued to deliver in his measured but engaged manner, pulling in the most neutral listener as Rovers took a 2-1 lead with a goal he made sound like Maradona skipping past six Englishmen at Mexico '86. As we approached the 60-minute mark and the next designated sponsor spot, the thought of Cullen neglecting his obligations became far more important to me than whether or not Plymouth could get back on level terms. I texted Sarah again, with imperatives in block caps, even as I pictured her sitting in a bar nearby, drinking and planning a new career. I thought about texting Fritz, but it was obvious he wouldn't be reading his messages while the game was on. Our late evening host, Pearl Garrett, had just arrived, so I readied her to deliver the message, in case Fritz didn't. Ten seconds to go until the hour. Plymouth had a corner. The ball, Fritz was telling us, had been cleared "clean out of the stadium and probably out to sea" by a Rovers defender. Now's the perfect time, then. A short break in play. Come on, Fritz!

Nothing, just the murmur of the crowd. It was like he was deliberately leaving a silence. I switched us back to the studio and Pearl, with a smile, told our listeners that, "Plymouth Argyle versus Bristol Rovers is brought to you by Chutzpah Fried Chicken, five-star fast food in a batter that beggars belief!"

And back to the stadium. Much crowd noise, because of course Argyle had scored from the corner. The ball may have been cleared out of the stadium, but a ball-boy had been on hand to offer a swift replacement. "A heavenly-honed header that sought its rightful home in the bottom corner of the away team's cage!" Cullen was crooning. I put my head in my hands and ignored another call from Sir Harry Vallance.

There was a meeting at 9am the next morning. It was supposed to be a half day for me, starting at 2pm. I had to cancel a doctor's appointment it had taken me six weeks to secure (a stress-related skin problem), and I had to let my mum know that I couldn't pick up a print she'd ordered from some gallery in Ealing, of all bloody places, and which she didn't want sending by post in case it got damaged. She'd been going on about it for weeks. I sent her a text, and ignored the eight texts that she immediately sent me back within the next five minutes. I wished that I had one of those mothers who was too old to understand smart technology.

Sarah had cancelled her hotel in Plymouth and driven all night to make the meeting. She looked a wreck. Before the meeting, I tried to apologise to her, and to brief her on what she should say to Millie from our commercial division, and Trent from Chutzpah, and to Sir fucking Harry. She just said nothing at all, wouldn't even look at me, like she knew she was going to have to take all the blame because she was the lowest paid and the lowest ranked, and that was just how it worked. I should mention that I suspected myself of being in love with Sarah, despite her having a steady boyfriend, Gabriel, whom she mentioned, but didn't talk about too much. There was a part of me that wanted to tell her that I was going to take all the blame and resign, just to try and make her happy. But she probably thought that was the very least I could do, and would still be pissed off at me, while likely not giving a second's thought to leaving her boyfriend.

I had met Gabriel at drinks after work one Friday. Annoyingly, there was absolutely nothing about him to dislike. He was bright, witty, considerate, interested in who you were, and didn't appear to be even mildly possessive of his beautiful, funny and intelligent partner. What a bastard. He was a biochemist, the kind of job that's supposed to make people boring. He should have been in a lab all night, possessed by his research and neglecting Sarah, who was going to resent his lack of attention sooner or later. But he wasn't, he was really into football and cricket, just like Sarah, and he seemed to be better informed than most of the people I worked with. Soon Sarah would be telling him that the Head of Sports he'd got on so well with down the pub had turned out to be a twat who yelled at her as soon as the going got tough, just another wanky male colleague with a big trap and no management skills.

I was going to have to find someone else to fall in love with.

That wasn't going to be Millie Shawaz, a single mother in her early 30s who only ever spoke in order to get straight to the point, and who seemed to be constantly about to slap me. As if she knew every filthy thought I'd ever had about her and her red high-heels. She threw down a file marked 'Chutzpah' on to the table almost before she'd entered the boardroom. It slid across the smooth hardwood surface and landed right in front of me, nudging my coffee cup and causing just enough drops to spill and worry me. Sir Harry and Trent from Chutzpah had yet to arrive. My half-apologies to Sarah were cut short.

"I work my fucking arse off for six months to get a major client, then you fucking morons lose them in the first 15 minutes of a League Cup tie."

"Good morning, Millie."

"I hope it turns out better than good, for your sakes. Did you get me Fritz Cullen on the line?"

"Fritz is not making himself available."

"Fritz is not making himself available," she mimicked. "Why can't you talk like a fucking normal person instead of a linguistic aggregator? You mean you can't get hold of Fritz. How hard have you tried?"

"I've tried his mobile a dozen times," I said, sounding defensive, because that's how Millie always made you sound. "His hotel says he's unhooked his phone and that they can not knock on the door of a client who has hung up the Do Not Disturb sign."

"Why didn't she ..." Millie pointed at Sarah, staring out of the window at the overcast capital, " ... stay there to demand some answers?"

"That's not her job," I said, and for a second Sarah stirred and half-looked in my direction. "And anyway, Fritz doesn't seem to believe in staff who aren't silent and servile." I was quite pleased with this turn of phrase. "She did everything that she could."

Sir Harry had arrived, and was listening in. "That's why we should have sent Jamie!" he roared, as I knew he would. "It needs a man to talk to a man. Where is Jamie?"

"Not in yet," I said, managing not to add, "as usual". Jamie came and went at random times, with variable excuses nobody cared about. We were auditioning for a new drummer. Fuck off.

Sir fucking Harry ignored the absenteeism of his crony-appointee and sat down. "Trent Warren's on his way up," he growled. "You're all going to have to crawl up his arse and promise him whatever it takes."

"This is pointless without Fritz Cullen on the line," said Millie, and she was right. We could pledge a tattoo of Chutzpah Fried Chicken across Fritz's forehead, but it wouldn't mean a thing without his assent.

"We have to butter him up anyway," said Sir Harry, then he looked around the table at each one of us and added, "Make this work!" I wondered if Sarah was thinking the same as me, that knighted cunts like Sir fucking Harry were revered exactly because they chose these empty imperatives that managed to impress the kind of people who yearned to be Sir so hard that they could barely get a bonk-on without imagining that the king was stroking their neckbone with a cold metal sword and commanding them to kowtow and lick his royal ring.

Here was Trent now, doing his best to look pissed off, but I had a theory about Trent. He bustled in, barely a greeting, just as we were expecting. Trent knew all too well that he was expected to be mad as a goaded steer at Spark FM. Mad at Fritz Cullen and the lackies who couldn't brief him to fulfil the simple obligation to mention the wonders of fried chicken once every quarter of an hour. I reckoned, though, that it was all bluff. Trent did not actually give a fuck. He hated his job. I bet that at home he had a room full of guitars or keyboards or something, and every morning when he left the house he almost cried that he could not stay at home to play them. Yet somehow he had to pay for all those guitars, and the only way he could do that was to go into Chutzpah Fried Chicken every day and arrange deals with the likes of Spark FM, and then when things didn't work out, he had to spend his Tuesday evening on the phone to me, acting like Fritz Cullen's commercial negligence was the most important thing happening in the world right at that second.

And that was why I quite liked Trent, late-20s, a little overweight and already going bald, but way too sincere for this job. I could see right through him. He would rent his arse out not be here right now. He wasn't a big enough twat to really give a shit about fried chicken sales.

"Do we have Fritz?" he asked, and tried not to look relieved when we told him no. "So what now?"

"We will sit down with him and hammer out exactly what his contract means," I said. "We have to make that clear to him. I thought it was clear, I really did. But it seems that the message didn't get through. That's on us, Trent."

"We will give you a month's free advertising to make up for last night," said Sir Harry, and I saw Millie flinch just for a micro-second. He was supposed to be staying quiet and letting us take care of the problem, but he could never shut up. He'd spaffed his load way too soon, and Trent was smart enough to exploit the poor performance.

"Three months," he said. "And Fritz Cullen has to be the man behind the message."

"Like I said, we will talk to Fritz." And just then, as though summoned by the gods of outrage, my laptop buzzed and Fritz joined the call from Plymouth, live from the breakfast buffet. Sir Harry gave a satisfied nod to Trent, as though all would now be settled.

"I understand there was a problem with my commentary last night," said Fritz. "How can I help?"

"First of all, good morning, Fritz." Sir fucking Harry, creeping like a malignant vine. "I trust you slept well."

"People with a clear conscience always sleep well, Harry," said Fritz. No 'sir'. You had to love him. "Now what can I do for you before I settle down to some scrambled eggs and a look at the sports pages?"

"Well, first I just wanted to say that, overall, you did a tremendous job last night," oiled Sir fucking Harry.

"Of course I did, Harry. That's what you pay me for." There was a solid irony to every word. He knew exactly what the problem was.

"Indeed. Now, there was just one slight problem. We've got Trent Warren here from Chutzpah Fried Chicken ..."

Fritz Cullen roared with a laughter forged from iron and steel, but which had nothing to do with joy. The patrons of the Royal Standard Hotel in Plymouth must have choked on their bacon.

"Chutzpah. Fucking Chutzpah. A little birdie tells me that you managed to tune out the commentary just at the very second Plymouth equalised. Can you confirm that?"

Harry nodded to me to talk. "Yes, well, this is exactly the problem we wanted to talk about ..."

"You fucking amateurs!" Fritz's laughter had swiftly morphed into contempt. "You broadcast 90 minutes of football, and you miss the most important moment of the game because you cut to an advert for fried chicken. Look, I'm prepared to go through a few teething problems while we get used to each other, Harry, but that's really not on. It can't happen again."

"Yes, well, like I said ..." I began again, flustered and on the back foot, but Sir fucking Harry cut me off.

"Fritz, I wonder if you can maybe come into the studio so we can talk ..."

"Not in my contract, Harry. I'll be going home right after breakfast, to my wife and my three lovely Labradors and my three wonderful children in a quiet Worcestershire village." He made it sound like a manifesto for life. "That's where I do my research for the next game, in peace and tranquility. That's where I recharge and refuel on inspiration. I put a lot of time and effort into my work, because I am a professional, do you understand? That's why you brought me to Spark FM, am I right?'

"If I might just say something ... " Millie began, but Fritz wasn't having it.

"We have to be serious about the way we cover football," he charged. "You want to build an audience? You build an audience with quality coverage by serious people, not fried fucking chicken. Do I make myself clear?"

There was silence. Millie looked furious, visibly breathing in and out so deeply that she looked like she was about to rise, roar and explode. Trent was suddenly vacant, like he'd lost the will to live, not just because he knew the commentator was right, but because Fritz had exposed the sham of his sorry career and life. Sir Harry was staring at me, like now was the time for my decisive intervention, as though I really was the man to inform a titan like Fritz Cullen that he'd got it all wrong, and that unless he got on board with the message of Chutzpah Fried Chicken, our contract would have to be torn up.

Sarah, meanwhile, was still looking out of the window, but now wore just the shadow of a smile. Something pulled at me inside, a sensation so strong that I almost cried out loud. The silence could only have been three or four seconds, but I sensed that it had just changed my life. I was a hopeless case, and unless I had the courage to leave this room, then I always would be.

Fritz had hung up and gone back to his scrambled eggs.

"We're done here," I said, and stood up, slapping my laptop shut.

"We most certainly are not," said Millie Shawaz. "We have a client here with a lot of questions, and we are here to give him some answers."

Trent shrugged and actually smiled. "It's look more and more like a case for our lawyers. If you break the contract, you have to accept the consequences."

Maybe I got Trent wrong. He doesn't play the guitar at all. He's just your standard mediocre twat.

"Let's start this again ... " said Sir fucking Harry, but I was at the door by now and said, "Let's just not. Fritz is right. How serious are we about sport? Who could find a single football fan in this country who's happy to have their match commentary interrupted by someone, even Fritz Cullen, or especially Fritz Cullen, telling them that Chutzpah Fried Chicken is fried in a batter that beggars belief? It's inane. It's absurd. And we're idiots for thinking that a football man to his core like Fritz was ever going to play along. And besides, we shouldn't be pushing this shit. Everyone knows it tastes like shit. Everyone knows ... ". And here I pointed at fat, balding Trent. "Everyone knows you exploit your workers and underpay them and you won't let them join a union. You murder chickens by the million, and the floods of chicken shit from your chicken shit chicken farms fuck up the soil and the rivers nearby. But because you have people like Sir fucking Harry here and his right honourable fucking friends in Parliament and the House of Crooks getting lobbied and paid off, then you get away with it. And worse still, we missed the most important goal of the game!"

Millie and Sir Harry were both on their feet and touching the darker shades of red. Trent sat back, condescendingly bemused. Sarah was all wide-eyed, almost laughing. Then Jamie popped up right behind me and said, "Does this mean I can have his job?"

I turned and stared him right in the eye. "The only thing you're fit to do is suck Sir Harry's cock, and I doubt you'd even show up on time to do that." Then I ran to my desk, and by the time I'd picked up all that was precious to me, three security guards were standing there too.

A year or two later, I bumped into Sarah and Gabriel at a pub gig in Crouch End. Gabriel had obviously heard the story, and looked more than incredulous as we re-capped that morning meeting, like I'd been an idiot to scupper my own career. He was probably right. Of course, I wanted to hear what had happened in my wake. In the short term, lots of shouting, agony and anguish. Both Jamie and Millie got fired, but Sarah somehow survived, and that turned out well for the company. Sarah it was who discovered and then brokered a compromise — using AI software, she'd engineered Fritz to voice the ads without him ever having to pronounce the actual words. With the commentator's permission, they'd give him the signal for silence and then invert the ad slogans from the studio when the ball was out of play. No one noticed, no one complained, and Chutzpah Fried Chicken hadn't a clue. Their partnership with Spark FM now flourished on love and money. Sarah had become Fritz's personal assistant, on a proper wage, and occasionally he managed to talk to her like an actual human being.

"And what about you, Michael?"

"I knew Sir fucking Harry would make it impossible for me to get another job in broadcasting. I've just qualified to be a German teacher."

"Oh," she said, and they both looked at me to see if this was a good thing or not.

"The first thing I did was to start enjoying football again," I said. "The second thing I did was to become vegan. I'm sure it's affecting Chutzpah's profits."

"Got a girlfriend yet?" said Gabriel, which I thought was a bit much given it was only the second time we'd ever met.

"No," I mumbled.

"I can give you Millie's number," said Sarah.

"Millie?" I said.

"Come on, we could all see you fancied her. She was like a mum-goddess to you." She and Gabriel were laughing, like the whole world was in on this.

"Fuck off," I said, and I wanted to tell her that she was the one I'd loved. Still loved. Still thought about every single day. That she was the reason I was applying for jobs in Scotland and Ireland, aside from the fact that you couldn't live in London on a teacher's salary.

"She landed on her feet after Spark. Head of Global sales at..."

"Stop, Sarah, please" I said, and she did, jolted by my tone. We stood for a few seconds, staring into our drinks.

"One thing," she said finally. "A while later, one night when he was in a talkative mood, I told Fritz Cullen about that meeting."

"And?"

"He said, *Good man, that.* That was it."

I just nodded, but inside I was glowing. For the love of Fritz. Good man. It wasn't exactly a eulogy. But it was enough to send me home with a quicker step, and helped me get out of the bed on the many moribund days to come.

Managing Kids

The wages that these lads are on, they had some bloody nerve. A delegation of three players trooped into my office and said they were representing "all the first team squad". And the message was that they did not wish to be considered for the FA Cup game on Sunday. They were tired and needed a rest. It was the Europa League first leg on Thursday, then the FA Cup on Sunday up north at Carlisle, and then all the way to Greece for the Europa League second leg a few days later. They just couldn't promise that they'd be able to give 100 per cent. It was for the good of the team, they said. It was the chance to give some of the younger boys a run-out. The experience would do them good.

I sat back in my chair and swivelled a little. I let some silence do my talking for a minute or two as I stared them in the eye, one by one. I am beyond incredulous, I wanted to let them know, but without shouting, without even speaking. One Englishman, one Spaniard, and one Brazilian, all of them seasoned internationals. Combined pay of God knows how much, I can't even get a grasp on their salaries anymore. Professional players at the peak of their fitness, at one of Europe's most revered clubs, and still in the running for three trophies. And now they needed a rest. Bless them.

Ten or 15 years ago, I'd have chased them down the hall. I'd have yelled at them and thrown things. If I did that now, I'd probably be clearing my desk by tomorrow morning. It's all about player power these days, and this is what player power means: having the money to moan about every tiny thing. Or getting their agents to do the moaning for them.

The press was already on my back after two successive league defeats. That's all it takes nowadays, a run of two losses, and a club like ours is "in crisis". Idiots with computers start speculating about my future. Other idiots with calculators start working out how much it will cost us if we miss out on qualifying for the Champions League again. And almost inevitably, someone will spot the club's owner, a foreign gentleman whose name and country of origin I can never exactly remember (it ends in '-stan' and has a lot of oil), in a European capital city, where he's presumed to be courting a new manager, usually a Dutchman or an Italian.

I'm old school, as you've probably gathered. I've maybe got five years left in me at the top of the game. I don't have a coaching badge, or a licence, or whatever the hell it is. There was no call for them 30 years ago when I quit playing. If you had half a brain, you just went straight into managing. I'd seen and played every possible situation by the age of 35, I didn't need tutoring by some berk drawing lines with arrows on his laptop.

"You wouldn't get a job in Germany without a licence," I was told when Villa sacked me. A very short meeting with the 12 gentlemen of the Board.

"Why would I bloody want to?" I said. "Anyway, I've got a lot of time for the Germans. We've more in common than you think. They lost two World Wars and I've lost two League Cups."

"Boss?" said Terry Barnett. I'd swivelled my chair so far around that I was now looking out the office window, thinking about Villa and QPR and Bolton and Southampton too. They all 'let me go'. I managed teams to promotion and then qualification for Europe, and I kept getting to the bloody League Cup final and losing, but I'd never won a major trophy. I'm proud to say I never walked out on any of them when things got tough, or because I was offered a fatter wage elsewhere. There's no return loyalty in football, though, no one's naive enough to expect that. It'd start with a bad run, then a few fan banners and chants from the stands, and then one board meeting of sparrow-headed, pig-bellied, suit-wearing morons later and you'd be gone. Never mind having the chance to re-build a team or forge a coherent style of play.

"Are you gentlemen aware," I said to the Englishman, the Spaniard and the Brazilian, "that this club has not won a trophy for 17 years?"

Terry nodded, he looked almost guilty. He'd been here for much of that time. The other two, who'd only come the summer before, probably had no idea. "We're aware of that, boss," he replied. "But we feel that if we maximise our energy ... "

"Terry, don't use words like maximise in my presence," I said. "I might be tempted to knock your head off and practice my volleys." I smiled at him, but he didn't smile back. There'd probably be an official written complaint from his agent that I'd physically threatened his client.

"The lads think it's a case of concentrating on the big prize," he went on. "A lot of us are carrying niggling injuries right now. We feel that fourth place is more important, in the long run."

"Do the lads think that it's more important than winning the oldest cup competition in the world? It seems daft when we already made it through the third and fourth rounds. We're almost half way to Wembley."

He still wouldn't give me a direct answer. All that bloody media training they get nowadays. "It's not a case of trophies, boss, it's the prestige of being in the Champions League. For the club and the players."

"Scared you won't be worth as much next season?"

That shut him up. Fernando and Silvio were staring at their shoes. You could see they'd only been brought in for moral support and were too shy to speak. Terry was the captain. He was captain of England too. Some called him the backbone of the English game. Others called him a whining git who specialised in under-achievement, and whose self-pushed reputation far outweighed his talent.

"If I was truly in charge of this club," I said, "I'd kick the bloody lot of you out. Your paymaster — that bloke who occasionally comes to watch a game — would probably reverse that decision, though, and kick me out instead. As it is, I certainly don't appreciate your interference in my team selection. If you're on the team sheet for Sunday, you'll play. It's only bloody Carlisle, you'd think you could manage that without your poor tired bodies having to put in too much effort."

They nodded, and shuffled out. I sat shaking my head. Then I called in the youth team coach Arie van Heeken and asked him to brief me on the best up-and-coming players.

When he was done, I said, "On Friday afternoon you will tell them that on Saturday they'll be taking the plane north, and on Sunday they'll be making their first team debuts in the FA Cup."

He looked at me like I had gone insane. "Is this some kind of a joke?"

"Arie, I've never seen you laugh once in the eight months I've been here. Do you think I'd waste my breath trying to cheer you up now?"

"I really don't think they're ready," he blustered. "Maybe one or two of them only. It could be a disaster."

"Today is Tuesday. You and I will take them tomorrow all day, and on Thursday morning, and all day again Friday. Believe me, by Sunday they'll be ready."

On Thursday, the first team could only draw 1-1 at home to AEK Athens in the Europa League. "I thought it was Sunday you wanted a rest, not tonight," I said. That was my post-game talk in full. The dressing room was very quiet.

On Friday, I released my team sheet to the media. Saturday's papers were full of it. How dare I devalue the FA Cup like this, foaming columnists wanted to know, (but secretly delighted they had something to pontificate on)? And what about the Carlisle fans who'd paid five times the normal asking price to see Terry Barnett? At the pre-game press conference, I said that Carlisle United ripping off their fans was not my area of responsibility. That meant we received a very po-faced reception in Carlisle. It didn't matter, because on Sunday our youth team spanked them 5-0, live on national television. Monday's writers changed their minds and decided that I'd pulled off a master stroke.

By the Cup quarter-final three weeks later, we were out of the Europa League, having lost 1-0 in Athens. "I should have put out the bloody youth team again," I told them. In the final eight of the Cup, we were at home to Liverpool, and everyone assumed that the side would be back to full strength. This time, there was no delegation sent to ask for a rest. But I gave them one anyway. I sent the youth team back out, and the press were at it again. He's gone mad. Playing youth against Carlisle was one thing, but against Liverpool? Why was I deliberately trying to throw our Cup chances in the bin?

It was indeed a very tough game, and we deserved to be beaten. We were 1-0 down with five minutes to go. Liverpool had missed enough chances to win by seven or eight, and then we were gifted a very dubious penalty. Johnny Granville, this cocky local lad who'd scored three at Carlisle, took a bit of a dive and the referee went for it. The Video Assistant Referee didn't see enough reason to intervene, and we'll never know why. Johnny got up, brushed himself off, did one of those annoying dummy runs up to the ball, then rolled it into one corner while the goalkeeper went the other way. His celebration got a little out of hand, and as he'd already been booked he got a second yellow for ripping off his shirt and so he was off. He'd be suspended for the replay.

Not that it mattered. According to the press, I had to bring back the 'real' team for the return at Anfield. Otherwise we'd get battered, especially without this young prospect, Granville, now suspended. The day before the game, I posted an unchanged line-up, except for Steve McHale coming in for Granville. He was 16 and built like a pipe cleaner, but was incredibly robust. He'd barely even played for the youth team yet, but I'd seen him in training every day. No one could get the ball off him. He had no idea how good he was, and he looked terrified when I told him he was starting at Anfield. "Just run at them," I told him. "They won't be expecting it. By the time you're past them, it'll be too late."

I had another visit, from the same three players.

"Boss," said Terry. "The lads think you're making a big mistake. These kids are gonna get murdered at Anfield. It'll destroy their confidence."

"Has the FA Cup suddenly become important again?" I asked. After the Europa League defeat and a switch back to a flat back four, we'd been doing okay in the league, holding on to fourth place by three points.

"We just want to let you know that … "

"Thanks, Terry, I've heard enough. Enjoy the game. Take another nice rest in the executive box. Or if the journey north is too much for you, watch it at home with the missus. It's not as far as Carlisle, I know, but still quite a trek." I gestured at Fernando and Silvio. "Invite these lads over and show them some traditional English hospitality. Phone out for a curry."

We went to Anfield, and these young players had learnt a lot from the first game. They won 2-0 and they deserved it. Steve McHale scored them both, the first one after dribbling past four players. He'd looked too skinny to be taken seriously. In 20 seconds, he became an international sensation. Even Arie broke into a smile and hugged me.

We got a lucky draw in the semi-final against the surprise team of the competition, Huddersfield Town. The other game was Chelsea against Manchester City. The youngsters were thrilled to be playing at Wembley, even though, if you ask me, playing a semi-final at Wembley's a bloody nonsense. Still, it would ease any nerves they had for the final. After winning at Liverpool, they were now full of self-belief. Even when they went 1-0 down early on, they picked themselves up and got on with it. I put Johnny Granville and Steve McHale up front, and they played off each other well. Right enough, you could see that Granville was going to be a pain in the arse to deal with, shouting at the ref and at his team-mates all the time. But that will all be someone else's problem. In the end, we won 3-1. All of a sudden, I was the manager-in-waiting for the England job.

The 'real' team meanwhile secured fourth place, and so we'd qualified for next season's Champions League. They had a big champagne party for that, after drawing 0-0 at Everton on the second last day of the season while Arsenal lost, but I steered well clear of it. I don't believe in opening champagne for getting fourth place after a 0-0 draw. Besides, the players weren't talking to me any more. I'd issue instructions, and they'd nod, and more or less carry them out. I think they actually upped their game to show me what they could do. Whatever works. An honest take would be that fourth place was exactly what this team deserved.

"What a wonderful surprise!" I said to Terry, Fernando and Silvio as they filed into my office one final time. "All the way up the stairs and down the long corridor — I hope you gentlemen are not too tired. Now, what could I possibly do to assist you?"

"It's about the final," said Terry. The captain and his publicity goons had been working their contacts in the gutter press. Now there were columnists proclaiming that, although the youth team had undoubtedly done very well so far, they couldn't possibly expect to beat Manchester City in the final. These sages also pointed out that I would surely not risk this opportunity to win a major trophy at last. Because, at my age, might this not be my final chance? (Talk of me getting the England job had lasted for about a day.)

"What about the final, Terry?" I asked. "If it's another rest you're needing, you know I'm always happy to oblige. You must all be exhausted after securing fourth place."

"We all want to play," he said. "We feel we deserve it. We got this club into the Champions League. Our policy of taking a rest in the Cup has worked. We feel it's our due to cap off the season."

"Your policy?"

"Yes, it was our idea to put the youth team out in the Cup."

I had to laugh. "Well, thanks for that. Credit it where it's due. It's such a good idea that I've been using it again and again. Why would I stop now?"

The three players held their silence.

"Also, the last time you played Manchester City, you lost 3-0 and we didn't manage a single shot on goal."

"That was in the league, at their place. This time will be different."

"Let's hope so," I said.

"We won't let the club down."

"And why would you?"

Silence again. I looked up at them.

"Well," I said eventually, "it's a huge relief to learn that you are all available for selection. As you saw against Carlisle, Liverpool and Huddersfield, this club would be nothing without its senior players."

Terry sighed. "We think you've made your point now, boss."

"And now you get the chance to make yours. You can play the youth team, and whoever wins gets to play at Wembley."

The captain looked at the other two, who both shrugged. "You're turning it into a circus," he said. "This isn't the way to run a football club."

"No media," I said, ignoring him. "We play behind closed doors. It's my only offer. And, of course, if you're too scared to play your own youth team, I'd be absolutely certain to make sure that such an embarrassing fact never made it to your good friends in the press, who in any case would not stoop to publish such tittle-tattle."

"We'll have to talk to the lads," the captain said, and stalked out. Fernando and Silvio and followed him, avoiding my eye. Ten minutes later they sent word that, although they "strongly disapproved" of my management techniques, they were not going to shirk the challenge. Like I'd given them the choice.

On the morning of the secret game, a few days before the Cup Final, I just happened to be having an informal chat in my office with a well-respected football writer, Sam Percy, who writes for one of the broadsheets. When we'd done, I might have inadvertently invited him to walk down the corridor to one of the executive boxes overlooking the stadium, just in case he saw something interesting. And so Sam watched the first team fall apart and get comprehensively outplayed by youth, which won 4-0. Foolishly, I forgot to ask Sam not to mention it in his column the next day.

The senior players are refusing to go to the final tomorrow, and now even the press has turned against them. The owner keeps trying to call me, but he's several thousand miles away and can't leave his country because the airport's closed. There's a revolution going on, rapidly morphing into a civil war. The blethering hacks are now all saying that maybe we really do have a chance against Manchester City.

I think we do too, of course, though I'll be surprised if we win. But this is not about the club's first trophy for 17 years, and it's nothing to do with my record as a manager. This is about helping young men to grow up. It's a struggle, but until they cast me out, I'll do the best I can. There needs to be at least one adult here in charge of the kids.

The Last Amateur

Among football folk in southern Lanarkshire, it's now agreed that Jackie McMurray is the greatest amateur player of all time. If you support the Thankerton Swifts, chances are that you'll say Jackie's the greatest player of all time, period. Not just because of his swerve, his flow, his effortless touch, his authority, his lobs and his lightness, his bottomless trove of egregious goals and concision assists. Not just because he took the Swifts from village to League football in little under a decade. To those of us scrapping for just a slip of reflected pride, he became the greatest player because of what he stands for.

"Take me down off that pedestal now," Jackie would say, in his gentle fashion, but upset nonetheless. He's no fan of lists that rank individuals in a team sport. Neither is he keen on football's exhaustive discourse, whether by numbers or perceived heroism. Even if he pays attention to stats and tactics, he certainly won't talk about them. You know that quote, he'd say. The one that compares writing about music to dancing about architecture. Same thing. You don't talk football, you play it.

There are those who criticise Jackie for not smiling enough. They say that for someone who goes on so much about the joy of football, he shows precious little delight on the field, and not much more when he's coming off it, despite having scored five times. They mistake modesty for arrogance, and forget that we Scots are not so well schooled in success. We've still to erase decades of disappointment from our souls before we can start any foolish, unfettered hollering.

None of us here in the village will tolerate criticism of Jackie. You can only adore every pale and hardy inch of him. Even those desperate to find a rogue nugget in a goldmine of goodness have given up and succumbed to eulogies. 'Between Maradona and Messi, you'll find McMurray' was one banner you could see for a while at Sheriflats Road. Jackie had a word with someone on the board, though, and the banner was never seen again. Archie Breslin, who covered the team a lot back then for the *Daily Record*, was the only hack who dared to ask him if he'd anything to do with the slogan's disappearance. "It's just nonsense, is it not?" Jackie asked back, dry and on the level, but serious enough, and right in Archie's eyes. There was no follow-up question.

At least Breslin squeezed an answer out of the player. If a journalist had the courage to ask Jackie if there was any truth in the transfer rumours, he would say nothing. In the early years, he'd answer, "You want me to talk about rumours? Why would I do that?" Even earlier, when the club was just setting up in the lowest of leagues, Jackie was cheerful enough when he trotted out his standard line. "I was born in this village, and my father founded this club especially so that I could stay in this village. I don't want to leave, and I never will. I'm a bairn of the Clyde." And that's how the club took up its nickname.

At one point you could barely move in Thankerton for journalists who'd travelled around the world to hear and then re-tell the story of the Bairns of the Clyde. How James Edward McMurray started an under-7 team in the village on the concrete court at the playground just so that wee Jackie could toy with lads from Symington, Libberton and Carnwath. No one else in the village was any good, bar the Fraser twins, Lizzie and Mags. But it didn't matter, because none of them would get the ball anyway. At 15-0, James would substitute his heir and give the others a chance. Final score: 21-12, with a hat-trick each for the Frasers.

It wasn't long before word spread and bigger clubs from Biggar, Lanark and Lesmahagow came looking to lure the wean away. "He's only eight," said James Edward McMurray, a headmaster in Carluke during the week. "He's nae goin' anywhere." "But you don't even have a proper field," came the retort. "We're working on it," he assured them. And by the time Jackie was 10, his dad had convinced the county council that Thankerton needed a full-sized football pitch. That James was married to Jean Scobie, a local farmer's daughter, was a big help. They got the field on Sheriflats Road for free, the council just flattened it somewhat and painted on the lines. Though Douglas Scobie, Jean's old man, was heard to mutter, "We'd better get a nice cut of the fee when he goes to Celtic." With that eventuality in mind, he stumped up for goal posts, changing rooms and a shed. Willie Gallacher, the taciturn postie, spent hours after his shift every day keeping the place in trim for 50 quid a week.

So far, so bucolic. But where's the conflict? When Thankerton U11s, then to become the U12s, then the U13s, started winning all the leagues and county cups, it was the Fraser twins that took the brunt from aggrieved losers. "They should be playing with the lassies," was a common retort. Mags was in goal and Lizzie played at centre back, and so the odd few times Jackie wasn't dancing through defences, they stopped damage at the other end. Lizzie loved to dump opponents on their behinds and leave them dazed and confused on the grass. Her ma, Big Annie, would chime with laughter that you could hear in the Highlands, while the dads of the lads would look on with fury at the humiliation.

For a while, when they were 10 or 11, Jackie and Lizzie were sweet on each other, or so it seemed. They'd hold hands and smooch in the centre circle before kick-off, and the other team would point and hoot. James outfitted the team in pink from top to toe, the club's first kit to this day. Then the Swifts would bruise and batter the mockers in the form of a 27-0 humiliation. Years later, Lizzie told the *Record* it had all been a ruse. They hadn't been a couple at all. In fact, the two would tussle at practice. Lizzie was the only player I ever saw who had the measure of him — she'd go in with her full force and floor him. Jackie would just get up and go back for more, no hint of a grudge in his face, but he wasn't exactly smiling either. Lizzie's success rate was maybe 40-60. No male player, pro or otherwise, ever came close to that.

When enough angry wee das and protective mas had complained to the league, officials were sent to take a look. They couldn't help but be impressed by James Edward McMurray and his son, and by the Fraser twins too. After the game, they accepted an invite up to the Scobie farm for high tea and a dram or two. Big Annie took Wullie Muir, the head of the Lanarkshire FA, to one side and said, "We've not got a car, you understand? If they dinnae play for this team, they'll play nowhere." She placed a firm hand on his right thigh that left a two-week bruise, adding, "And down the line, that will be Scotland's loss." No further action was taken, and the twins played for the Swifts until the day they turned 17 and left to play for Glasgow City instead.

Instead of the three players getting lured away, new talent started turning up in the village by the Clyde. Footballers from teams all over Lanarkshire who'd been humped by the Swifts would shyly jump out of a car just before training and ask if they might please join in. James Edward McMurray was not the kind of man to say no. If they weren't good enough, they'd not bother coming back. If they somehow fit in, they'd be asked if they fancied signing on. Sometimes a strutting dad would ask to speak to the coach. "That'll be me," James would say, all smiles. He knew nothing about the game, he'd been brought up a rugby player in the Borders. "What formation are we playing today?" a new recruit might ask. "Ach, sort it out among yourselves," James would reply. "Jackie and Lizzie will tell you where to play. Just get out there and enjoy yourselves."

When the team were at U16 level, James finally had a sign painted for the entrance: Welcome to Sheriflats Road, home to Thankerton Swifts. SCOUTS NOT WELCOME.

When the team, now unbeaten in seven years, reached U17 level, James asked his son what he wanted to do next. Frankly, he was tired of the solicitations from Glasgow, London, Manchester and Milan.

"Dad, we need to start a men's team," said Jackie.

The following season, the team left youth football and won the district league with maximum points, conceding just nine goals. They only let so many in because the Fraser twins had gone. Jackie scored 137 times. If James hadn't subbed him out on 75 minutes every weekend, it would have been more. "Whit's the point?" some teams would say, and then forfeit their games in Thankerton. James sent out the word for opponents from higher up, and they came from Arbroath, Dundee and Dumbarton, hoping to hook the prodigy. They'd lose, by several goals, and James Edward McMurray used the money they took at the gate to build a clubhouse and a stand. Jackie left school and enrolled at Glasgow University to study economics and history.

"That'll be him away then," we said, worried that we'd be left with an abandoned football ground on our hands. But Jackie mainly stayed at home. He took the bus into Glasgow for his studies, but he was always back in time for training and games. Crowds of one to two thousand were showing up to watch. We locals got in for free, the rest had to pay. Players started asking for money, so Jackie and James called a meeting.

"At this club we play for pleasure, for pride and for the love of the game," the 19-year-old central midfielder announced. "There is no money to play in an amateur league, and as long as we play in an amateur league, that's how it will remain. All money goes back in to the club, and any profit goes into community support. You are free to leave if that doesn't suit. Good luck finding another club that gets a four-figure crowd to watch you every week." Somebody muttered, "Founded in 1996, stuck in 1896." Yet not a single player left the club that day.

As the ground grew, so did the crowds. Everyone loves to follow a winner. Soon they were running special buses from across the county, because the village could no longer cope with cars. Some of us said we couldn't wait for Jackie to sign with a pro team so that all this would go away, and then Saturdays in Thankerton would be quiet again. All the while, offering our spare rooms or even the sofa-bed for 100 quid a night, breakfast not included. And every year, the beaten teams and the voices of sport called Jackie McMurray a playground bully who'd get found out at the next level. At the next level, he'd score a century of goals again, and the Thankerton Swifts would win the league with a one hundred per cent record.

The *Daily Record* started a campaign. If no one could persuade Jackie to sign for Celtic or Rangers, then they would persuade him to move in the interests of the nation. Was Jackie not a patriot who would surely want to play for Scotland one day? The campaign went flat when the player declared that he had already turned down annual invitations from the Scottish FA to train with respective youth squads, because he did not agree with national boundaries and the outdated policy of dividing people by borders due to language, geography, religion, skin colour, or any other reason. Also, FIFA was a corrupt, undemocratic body lacking accountability and transparency, which violated its own statutes on human rights. Jackie McMurray would not play in any competition organised by FIFA. The pompous wee shite, I heard someone say at the village pub when they announced it on the local news. The fight in the car park went the full distance, and I got a big row from Moira, my wife, for coming home with a broken nose. "At your age," she said, shaking her head. "Ya bloody eejit."

The *Record*, all hurt now, labelled Jackie 'The Amateur'. Jackie said that it was a label he'd wear with pride, but that he also had enough pride not to talk to the *Record* anymore. "I'm going off the Record," he said, with half a smile. In the row that followed his self-deselection from the Scottish team, he did agree to an in-depth interview with *The Scotsman*'s Stuart Cairns. I'm going to pull up a wee extract:

Cairns: You say that as long as Scotland is a member of FIFA, you will not represent your country. But who would Scotland play against if they weren't in FIFA?

McMurray: There are plenty of other countries that aren't in FIFA. And maybe other countries would follow Scotland's model example and leave FIFA too.

Cairns: Seriously? You think that Scotland has that great a standing as a football nation?

McMurray: We might, if we left FIFA.

Cairns: You criticise FIFA due to its lack of democracy and transparency. How is that any different to the Scottish FA? Your team plays under its umbrella too.

McMurray: I would never do anything to damage my club.

Cairns: Yet you don't mind damaging your country.

McMurray: How am I damaging my country? I'm just playing football for the village and the club that I love. You can hammer me for holding a set of beliefs and sticking to them, if you like. That's your freedom as a journalist. It makes no difference to me if you do that. But it will not persuade me to change those beliefs, otherwise they would no longer be beliefs. They would just be empty words, like FIFA's statutes on human rights.

Jackie wouldn't let the Swifts trade on his blossoming fame, and he forbade all merchandise that used his name and image. With one famous exception. After the *Record*'s anti-Jackie campaign (they denied that's what it was, but that's exactly what it was), a design student at the University came up to him in the library one day and showed him a t-shirt she'd made up. On the front was an image of Jackie scoring an overhead kick framed above and below by the words 'The Amateur'. On the back, in speech marks, "I'm going off the Record." The designer, Sheila McGiel, said she'd offer it to the club for free. Whether Jackie accepted the offer because he loved the t-shirt or had been taken in by Sheila McGiel's killer smile was an open question. We saw a lot of Sheila in the village over the coming months. We were all very taken too by her cheer, and her thumbs-up attitude. The t-shirt sold in tens of thousands, around the world, via Sheila's website. She and Jackie would spend whole evenings packing them up and hand-writing the addresses, until it became too much and they moved the operation down to the pub, where we all helped out because we all wanted to please Jackie McMurray, and Sheila McGiel too.

"See, you're commodifying the lad anyway!" Archie Breslin crowed at the very next press conference. "We need another new stand and a car park for the coaches," James Edward McMurray replied. "Next observation, please."

Because of the growing ground and the cracking crowds, and because Jackie McMurray was hammering every team we played, the Thankerton Swifts were given a leg-up to the Lowland Football League, skipping a handful of promotions. Jackie answered the customary summer question of, "Is he really *that* good?" with 51 goals before Christmas. His co-players were now on part-time contracts, with training three nights a week. People started coming to that too, wanting a glimpse of the myth, but if you didn't live in the village you had to pay a fiver to get in. Sheila had a stand selling t-shirts, I had a stand selling pies and Irn Bru, because it's hard these days to make a living with ghost-written hagiographies.

Now it was time to nail the hypocrisy of the Bairns of the Clyde. It was all about money after all, right? Archie Breslin quoted an entire interview back at Jackie in a press conference just before a Scottish Cup game against Partick Thistle.

"You once said, Jackie, and I quote this word for word, 'Sportsmen and sportswomen should play sport because they love the game. Love is tainted by money. You can not kiss the badge that pays you. You can not compromise the club's financial position by taking out in return for putting back in. That way, you will weaken your club, not strengthen it. You strengthen your club by performing to the best of your abilities. What you take out are the joys of victory and the pleasure you give to the fan.' Yet now you are in a team with players who are directly contradicting all of that? What do you think of those team-mates? Are your conflicting approaches not damaging to team spirit?"

Jackie had announced an end to his boycott of the *Record* at the start of that season. "I'm not one to bear a grudge forever, it's too heavy," he said. Now, though, he always waited a long time before he answered a question from Archie, like he was considering whether to answer it at all. Journalists knew better than to hurry him. Whatever he said was usually worth waiting for. "Well," he'd always begin, "I think the answer to that is fairly obvious."

In this case, he went on, "My team-mates represent one approach to sport, and I represent an alternative approach. I'm not going to try and make my team-mates feel morally inferior. I presume that they respect my position, otherwise they would not have joined the club, and they wouldn't pass me the ball or congratulate me when I score. They need to feed themselves and their families, whereas I now have a job teaching economics. Why would I want to make money out of football as well?"

Answer the question with a question. The only response to that would have been to say something like, "To get rich", but while Archie Breslin was devious, sneaky and hypocritical, he certainly wasn't stupid enough to give an answer like that.

After Jackie put the Swifts 2-0 up against Partick, a Thistle defender took him out of the game with a brutal tackle that only yielded a yellow card. Partick won the game by four goals to two. That was the day when we started to wonder if football was such a good thing for Thankerton after all. The referee needed a police escort to get away, and the Thistle bus was damaged so badly that they had to send for a replacement while the team sought shelter up at Scobie's farm. On crutches, Jackie thanked the Thistle players for their patience while his grandmother served them organic mutton broth. The player who'd taken out Jackie apologised, face to face. "It's us who should be apologising," said Jackie. He renounced the violence of the home fans and told them that anyone who couldn't accept defeat would be banned for life, even if they lived in the village.

Defeat — we just weren't accustomed to it. We felt hard done by. I have to admit, I swore at that referee from behind my pie stand as he was running with his linesmen into the changing room. I was summoned to the new boardroom for a talking to by James and Jackie, just the two of them. They sat me down with a cup of tea and some shortbread. I admitted everything and begged for mercy. The pie stand was my living now. The club was my life. I spent all day looking forward to training. I spent all week waiting for Saturday. I spent all summer in a state of agitation.

"That's not really how it's supposed to be, William, is it?" Jackie said. "It's just a wee game of fitba. The referee's doing his job. How would you like it if a fan came up and screamed in your face that your pies tasted like mud and that you weren't fit to make them?"

"It's happened," I said.

"Has it really?"

The way he looked at you. Called me William instead of Wullie. I had to admit that, in fact, it had never happened. That people only had nice things to say about my pies. But that was because I was conscientious and made the best pies. Quality meat, properly sourced, with a light pastry. If the referee had applied the laws of the game like I applied the laws of cuisine, then we'd perhaps never have been in this situation. Even from the pie stand, I could tell it should have been a red card.

"We're still not sensing the right attitude here, William."

And so I had to dredge up the right attitude and apologise at great length in order to keep my pie stand, and write a letter of apology to the referee, and then they had me refereeing a U11 game, in which I made several bad decisions, followed by another interview where Jackie asked me how it felt to be a referee when even 10-year-old players are getting on your case because you haven't a clue what you're doing.

When I walked away from the ground that morning, there was part of me saying that was the last time. I'd get out of the club and out of Thankerton. I could sell my pies anywhere, they were good enough. And who did they think they were, questioning my commitment to the club? Just because I cared that we'd been knocked out of the Scottish Cup. What was the point of this team if no one cared about it?

By the team I got home, some of my steam had evaporated. When I tried to explain to Moira that we were going to be up and moving somewhere else, she interrupted me and said,

"Hawd yer maw, ye eejit. Where are we going to move to? The Yetts o' Muckhart? Get over yersel. All they're asking you to dae is not yell at the referee. If ye cannae manage that, ye need to see a doctor."

The year we lost to Partick in the Cup was also the season we were promoted into the Scottish Football League. Our very first game was an 8-0 away win at Stranraer, with Jackie scoring all eight goals. After a lull in coverage, when Jackie's indifference to world glory seemed to have finally found some acceptance among the Scottish press and people (and the scouts at Inter Milan and Barcelona had given up wasting their money on flights to Glasgow), the campaign to take him away from the Swifts sparked back into life. It was absurd that such a talent was wasted on the Scottish fourth division. And why could teams like Forfar Athletic and Albion Rovers not be spared the indignity of getting whacked by such a monstrous talent? This was McMurray's ego trip. He simply got a kick out of flattening minnows. What was his problem? Why could he not help Rangers or Celtic win the Champions League?

"My team is Thankerton, as I may have stated before," came Jackie's pacific response. "However, as you're mentioning those teams in Glasgow, it is certainly my hope to play against them some day for Thankerton, and for our village to perform to the very best of our abilities and hopefully achieve a positive result."

Albion Rovers weren't complaining either. They moved their home game with the Swifts to Hampden Park and sold 50,000 tickets at an inflated price, as well as foreign TV rights for a tidy sum that would, in the words of their chairman, "see us alright for the next five years. It's not like anyone else is helping us out."

After the Swifts won 5-1 (with a hat-trick and two assists for Jackie), the press wanted to know what he thought of the Wee Rovers making money off his name.

"That's not how I see it," said Jackie, "and it's really no concern of mine what Albion Rovers do as a football club. I do understand, however, why they would act as they have. The people that run their club take decisions in the best interests of that club because maybe they love their club. They care about their local side and want it to survive. They're looking out for themselves so that they can keep playing football. I don't see how anyone could possibly quarrel with that."

Now the problem for the media became that Jackie was apparently too clever by half. "Why does he have to have an answer to everything? Who the hell does he think he is?" Meanwhile, the university had to bring in extra security because football fans from the continent were trying to crash his lectures and take pictures. Sheila McGiel was offered contracts to model, to sing, to endorse. She would be doing no such things, she announced. She and Jackie were planning to start a family and were converting an old farm house for the future. There would be no time for anything else. Oh, did that mean they were getting married? No, she replied. Neither of them believed in marriage. They preferred to be in a polyamorous relationship. She said this in an interview with *People's Friend*. The journalist missed the significance of the remark, having no idea what polyamory was, and not having the curiosity or the common sense to ask. I'm sure that Moira and I weren't the only ones googling the word when it all became public. The diffident publication assured the world that this was indeed the quote, and that it was not a typographic error. They claimed that they had not made a big deal out of the quote because "we are not that kind of magazine".

"My goodness, whatever next?" said Moira. She looked at me and said, "Dinnae go gettin' any ideas, Wullie."

"I don't think Sheila's interested in anything besides my pies," I said.

"Not just her. Anyone else. I've seen ye havin' a gawk. Just remember there's a sparrow's nest underneath yer baw sack."

It's hard to say in retrospect why Sheila made this information public. Jackie didn't seem exactly pleased to be now fielding questions about his apparently adventurous sex life, but at least it made a change from justifying his refusal to sign for Bayern Munich. He was also too much of a gentleman to show any public displeasure with his partner, while patiently explaining to the dunderheaded outside world why their life choice was hardly a matter for such astonishment.

"Sheila and I feel that the best way to keep our relationship on an even keel is to be perfectly open and honest about our desires and our feelings for other people," he told the press after an 11-2 home win over East Fife (nine goals for Jackie). "We are not enslaved to each other, we are individuals. That's all I have to say about this very private matter. Has anyone got any questions about the game?"

What was there to ask? Did you think you should have got 12? Are you disappointed at conceding two? There was silence, though that pause held a gag that every juvenile-minded hack in the room wanted to make about scoring. The jokes had already been doing the rounds in the previous days. They morphed into terrace chants over the coming months, but Jackie "answered the chants in the best possible way", as the TV commentators intoned. Goals, goals, goals. And a run in the Scottish Cup that took them all the way to the semi-finals and a plum tie against Celtic at Hampden.

Some called it the biggest game in Scottish football since the 1978 World Cup in Argentina. This was the ultimate test of McMurray, at long last. How would the prodigy, now 24, measure up against the nation's best? How would Celtic cope with his speed, his craft and his beatific agility? Despite the stated modesty of just wanting to do his best for his local team, the Amateur had drawn the world's attention to the unspectacular, some would say inherently mediocre, plain of Scottish football. Now the world wanted the finish that the story was crying out for. The script had been written, Jackie just needed to sign off on it by scoring the winner in the 90th minute, preferably with a crashing volley or a flying header.

He was ordered off after half an hour. The only card of his entire career.

The crowd was shocked, even the Celtic support. They'd wanted to see him play and maybe even shine as much as everyone else. A 3-2 win for the Hoops, with McMurray scoring twice for the Swifts — that would have been their ideal result. Instead, they'd watched as their defenders tied the striker up with borderline legality — holding, pushing, outright shoving, discrete ankle-tapping, muttered calumnies. None of that was enough to throw Jackie off his game. In that time he'd hit the crossbar and both posts. One of those days — as close to an off-day as he was likely to come. But a Czech and a Croatian centre-back, both regulars for their national teams and with years of experience at the top level, come equipped with all the tricks, aided by a referee who seemed determined to show that he wasn't blinded by the international celebrity of this bloody Amateur fellow. A referee who maybe wanted to show himself too. A self-important poser. Ach, I know, our club doesn't criticise officials. But it's all done now. This bastard with his wee black whistle knocked Jackie's career off course. Knackered our upstart village club, right enough.

The score was 0-0. The Swifts had a corner. The Czech lad, Strykhova, had his arms all around Jackie, who made an attempt to set himself free just as the ball was coming over. He raised his left arm, and stricken Strykhova went down clutching his face. Bobby Knox, this referee I was just telling you about, sprints over there like it's a medical emergency, brandishing the red without even talking to his linesman. Jackie looked at him for just one second, surely the nearest he ever came to a murmur of dissent. Then he walked off the field without a word passing his lips. No one jeered him off, not a soul. Say what you like about Glasgow fans, and I've said it all, none of it good. But that day, they were in tune with the moral imbalance of Bobby Knox. The game died. Thousands left at half-time, fans of both teams.

Anton Strykhova, this strapping tractor of a player, was miraculously okay and able to play on. Celtic won 3-0. They were to play Rangers in the final. How about that for a change.

Jackie: "I raised my arm and unwittingly struck the defender in the face. For that I would like to apologise."

Bobby Knox: "In my opinion, McMurray deliberately struck his opponent in a clear act of violence. This will be the tenor of my match report." Shortly afterwards, he was appointed to the UEFA list, even though all the replays showed that Jackie had merely been trying to make space for himself, had barely touched Strykhova's cheek, and that the defender had gone down with the kind of professionalism that Jackie himself abjured. A year later, it emerged that Knox was the member of a small religious creed that believed adultery should be punishable by stoning. Not that there was necessarily any connection between those beliefs and his red card for Jackie. But you can't stop people making connections. Bobby Knox will never be welcome in Thankerton.

The Bairns of the Clyde continued to move up the divisions, but were also badgered by bad luck in the Cups. Again and again, teams would take Jackie out, and his body began to suffer from wear and tear. Thankerton would progress to the final eight or four of the FA Cup or League Cup, then Jackie would come down with a bug or a niggling injury. Just as he was hitting his late 20s, when he should have been in his prime, his body began to suffer. In a League Cup semi-final against Aberdeen, he put the Swifts 2-0 up after 15 minutes, only to suffer a severe cut to the head when he was pushed into the ad hoardings by another lumpen centre half. That was him out the game, and the Swifts out of the competition on penalty kicks after a 2-2 draw. Two days before playing Rangers in the FA Cup quarter-final, he tore his ankle ligaments while running for the bus in Glasgow, worried about being late for training. The damage kept him out for six weeks, de-railing the Swifts' promotion bid to the Premier League at the same time.

I was manning the pie stand at training a couple of weeks after his fall. Not that there was anyone there, no one came from outside to watch the Swifts train if Jackie wasn't playing. He was standing on crutches talking to his dad near the main stand, a muttered conversation that I crept a wee bit closer to hear under the cover of darkness.

"You cannae take a decision like this from one day to the next, son."

"You always said I could."

"Aye, when you were a laddie."

"No change, dad. I'm still a laddie when it comes to fitba. And I'm done. Sheila and I've got a second on the way. I need to focus on my job and my family. It's no fun any more. I was lying there on the pavement in Glasgow almost laughing. Laughing with relief, dad. It was like I got jolted awake. Why the hell am I running? What am I running for?"

There was a pause in the conversation, and then I heard James McMurray let out a heavy sigh.

"Just do me one favour. Don't announce it until the end of the season. Let's see if we can go up first."

"I can do that, dad, but we'll no go up now. We need nine points from four games, and we still have to go to Dundee. I don't want to make out that I'm the major difference here, but we're not going to win at Dens Park."

"Let's just see." Though you could hear the truth of the matter in his voice too. We had no chance.

"Even if we do go up," said Jackie after a short silence, "I just cannae be doing with it all. Players going down for nothing. All the screaming and fury and upset. The same stupid questions every week."

There was a silence. James McMurray knew his son as well as the rest of us. When Jackie reached a decision, there would be no turning back.

I crept back to my pie stand and, you'll think I'm bloody stupid, but I started to greet.

There's still a pitch there, but as we slipped back down the leagues, various Junior clubs took the stands off our hands. There's one in Cambuslang, and one in Newtongrange. One in Bonnybridge and one in Cumbernauld. We gave them away for free, because otherwise they'd just have rusted into nothing, and we didn't want folk coming to Thankerton to make art out of our decline. Jackie, meanwhile, was no more to be persuaded out of retirement than he could have been talked into signing for Liverpool. He and Sheila kept their lives closely out of the public eye until the public eye lost all interest and shut for good. Media attempts to unearth lovers involved in their polyamorous lifestyle were so unsuccessful that we wondered if Sheila had set the whole thing up as a prank. Retroactive documentary film makers and unofficial biographers found the village closed in solidarity to all their approaches. We had our pride, and all that consisted of now was in being unhelpful. It was the village in-joke to send people looking for directions to the McMurray farm instead down to the banks of the Clyde "to look for the bairns". Jackie's colleagues in Glasgow were briefed to act in exactly the same obstructive manner.

The Thankerton Swifts play on Sunday mornings in the Football Central Amateur League. If I can be bothered, I'll walk up to see the second half. "Did ye no bring any pies wie ye, Wullie?" someone will ask, if there's anyone there at all. There's the odd groundhopper, disappointed to find nothing more than a pitch with a fence and a clubhouse. As we fell back through the rankings, our crowds dwindling to three and then just two figures, I made just enough money to retire thanks to the fattened years of Jackie's peak.

You'd think we spend our days talking about the times we got 10,000 every week and sold the place out. Beating Falkirk 5-0 in the League Cup on a glorious floodlit night in the rain. The time we drove to Arbroath in the fog and watched Jackie hit six without breaking sweat. It's still too raw, though. We always defended Jackie, and we always will. What a genuine stalwart of granite integrity. What an immovable force for all that's decent in sport and humanity. You don't find people like that in the game any more. If they were ever there to start with.

And then you watch Scotland on telly struggling at Hampden, losing in Latvia. And you can't help but think. You just can't help but think.

Bad News
for the Brute

The Brute is late, of course. It's part of his shtick. I've tried being later than late, but it's like he's tracking me. Now matter how long I delay my arrival, he's always second to show. He's reliably late, and never apologises. It used to annoy the hell out of me, until I stopped letting things I couldn't influence annoy the hell out of me.

Now I just take it as read that our meetings will start at least an hour after they're scheduled. Today was set for 10.30am. I came just after 11. The Brute swans in just before noon, announcing that it's the perfect time for lunch. "But not this place," he gestures at the club reception and beyond into the canteen, which would be perfectly fine, but it's not somewhere The Brute would deign to be seen. It's self-service, to start with. The Brute needs to see someone running around and fulfilling his requests for medium sparkling water, or Nordic sea salt for his bream, or a bottle of Petit Chablis that's just slightly less chilled than the one they've brought him. He has refined the art of being just enough of a pain in the arse to impress upon the serving classes that they are beholden to a man of wealth and stature. It's a fine way to conceal a wholesale lack of talent.

We could have easily found a quiet spot to talk in the canteen. There are not many people around as it's the last day of the summer break. I've had two weeks off after the World Cup, where I scored three goals and we got knocked out in the quarter-final on penalty kicks. I was nominated to some tournament Best XIs, but not by anyone serious, just a couple of home papers and fan-boy websites. Part of the news vacuum has been filled by rumours of my presumed desire to move to a bigger club on a contract to befit my new standing on the global stage.

The Brute is likely hoping that someone will see him meeting me here to stoke the stories. In a theatrical whisper, he tells me that we can't talk here on my home turf when other clubs are "interested". The team where I've been these past few years habitually finishes between ninth and 14th, but we've won a couple of domestic cups in the past few years, so I've played Europa League. The Brute tells me that I'm better than that. "You need to be playing Champions League. Player of your consistency. Never injured. Never in trouble. Never does anything fucking stupid. International squad player." I never press him. I've always been happy enough here. Reports linking me to the Big Four or "the continent" come and go. Am I interested? Whenever the rumours start, I make myself scarce. By the time I answer The Brute's messages or call him back, he's distraught. "Where were you? Juve's lost interest." Or the transfer deadline has passed. Oh well.

We take The Brute's car into town, he's on the phone booking us into Facundo's, even though it's a Monday lunchtime so he hardly needs to bother. He just likes the opportunity to talk. It's not just a simple reservation for two people to eat spaghetti at a table. Our table has to be in a quiet corner. The tables next to us have to be kept free — don't worry, he'll pay if the restaurant has to turn anybody away. Then he starts to ask them about today's specials, like that can't wait.

One thing I do actually like about The Brute is that he knows fuck all about football, and he doesn't pretend to, so at least we don't have to talk about that. He's never played it — "too fat", in his own words. He'll be in the stadium often enough, but always chewing the ear off whoever's unlucky enough to be sitting next to him. Avoid The Brute is a game played by all his clients whenever he's in town. He does his job well enough, so we let him get on with it. My team-mate Lars is also on his books, and always tells him, "We trust you one hundred per cent. So the deal is, take your cut and keep your big mouth shut." The Brute laughs, the laddish bants makes him feel like he belongs, and he calls Lars The Dane of My Life. He thinks Lars is hilarious, and Lars thinks he's a moron.

By the time that The Brute has given Facundo's all his instructions, we're almost there, and of course we walk into a completely empty restaurant. The head waiter plays the game, and he and The Brute act like they're bonded by years of brotherly love and loss. We are shown to the desired table in the corner, and already The Brute is scanning the menu. I've never known anyone so quick to order, he's always after stuffing his maw, but at least that gives you the chance to get a word in. He's not once asked me how I am, how was my break, where did I go, was I disappointed that we didn't win the World Cup (honest answer: no). He orders calamari to start with, and a steak for his main course. Eventually, there will also be profiteroles, a basic daily human right in The Brute's universe. I'm not even slightly hungry, so I order a small mixed salad and a mineral water.

"It's on me," says The Brute, like I'm skimping on a steak because a footballer's wages are so low these days.

"Thanks," I say.

"I mean, you can order more than a weak salad and a glass of water."

"I know what you mean, Bruce."

"So what's it going to be?" The waiter is standing there, unsure whether to leave or not.

"A small mixed salad and a glass of mineral water, please."

The Brute shrugs and gives the waiter a "what can you do?" look, like he's embarrassed that the bill won't be large enough for a man of his bank balance.

"So, I've heard from Spurs, Arsenal and Borussia Dortmund ..." he begins, with the waiter still in hearing distance. So much for his discretion. It'll probably be on the web in 15 minutes.

"It was great, thanks," I say, interrupting.

"What was?" The Brute's confused.

"My holiday."

"Oh," he says. "Right. Where did you go again?"

"Mountain-hiking in Turkey. I did part of the St. Paul Trail. Going to go back and finish it someday."

"Wait, isn't that against the club guidelines for off-field activities?"

"Don't know, I didn't read the small print. Just thought you might want to know that's why I didn't answer your messages. I was out of reach. But anyway, here I am, alive and healthy, so all's good."

"Right," he says, and you can tell he wants to keep banging on about Arsenal and Spurs, but I've taken the wind out of his throat and stalled his verbal momentum. Does the client really want to talk about summer holidays? Can't we put that behind us now and focus on doubling everybody's wages?

"Ever been to Turkey?" I ask.

"Only that time I fixed up Glenn Hackleton with Fenerbahce..."

"And he left after six weeks when he was released on bail after getting arrested following a fight in a night club, and the kebab-scoffing bastards still haven't paid your commission. Finished your story for you."

This gives the Brute some pause for thought, which isn't something that happens often.

"You alright, mate?" he asks warily. Not out of concern, rather asking if he's going to be alright if I keep on like this.

"I'm great, thanks," I reply. "Feeling fantastic after that hiking holiday. All on my own. Just me and a rucksack and a pop-up tent. Some days I actually cried, I was so fucking happy."

Now there's actual silence, an absolute first with The Brute. He's saved by his phone ringing, which he usually ignores if we're at lunch, but today you can tell it's a lifeline. He looks at the screen and announces, "Gotta take this." He gets up and paces around, but close enough so that I can hear. It's the usual baloney.

"Nah, 25 per cent, that's not negotiable ... I know, I know ... You're not listening, Steve. Make sure he knows what he's getting for that ... we take care of everything ... there's not a player on my roster who's unhappy. Tell him that ... yeah, I know, but tell him again. Every big club in England, I'm balls deep in every last one of them ... yeah, I know, fucking [he names the town we're in]... hopefully for the last time. Lars is good for Atletico, just need to agree terms. Now I have to shift His Royal fucking Highness here ... "

Fair enough, he has a nickname for me too. Plus, I didn't know Lars was going to Spain. Good for him, I suppose. I want to go to Spain too. But not to play football. We had a Europa League match there a couple of years back, in Sevilla or somewhere. We beat them 2-1, and I almost wished we hadn't. The fans were at the players like they genuinely wanted to tear their limbs off for losing. I was in shock. It wasn't just a few idiots like you get in England. Thousands of them, having a mass feral fit. Like this defeat meant the end of the club and the town, the whole place was going to be pillaged and set alight.

The Brute has finished telling Steve how it is, and slides back into his chair and his element.

"So, three goals at The World Cup, mate. Every one of them put another £10 million on your price tag! I'm not kidding, don't look at me like that. Before summer, we were talking maybe 25, 30 mil. Now we're looking at 60!"

"I don't want to go to Arsenal," I say.

"Tottenham fan at heart?"

"When have I ever said that? I don't want to go to Tottenham."

"Useful to know. So, the Bundesliga? The only snag is that they're not paying our kind of prices and wages. I've put out feelers at Dortmund and they're talking more like 40. I've laughed at that, of course, and so has your chairman. But, we can push them higher. And your wages will go up a bit, but nothing like what you'd get in north London."

"I don't want to go to Borussia Dortmund," I say.

"Bayern? I have a contact there."

"No."

The Brute lets out a sigh of impatience, at last, as the waiter brings his calamari and a glass of white wine. "Well, while I dig into this, maybe you can give me a list of the clubs where you do fancy going, so that I've got something to work on and I'm not wasting valuable time ... a grind of fresh pepper, maybe? ... calling up contacts and working up deals that are never going to happen." He squeezes a wedge of lemon over his food and puts his head down to eat, not waiting for the grind of pepper. He's slightly in the huff.

"Let me think about it for a few minutes," I say. "Do you mind if I get a couple of minutes fresh air? Watching you eat makes me feel a bit ill, and we royals are very sensitive to bad table manners." Before he can answer, I'm up and out to the back patio, where only two of the tables are set up, but there's no one eating here yet either.

It's a cool, overcast day, but quite pleasant and breezy. I look up at the clouds. I feel bad about that last comment. I've let his nickname annoy me after all. I contemplate just climbing over the wall and walking away. I look through the window at The Brute shovelling down his squid. For one second, I want to run in and throw the table over and kick him and his bulbous arse out of town. Then a weird kind of sorrow comes over me and I think of The Brute zipping from town to town, always talking, always eating, always masking the isolation of his soul with numbers, riding the wave of fiscal success until he's beached, bloated, no longer breathing, the arteries blocked with fatty cash.

"Sorry, that was out of line," I say when I sit back down. The Brute has finished his starter. My salad's waiting for me.

"It's alright, mate. I am a fat bastard, after all." He tries to laugh, but it's not working. "Thought of any clubs?"

"No."

We stare at each other across the table. I wonder if he's going to ask me something like, "Is that what World Cup success does to a player? Makes him mean and arrogant?" But that's too deep for The Brute. Instead he says, "If it makes a difference, I can reduce my cut from 25 to 22.5 per cent." And I laugh, very loudly, and he looks hurt and confused, like really hurt and confused.

"I appreciate the gesture," I say. "It's not about that, Bruce. It's not about your cut."

"Is it the overall deal? The Saudis are off the scale right now with wages. I could get you in there, no problem, they'd love a World Cup international."

"No," I say. "I'd rather cut off my hands than play there."

"America? You're not Messi, but you'd be a big catch. Couple of clubs there right now are happy to splash for the right names."

"No."

The Brute emits an exasperated whoosh, throws his arms in the air, and sits back in his seat. The steak comes, thankfully, and we both set down to eating for a few minutes. My salad's soon done, though, so I take the chance to talk while he mauls his main course.

"I've been earning a fantastic amount of money the past few years," I say.

"Yes, but..."

"I know, Bruce, nothing like as high as I could be. Nothing like what they pay at Spurs and Arsenal and even humble little Borussia Dortmund. But I've bought a house and paid for it. I bought my parents a house and paid for it. I bought my brother a house and paid for it. And I've still got more cash than I know what to do with."

"I know some very good investment brokers..."

"Stop. Just eat and listen to me."

The Brute shrugs and keeps on masticating.

"I could go to Arsenal and treble my wages, or whatever. I don't care about Arsenal. Even if I played for Arsenal and was on a million quid a week, I still don't think I'd care if we won or not. It would be the same at Tottenham or Borussia fucking Dortmund. What I care about is that I'd hate it, because I'd be getting paid a million quid a week, or whatever, and all these people there would be expecting me to play like someone who earns a million quid a week. The money doesn't make it worthwhile. Every day, every game, worried that you'll be shit, because I'm not really that good to start with, or not as good as they'd want me to be. Or not good enough at all. You miss an easy chance. For Arsenal against Spurs. Arsenal fans turn on you. Spurs fans delight in your failure. I've missed an easy chance for Arsenal against Spurs, and because I get paid a million quid a week to not miss that easy chance, people around the world, not just North London, people around the whole world are looking at me and pointing, and there's only scorn, anger, hatred and mockery. And there may be players who can take it, but I'm not one of them. Here, in this town you think is such a provincial shithole, here — even though I'm supposedly his Royal fucking Highness — here, no one gets that upset. We won the League Cup and the FA Cup and we played in Europe, and no one here had ever done that before, so they love us, and they forgive us if we miss an easy chance, even though we're already earning more in a week than they earn all year. And even here, that's starting to change, the expectations have been raised by those silver trophies, because Arsenal fans say, yeah, but it's just a one-off, it's just a phase, Arsenal will be big and glorious forever more, but not you, and so our fans are starting to ask why we can't stay at the top forever, why can't we get into the Champions fucking League even though we've never been fucking champions, and frankly I've had enough of all this shit about sticking a round ball into the fucking net."

The Brute has stopped chewing. He looks almost catatonic, his mouth slightly open, the grey half-chewed meat peeping through his jaundiced teeth.

"So, in short, I'm quitting the game."

I'm worried The Brute might throw up for a second, but then he catches himself, chews furiously, pointing his fork at me. "No, don't be daft, lad. You can't do that. There's something wrong with you. I knew it as soon as I saw you today. But it's okay, we'll sort it out. We'll talk about it."

"I have talked about it," I say. "That's what we just did. I've told you everything. Pre-season training starts tomorrow, and I won't be there."

I don't tell him that I've only just made this ultimate decision right now, on the spot, and that it's the mere presence of The Brute himself that's helped me get here. Of course, I've thought about it. Sometimes, it terrified me, some other days it excited me way more than the thought of lifting the World Cup. Now, at this precise moment, I'm so high I could run down the street whooping and naked and throwing money to the wind.

"You're only 28! You're at peak earning for a football player. You just showed the world how good you are, for Christ's sake. Please, lad, come on, think about this properly."

"I'm going mountain-hiking. I'm going to jump into lakes without worrying that I've breached the insurance clause on my multi-million pound contract."

"Just do a couple of years in the Saudi League and quit then!"

"Can I take my boyfriend?"

"WHAT!"

I laugh so hard. I don't have a boyfriend, not right now, but it's the perfect way to stop The Brute. I should have waited until he took a slurp of wine so that I can write that he sprayed it across the table. I stand up and ask him to please tell the club that I am tearing up my contract, and that I would be happy if they re-paid my loyalty over the past few years by issuing a press release saying that we have parted on good terms and via mutual consent.

"And on my way out, I'll pay for lunch," I add. And I turn my back on The Brute, and I leave a one hundred pound note on the bar as I walk out. And so, I don't know if the Brute will finish his steak and go on to order profiteroles. I suspect, though, that he will manage both.

We Can't Support You Evermore

"Are you up for the challenge, Kyle?" Both men are on their feet, and there are gargantuan smiles, hefty handshakes, robust blows to the back and shoulders, all under the guise of congratulations. Kyle has a job, his first proper salary, no more cash in brown envelopes, this money will be paid into his bank account on the 15th. of every month. Then Kyle will be going places. More specifically, he hopes that he'll be going to places connected to the fact that his new company is the main sponsor of the local football club. The team that Kyle has supported since he was five years old and first stood on their bony terrace, watching his late step-dad dad turn into a bitter, despairing critic for 90 minutes on Tuesday nights and Saturday afternoons. (Which, as it turned out, was the nicer side of his personality.)

We need to protect Kyle's identity, so the team will only be referred to here as The Fletchers. That name harks back to an artisanal era in this medium-sized city when, you may have guessed, the craftsmen made and traded barrels. That no longer works as an industry, but it's a central tenet of the city's identity. There are barrels everywhere you go, but they're only for show. Barrel key rings, hats and scarves, and t-shirts saying Meet The Fletchers with a cartoon of four barrels — a mum and a dad barrel and two kid barrels, all in a row, humanised with cheery smiles.

That same expression is on Kyle's face right now, as he tells himself that everything's going to be fine. He's not a suits kind of bloke, it's true. He's not a meetings and emails kind of bloke, either. Nor is he into hosting 'sales events', which will be a big part of his new job. He's told the man who is shaking his hand that he is "passionate" about sales, and that was a colossal lie. Perhaps both men know it. Very few people can say with conviction that they love capitalism, that they're passionate about it. We're all just playing along due to a dearth of options.

Truth be told, Kyle would rather be a postman, out in the fresh air, a gently whistling human signifier of stability. He's always imagined an interview where he could say, "I feel this is a job where I could really deliver." His mum had other ideas, because Kyle was good in school, without even having to make much effort. At college, he wanted to study graphic design (no such thing as Postal Studies, unfortunately). Nonsense, said his mum. Business Studies. How about a language on top? Business Studies with Japanese. Fucking hell, even Kyle was impressed when he was telling people that, despite being bored by business and extremely challenged by Japanese. Still, the stories from his half-year studying in Japan form a big chunk of Kyle's anecdotal archive. He'd used a couple in the interview with the CEO, Trevor Dunsett, MBE, the main now pumping Kyle's hand and trying to crash his back in. "We're thinking of opening up an office in Tokyo," Dunsett has mentioned. "Is that something that would interest you?" Very much so, Kyle had enthused, though not really because of the expansion potential of VitaHerb (his new employer), but because he was still exchanging emails with a girl in Nagoya called Miyuki. They'd met in a record shop, both studying the sleeve of the same vinyl re-issue of Thelonious Monk's Underground LP. He'd asked her to go to a jazz club with him the next night, and then they'd gone out together to gigs around the city for all his remaining weeks at the university. Not until the last night had they held hands. No kiss, she wouldn't allow it, and anyway, she'd just started laughing whenever Kyle put his face close to hers, the same way she laughed when picking him up on his poor accent and grammatical errors. That laugh, he still tells himself, had touched him way more than any kiss could have. And all the things that had yet to happen between them convinced Kyle that he was still in love with her, even though that last night was two years in the past. Two years and four months, to be more exact. But still, Miyuki "is my Japanese girlfriend", and if anyone asks when they last saw each other, Kyle says that in the digital age that's not so important, they can talk by video every day (even though they don't).

What's VitaHerb? There's only a long answer to that question, and it's a sales pitch. It's the answer to all your health problems, but how can that be? VitaHerb is an 'alternative drug' that you take twice daily, and it may prevent all kinds of disease (except that it doesn't), and it makes you feel good about yourself and life, and haters and naysayers who ask for clinical proof are just the sort of people you need to cut out of your life at the same time you let VitaHerb in. They're a growing company based in California, very much on the up, which is maybe why — as yet — their only western European office is in the town where the Fletchers play. There are offices in Minsk and Bucharest too, though Kyle's not exactly sure how many people work there. He doesn't yet know that it's half an employee per city, and that she commutes between the two.

Kyle's new title will be Vice President Recruitment, which he soon finds out is the same title of at least a dozen other colleagues.

"We are an egalitarian company!" proclaims Trevor Dunsett, MBE, when Kyle asks him what the next step up would be. "Your title's not important. It's what you make of it." Does that mean anything? Before Kyle can decide, Trevor's moved the conversation on to Strategic Targets. These targets have today become an important pillar of Kyle's life, now that he's signed the contract. It means he will be persuading fellow human beings (anyone 18 or over is fair game) that they not only need VitaHerb to lose weight and keep themselves alive, but they need to become roving ambassadors for VitaHerb too, which means paying the company an investment sum (otherwise known as 'cash') so that they receive in return (otherwise known as 'paying for') supplies of VitaHerb to sell to their friends and family too. They also get free t-shirts, jackets, badges and caps that say 'Live Happy to 100 – Ask for VitaHerb!' Kyle's not yet fully convinced that VitaHerb will guarantee what it promises, but when he sees how many people turn up at a 'Happy to 100!' sales event a couple of days later, he can't help but be mesmerised by the pill's apparent power to stir up such a crowd. As Trevor says, just because the gloomy, negative bureaucrats at the Food and Drug Administration have not approved VitaHerb, that doesn't mean it doesn't work. Just look at the hundreds of thousands of happy, healthy Americans who are already convinced! Who would you rather believe? Of course the government doesn't want you to live longer!

California's a long way from where The Fletchers play, but the west coast executives figured that sponsoring the town's soccer team was a smart move to get the company's name out there and have them identify with the local community. Office space was cheap and plentiful in the town of former Fletchers, thanks to Brexit, and Trevor Dunsett MBE was a cheap recruit too, thanks to a corruption scandal at one of his previous companies that no one in America cared about. They just needed someone with one of those posh British accents who happened to be a Member of the

Most Excellent Order of the British Empire, an accolade which for some reason the disgraced Trevor Dunsett MBE had not yet been asked to return. *The Guardian* wrote a piece about his new job, and what he was selling, and asked how he still could be a member of something Most Excellent, but who on earth still reads a doomy catalogue of Woke like *The Guardian* (as Trevor asked his American bosses)? Certainly not the robust and radiant consumers of VitaHerb.

"Now then, young man, how's it going?" Kyle has been at VitaHerb for a week, and he's been summoned into the office of the Most Excellent Trevor Dunsett. Kyle tells him about the induction course he's been on with six other new recruits, including the impressive sales event, and makes sure to say what a superb and invigorating week of instruction it's been so far. Does he need to reiterate that he's still passionate about sales? He decides that he does not — after all, he'd got the job now. He also doesn't mention how uneasy he felt when new recruits toured the building and were introduced to the Good News Team, 25 middle-aged women in a large room who countered any negative reviews of VitaHerb on the internet with concerted campaigns of testimony from very sick people (or relatives of very sick people), all of whom swore that VitaHerb had saved them, body and soul. Briony, the turbo-perky American woman in charge of the induction course, had praised this part of the operation almost as much as the miracle pill itself. The room was staffed 24 hours a day, "promoting visibility and positivity", according to Briony. "If we don't defend ourselves," she said, "then nobody else will."

Trevor Dunsett MBE is pleased to hear that Kyle's first week is going well. He tells Kyle that he suspected from the very first moments of his interview that Kyle was going to be the pick of the bunch. "You're a quickstep smarter than the rest of them," he says, winking at Kyle, who has seen no evidence from talking to his fellow recruits that he's in any way better, or smarter or quicker to step than any of them. They're all in the same position — graduates who've come back to Barrel-Town to live with their parents because no one can afford London rents any more. Three of them he hadn't seen since they were at school, but they avoided talking about that much because they wanted to feel they were going forwards, with VitaHerb, not backwards to falling asleep during double Maths.

"Now then," the CEO continues, "I'm taking you out of the induction course tomorrow because I need you to represent the company at a very important meeting." He asks Kyle if the name Bob Vickie means anything to him. Kyle, already thrilled, says that of course it does, Vickie is chairman of the team nicknamed The Fletchers. He's thinking of a lavish lunch with himself, Bob Vickie and Trevor Dunsett MBE, and then he's thinking about free tickets and away travel at weekends to see The Fletchers, who just had a very good season and and almost got promoted from Division Four (as we old-timers call it) . Kyle wonders if his status as an exceptional recruit will allow him to become the company's point of contact with the football club. He wonders if this could somehow become his main role, allowing him to skip the 'Happy to 100' sales events.

"It's like this," Trevor Dunsett MBE continues. "You may have read that the sponsorship contract is up for renewal." Kyle knows about this as well. The club is hoping for a better deal on the back of promotion, and Vitaherb's soaring local profile and burgeoning sales. His mind is racing ahead and has already appointed itself as part of the negotiating team, maybe even its head. Kyle is starting to believe Trevor Dunsett's hype about him being the top recruit of the bunch. Perhaps The Fletchers would be so impressed that they in turn would offer him a job as their Head of Marketing. If no such post yet existed, they would surely create it when they saw how passionate and exceptional he was. Kyle is suddenly so excited that he needs to go to the bog.

"Now, when we signed the first deal two years ago, we were new in this town. It was important for us to get our name out there, and in that respect it's worked very well." Trevor Dunsett MBE pauses for a second and looks Kyle right in the eye. "You said during your interview that you were open to any kind of challenge, isn't that right?" Kyle can't remember saying any such thing, but doesn't doubt that he certainly did. He would hardly have been offered the job if he'd said that a challenge was okay, right enough, but only within limits. Obviously, he agrees that he is up for any kind of challenge. Like negotiating a new sponsorship deal with The Fletchers? he almost adds, but manages to hold himself back because he wants to hear the words from the lips of his wonderful new boss.

"Here's the situation. In the US, VitaHerb has been making more money than they know what to do with." Yes! thinks Kyle. This is it. They want to not just sponsor The Fletchers, but pump money into them too. Premier League football within five years. Champions League within the decade. A women's team. Friendlies against the US national team. Tons of beautiful Californian girls roaming the streets of Barrel-Town …

"So the plan is to find a Premier League team instead to up the UK profile. I need you to sit down with Bob Vickie and tell him that we're very sorry, but we won't be renewing the deal this coming season. They'll need to find another sponsor."

Trevor Dunsett MBE is staring right at Kyle now, who feels himself sinking into the comfortable executive couch he'd been almost floating above just a few seconds before.

"Mister Dunsett …"

"Trevor, please. You know the company has a first names policy."

Kyle is swallowing hard. His heart's thumping and he might even start to cry. He dispenses with a term of address, he can't get the word 'Trevor' over his bottom lip. "I've been a supporter of the team all my life."

"You mentioned that at your interview, Kyle. You know the club, so of course you're the man for this job." Trevor is suddenly curt, borderline impatient. Still the testing stare. Yes, it's a test, Kyle. You must perform and pass.

"Could perhaps someone else who's not a fan of the team break the news to Mr. Vickie?" Bob Vickie was that rarity in running a lower league football club — an honest, competent and likeable individual.

"No, they can't, Kyle" says Trevor Dunsett MBE. "Because I've chosen you for the job." Kyle nods, in crass contradiction of his inner desire to shake his head sideways. "It's a simple task. First, you apologise that I can't be there, and tell them that I've been called to California for an urgent meeting. Then you thank them very much for their co-operation over the past two years, and then you tell them that we're done. You return to this office and confirm that you have completed the … challenge, let's call it. The meeting's at 10am." Trevor Dunsett MBE emits a spurt of a chuckle. "I presume you know where it is."

Kyle nods, stands up, nods again, thanks the CEO (for what?), then turns and leaves the room, dizzy with dread, and wondering if he quits now, would he still get paid for the week he's spent on the induction course pretending that he was passionate about sales?

That night, Kyle dreams that he's a postman. He knocks on the door of a large standalone Victorian villa. Bob Vickie answers the door, he smiles and invites Kyle inside. Kyle says that he couldn't possibly sully such a beautiful house by tramping his dirty boots along the polished hallway floor. Both he and Bob Vickie look down at his boots, and they are inexplicably covered with mud, there are even worms writhing through the thread holes instead of boot laces. Kyle is embarrassed, horrified, and thrusts a letter into Bob Vickie's hands. Bob, still friendly, opens the envelope and starts to read the letter, and then his face changes and he thunders at Kyle,

"You bastards!" Kyle starts to run back down the driveway, but suddenly there are Alsatian dogs coming at him from all directions, barking and snapping...

Kyle wakes up. It is 5.30am. He tries to get back to sleep, but all he can think about is having to go and see Bob Vickie at the football club. He imagines Bob Vickie saying, "Don't worry about it, we were lining up a better deal with another sponsor in any case." That's the only possible outcome Kyle can imagine that won't end up with both parties being extremely upset. Or, he could just not turn up. Quit the job through blatant absenteeism. Go straight to the Post Office and apply for a round. Don't tell mum. Just head out one morning in the new uniform, whistling. He's 23 years old, surely he can stand up to his own mother ...

It's 6am. He turns on the local news, hoping to hear how VitaHerb's offices burned down overnight. Everyone's safe, but the company will not be operational for a few weeks, all employees are asked to stay at home for now. There is no such story on the local news, instead a body has been found on an allotment, the police are not looking for anyone in connection with the body. No murder, just natural causes. It's how people die in Barrel-Town, no drama here. Kyle's final hope is that the body belongs to Trevor Dunsett MBE, but he can't imagine that Trevor has an allotment on the North Common. He gets up and turns on his computer, and the first thing he sees is an email from the CEO, sent just 10 minutes ago. So the allotment corpse definitely isn't Trevor's, but wait, maybe Trevor is emailing him to say that the company's changed its mind. In California, it's still the night before, perhaps they'd been in meetings all day re-considering the benefits of sponsoring The Fletchers.

"Hi Kyle," says the email. "When you go to your meeting this morning, don't forget that we are a business. You are smart enough to know as well as I do what that means. There is no room for sentimentality. We are not here to be friends for life with the people we do business with. In business, results are all that count. A bit like football! Look forward to hearing all about it, Trevor."

"Fuck off, Trevor," Kyle says out loud, then worries that somehow the email can transmit his words back down the fibre optic cable. Not for the first time, he googles VitaHerb, but not just the company name, he googles the words fraud, fake, and problems too. The Good News Team were doing a hell of a job. Whenever individuals on chat rooms and in message boards dare to slander the company's reputation (snake oil salesmen, Ponzi scheme etc.), a dozen outraged 'customers' have crashed in to refute all allegations and make personal attacks on the poster, within a matter of minutes. The concerted barrage looks so blatant that obviously the company doesn't care — it's less about saying that VitaHerb is a life-saving product, more about: whoever tries to badmouth us, we are gonna fuck you up and smack you down.

Am I working for conmen? Kyle asks himself, amazed that it's taken him so long to ask this obvious question. Is Kyle culpable in the con if he recruits dozens of people who want to believe that VitaHerb works? If people taking a pill with no medical properties are happier and feel healthier for taking it, doesn't that mean, in some sense, that it works? A psychological feel-good product, with none of the negative side-effects of approved medication. What is there not to like about that?

Kyle avoids his mum this morning, because she will sense that he's worried about something, and she will not stop asking him questions until she's found out what the problem is. True, she'd likely have some appropriate words and advice for him. She was not a bad mother, not at all, but she was a total mother, there was no escaping it and there never would be. Unless you waited in your bedroom until she was done in the bathroom, then waited in the bathroom until she was done in the kitchen and had gone to work.

She knocks on the bathroom door and asks him if he's not going to be late for his Induction Course, she knows it starts at 9, but Kyle calls back that he has a meeting, and it's not until 10. What about the induction course, she asks. Of course she does. She needs to know fucking everything. Kyle can't lie to his mother, not anymore, so he tells her that he's been taken out of the induction course for the day for a special meeting at the football club, and that causes his mum to say, "Ooh, that sounds promising!" but then she has to go. She asks him if he'll be home for dinner, and Kyle says he doesn't know yet, and his mum says, well can he let her know before noon because she'll need to go shopping in her lunch break, so Kyle says, I'll be busy, just don't reckon with me tonight, and his mum sighs and says that she'll likely be eating on her own again in front of the teatime news, and Kyle's tempted to say that 23-year-old men shouldn't still be having tea with their mum every night, but he doesn't bother, it's hardly going to make her less of a total mum.

Even once his mum has left, Kyle stays in the bathroom, sitting on the bog for another half hour, nurturing his nerves. Eventually, there's nothing left to shit, and Kyle thinks that at least he won't be holding in farts during the meeting with Bob Vickie. He doesn't linger in the kitchen, he's way too strung up to eat any breakfast, although his mum's left coffee on, and a plate and a spoon for cereal, and a packet of Harvest Crunch and a jug of milk, and a banana and a box of blueberries, and a piece of paper with a note that says Good for you! And then an arrow pointing at the fruit. Kyle has to laugh, because at first he thinks it's a note congratulating him for having a business meeting at the football club.

He puts the fruit back in its bowl, and wonders if all the people who took VitaHerb instead ate blueberries and a banana every day, would they be just as healthy?

Kyle walks to the club, he knows that it takes exactly 17 minutes on a match day. He sets out at 9.30am. Why does he not set out at 9.43am?

It's just in case something goes wrong on the way. Like, a burst water main that causes him to take a detour. A mourning procession for the unidentified person found on the North Common allotments. A horrific head-on automobile collision involving … wait, who's that bleeding and broken on the upside down SUV's steering wheel? It's none other than Trevor Dunsett MBE. Oh my God, this is terrible, I'll have to miss the meeting now helping out at this accident, and obviously the whole sponsorship situation will have to be put on ice for the time being. Until we see if Trevor Dunsett MBE is still alive and capable of working, and if he can even remember who he is after this terrible blow.

What are the chances, thinks Kyle, mooching about in front of estate agent windows so he's not too early. What are the chances that even if his boss was involved in such an accident, that his airbag wouldn't work? Bloody hell, look at the price of a terraced house, even here in Barrel-Town. He's going to be living with his mum until he's 30 at this rate. Seven rent-free years to save up for a deposit on a house that would still be mostly owned by the bank. Seven years of 'Happy to 100' sales events. Trevor Dunsett had not asked him in the interview where he saw himself in five years' or ten years' time. It was a shame, because he'd actually prepared an answer. "I will be wherever my passion, my industry and my diligence takes me, and that will be a long way up from where I am now." And yet now, he blushes even thinking about it.

Why do you want to become a postman, Kyle?

Dunno, just fancy it.

Where do you see yourself in five years' time?

Still a postman putting letters in letter-boxes, I should think.

Will you still be living with your mum in five years' time?

If nothing better comes along. Have I got the job?

Kyle arrives at the ground, still 10 minutes too early. That's a good thing, though, because it suddenly occurs to him that he doesn't really know where to go. He's been to this stadium hundreds of times, and he has no idea if the club has anything other than a metaphorical boardroom. There's a double glass door that says Authorized Personnel Only, but that's just for match days. He opens it and finds an unmanned reception desk. There's a bell, though, and he rings it. After three minutes, and two more rings, a flustered woman appears. Must have been having a dump, thinks Kyle, and wonders what she would say if he thought out loud. She was attractive, maybe he even recognised her, a couple of years below him at school, was it Gina Hussingham? Her sister Bridget had been in Kyle's class. Would Gina be the kind of girl who would laugh and think it was earthy and honest to talk about the fact she'd just had her morning dump? Kyle's not the kind to take a risk like that 15 seconds in. Instead he tells her that he's here to meet Bob Vickie, and Gina Hussingham says that won't do, Mr. Vickie has an important meeting with the club sponsor at 10, he'll have to make an appointment for another time. Kyle knows he should smile, but he can't, he gets a little flustered instead, in case they throw him out before he can even explain himself. He says that he is in fact from VitaHerb, and he's here for the meeting she just mentioned. Lovely Gina, who looks way better than she did when she was a hissing, knock-kneed 14-year-old who liked to smoke cigarettes and fight dirty, looks confused for a second, and then she turns professional. She smiles, apologises, and explains that she had been expecting Mr. Dunsett, and not for the final time Kyle explains that the MBE guy had to fly to California for an emergency meeting with the parent company. Which is good, it implies a crisis in the making, and Kyle thinks that might help explain the withdrawal of sponsorship. But the withdrawal of sponsorship is down to having too much money, not too little, so unless he lies about the reasons for cancelling the contract, Kyle will have to forget that excuse. There's no easy way out of this now, he thinks. His first ever official contact with the club he loves, and it's going to be dealing them a mean and unexpected blow.

Kyle follows Gina Hussingham upstairs, keeping his eyes down all the way. Gina says, It's Kyle, isn't it? Weren't you at school with my sister? Kyle confesses that he was, and duly asks what Bridget's up to. Sailing the world, working on cruise liners, says Gina. Absolutely loves it. And Kyle wishes that was his job too right now. He almost asks her which company, and where can he apply. He wonders if Bridget looks as good as her sister. There had been a party once, six or seven years ago now, where a girl he didn't know had come up to him and announced, "Bridget Hussingham wants to dance with you", and Kyle had done nothing about it. Like everyone else, he'd fancied himself in love with Michaela Zwieback, the stunning tall Austrian who'd turned up at the start of sixth form from Kitzbühel, living with her English aunt because her parents had been killed by an avalanche, speaking English like the fucking queen and top of all the science classes within half a year, fucking the best lookers on the rugby team, one a month. Bridget, Kyle considered at the time, was not in her league. And now, three steps away from the first meeting of his career, Kyle realises that he should have danced with Bridget Hussingham, not swooned over an unattainable Austrian girl who didn't even know his name. Bridget had had the courage to explore the world. Had she ever docked in Nagoya?

The meeting takes place in the club bar. Not just with Bob Vickie, but the entire board, eleven men and one woman. There's a massive spread laid on, there are two waitresses. Slender, grey-haired and still handsome Bob Vickie is also surprised to see Kyle, not Trevor. Same goes for the whole board, who are clearly expecting a delegation. Kyle feels humiliated, stupid, out-of-place, out-of-depth, he wants to tell them sorry, this is a massive misunderstanding, I can't go through with this, I love you all, I love The Fletchers, I can't be the one to do this to you. He could sob, and get their sympathy. He imagines Gina Hussingham sending Bridget a text message saying, 'You'll never guess who showed up at the club today, and what happened next!'

There's a funny atmosphere now, and Kyle knows that the club senses that something's not right. He wonders how many people from VitaHerb were here the last time they negotiated. Surely it had been a whole team. He wonders why Trevor Dunsett MBE could not at least have warned the club that Kyle, the office junior who hasn't even completed the corporate induction course, is here to talk about something so important to both sides. Kyle thinks that it might simply have been that Trevor is too chicken-shit scared to own the decision, and that he's sent Kyle in as a kind of sacrifice. Kyle is so upset at Trevor right now that he wants to tell The Fletchers that he is going to resign, and that he wants to work for them instead. Anything, he'll do anything. Assistant to the groundsman. And he knows the club is run on a very tight budget, so he'll work for nothing. He'll be an intern until they can find a space for him.

"It must be very urgent for Trevor to miss a meeting like this," observes Bob Vickie, observing Kyle, who knows this comment is a question. "I hope everything's okay." And then for a second, Kyle is annoyed with Bob Vickie and his leading observations. You're just as bad as us, thinks Kyle, getting a sponsor that's a Ponzi scheme conning people out of their cash in return for a no-miracles pill that supposedly contains elements of a rare herb found only in Borneo, but now grown in Californian hot-houses to meet the demand of all those satisfied customers who have been liberated of their health concerns. Why couldn't you find a sponsor that at least produces something, like … Kyle struggles to imagine alternative sponsors. Half the teams in the league are sponsored by gambling companies. How is that any better than VitaHerb? Cars, oil, Middle Eastern and Asian airlines aligned to governments that imprison and torture people. The more he thought about it, the higher VitaHerb rose on football's ethical scale. A scale that's measured in units from minus 100 to zero.

"He couldn't tell me what it was about," says Kyle, "but he was very concerned, and of course very particular that I should offer you all his sincerest apologies."

"And Roger couldn't have come instead?"

Kyle has no idea who Roger is. "I'm afraid not, Roger's on leave right now."

"Is he now?" says Bob Vickie. "That's odd, because I just talked to him yesterday."

Awkward pause. "Perhaps we should postpone the meeting until they're back," someone offers, and there are some murmurs of assent. Kyle says that he is absolutely authorised to act on behalf of the company, and that they should definitely go ahead, especially as they've put on such a spread. That's the kind of outlay a team like The Fletchers can't afford every week. All kinds of smoked hams and fish, and French cheeses, you could actually smell them.

Bob Vickie gives an avuncular chuckle and says that Kyle is right, we shouldn't let the food go to waste, even though there are not as many people here from VitaHerb as they'd been expecting. Kyle looks through the smoked glass window of the bar and out on to the stadium. It doesn't feel like his stadium from inside here. It doesn't feel like a stadium right now, all neat and still and empty. He wonders if he'll ever be able to come back here again. Bob has taken him by the arm and is leading him to a chair, someone's dimmed the lights, Gina Hussingham brings him a plate of food, and now there's a presentation on the big screen. VitaHerb and The Fletchers, a Partnership Forged for Barrel-Town! For the next 15 minutes, Kyle watches the highlights from the last two seasons. Not much football, but lots of people in suits shaking hands down on the field, up in the executive boxes. Shots of VitaHerb HQ, with sonnets of praise for its role in boosting the local economy. Bob Vickie is interviewed, saying that without VitaHerb, there is no way that The Fletchers would have challenged for promotion last season. A run to the fourth round of the FA Cup, with their defeat to Everton having been shown live on Sky, had not only bolstered income, but had upped the profile of the town, the team and the company. We are working together, and it's working very well for both sides, says Bob Vickie to the camera. Kyle cannot even think about touching the plate of food. He has never had a proper girlfriend (even though he maintains that Miyuki in Nagoya really is his proper girlfriend, they had held hands for a few minutes 28 months ago), but Kyle knows this must be how it feels before you are about to dump someone. And that someone has no idea what you are about to do, because that someone thinks the relationship is going really well. Would Kyle's relationship with Bridget Hussingham have gone really well if that dance he refused had turned into something more lasting? Or would she have done this to him. "I'm really sorry, Kyle, I've found someone bigger and better. A Premier League fuck-buddy who's going to take me to all the places that you can't afford. Don't take it personally, it's just good business."

Kyle wants the film to run and run, no matter how uncomfortable it is. What comes next is going to be much worse. He wants the lights to stay down, keeping the dozen board members as silent silhouettes and preventing the next event: Kyle versus The Club he's supported all his life. He never even had a 'big' team like every other fucker in the school yard with their Liverpool and Man United shirts and bags and hats and badges and scarves, and their shitty debates about how good the latest 25 million quid left back from Ecuador was. How often had Kyle got into disputes with them about supporting your local team. How he'd loved to abjure the Champions League on a Tuesday night to go and watch The Fletchers lose 1-0 at home to Accrington, just so that he could bang on about it at length the next morning. And in all those years, he's thinking, how many of my class-mates said, Kyle's right, I'm binning all this replica gear I got for Christmas and am off with him in the rain to pay fifteen quid to watch professional shite. And Kyle also remembers how he would stand on the terrace for that dreadful defeat to Accrington and wonder what the chances were that Michaela Zwieback would show up there too, on her own, a fan of The Fletchers since the day she arrived in mourning from Kitzbühel, hoping to find something to fill that gap, a football club to love, and now here's Kyle too, chatting and laughing with her about fourth division losers, and how she hates the Champions League too …

"So we were wondering what VitaHerb's reaction to our short film is," Bob Vickie was saying as the blinds were raised and the lights came on, and everyone could see that Kyle had not touched a thing from the lavish breakfast buffet. "We feel that it very much sums up the spirit of our excellent co-operation, and we are of course all wondering how VitaHerb sees our relationship going forward."

Are you up for the challenge, Kyle? This is not like Bridget Hussingham's request for a dance. You can't just ignore it for seven years. You have to stand up. Put down your plate. Speak loudly and clearly. Convey the short and brutal message from Trevor Dunsett MBE. Stand tall and dominant. Let this little club know that they have been useful, right enough, but now you are moving on to bigger things.

Kyle stands up, his heart beating like a Pet Shop Boys 12" re-mix. Everybody is looking at him. Everybody is wondering what the fuck this kid is going to say. They're already disrespected, Kyle thinks, the message is surely just going to confirm what they must have started to think. It's like they were expecting King Charles and got the Earl of Tewkesbury's dim-witted nephew instead. But it doesn't matter. If they all keep taking VitaHerb, they will live happy until they're 100. Maybe even longer. Can I tell them that? They will think I'm insane, but that would be a good diversion. Wait, this is okay, I'm dreaming, but in fact he's fainting and falling, along with his untouched buffet breakfast. He hits the floor and blacks out.

"I don't know why you didn't tell me this morning that you weren't feeling well," Kyle's mum is saying. "I'd have kept you home. I know you're not the kind to make things up. I don't think you missed more than two days at Kelsey Comp."

It's only a few minutes since Kyle woke up in his hospital bed with a headache, his mum waiting besides him. It was just past midday. His mum had yelped and a nurse came running, but pulse and eyes and speech were all in working order. Now he's under observation, mainly from his mum. The rest of the A&E ward is empty. Another quiet morning in Barrel-Town.

"I felt fine when I got up," says Kyle, omitting to mention that he'd felt like running away to Scotland thanks to the the very first challenge that MBE-boss had sent his way. It isn't technically a lie, because he hadn't felt physically ill.

"You can't possibly have been," says Kyle's mum. She's sure about everything in life. When Kyle's step-dad had thrown a bottle which had smashed against the wall behind her at head-height, she had thrown him out and never once even looked like caving in to his weeks of simpering for mercy and a key to the new locks. "I was wondering if it was last night's chicken. Then again, I feel fine."

"Well, you haven't missed a day's work for nine years," says Kyle, because it was as much a part of his mum's mythic statistical canon as his two lost days at Kelsey Comp.

"Very funny," she replies. "I suppose you can't be feeling too bad if you're up to being a cheeky bugger already."

Kyle reaches to his bedside table and takes a drink of water. His mum continues to observe him with a look that says, 'What am I going to do with you?' He's touched that she's here, and he thinks about telling her what went down at the football club. And then he thinks how much she's worked to help pay for him to go to college, on top of all the student loans, and how weak he will seem if he says that he's going to quit his first job before he's even taken home a pay cheque. Before he's even finished the fucking induction course or hosted a single 'Happy to 100!' sales event. To confess that he is not passionate about sales. That he does not have a hard-on for hawking, and probably never will.

"I think it was nerves, mum," Kyle says. "My first meeting and all that, you know."

"Really?" she says. "But you were just there for the experience, weren't you. It's not like you were doing a 30-minute Power Point presentation."

Kyle continues to struggle with telling his mum the truth. The thought of the boardroom makes his stomach fall, all over again. "I was there on my own," he croaks.

"What do you mean? Did the others not turn up?"

"No, they weren't supposed to. They sent me there on my own."

Kyle's mum narrows her eyes, ready to interrogate him until she finds out how he's got his facts wrong. "They can't possibly have done that, you're just a lad barely out of his shorts. What was this meeting about?"

When Kyle tells her everything, minus the details about his regrets for ignoring Bridget Hussingham's dance invitation, or the blossoming of her younger sister, or his new career plan to work the cruise ships and maybe stop off in Nagoya to see Miyuki, his mum explodes into action. Before he can stop her, she's calling VitaHerb's central switchboard and demanding to speak to "whoever's in charge". Kyle tells her to stop, so she leaves the ward, phone held to her ear, and he can hear her pacing the corridor, shouting to various colleagues he probably hadn't even met yet about sending a virgin to be sacrificed, though not in those words exactly. Then a doctor shouts at Kyle's mum for making such a noise and she goes outside, and then half an hour later she returns, red-faced and indignant, and Kyle knows that he will never be able to show up at VitaHerb HQ again. Despite the humiliation, he feels a hundred times better.

His mum sits down on the bed. "Well, I told them," she says, much quieter now.

"You shouldn't have done that, mum."

"They shouldn't have done that to you!"

"I know, mum. But..."

"What? Were you going to stand up for yourself?"

"Maybe. At some point. Just not today. It's for me to decide. It's four years since I left school, you know."

"That's not so long," his mum mumbles. Then they sit for a long time, staring in different directions.

"Did you speak to Trevor?"

"No, they said he wasn't there. I just yelled at whoever they put me through to, until they passed me on to someone else to yell at."

Kyle let out a short laugh. "Great work, mum."

"I'm sorry," she says, and takes his hand. "I got a bit worked up. They should never..."

"I know, mum. I know."

Kyle feels his phone buzzing in his pocket. He's still in his new suit. There's a message from Trevor and it says: "You had one job. With the emphasis very much on the 'had'."

Kyle feels a surge of the passion that he couldn't summon for sales and begins to type back. "Fuck off you phoney fucking fraud, and hand back your MBE while you're at it." But before he presses SEND he shows it to his mum, who laughs, but then says, "Don't send it."

"Why not?"

"Be the better man. Plus, it's on the record. Just block him."

Kyle deletes the message and blocks Trevor.

"Good lad."

"I'm gonna have to get out of here, mum."

"We'll get you discharged just as soon as the doctor's given you the all-clear."

"Out of Barrel-Town, I mean."

"I know," she whispers, gripping his hand now, and smiling despite the sudden eye-drops.

Or get a job as a postman and marry Gina Hussingham, he thinks, and get a season ticket for the Fletchers, and then one night fire-bomb the VitaHerb building.

Eventually, Kyle achieves at least one of those goals.

***

That's not how it happened. Let's try again.

Kyle stands up, his heart beating like a Pet Shop Boys 12" remix. Everybody is looking at him. Everybody is wondering what the fuck this kid is going to say.

He pauses, because something is happening to his body, starting in his head and flooding downwards, like a miracle elixir. Enlightenment overwhelms every last one of Kyle's bones and organs, like he's just been cold-loch dipping or done intensive yoga. He suddenly thinks that he knows exactly what to say. The audience no longer terrifies him, it's now a welcome vessel for his sermon. He can barely wait to tell them the news.

"My name is Kyle Moore," he begins, "and I've been a fan of The Fletchers since I was five years old." His voice sounds like it's being transmitted from an alien plain of certainty and confidence. He likes it. He embraces it and claims it for himself, and for all the meetings to come. "I've been sent here today from VitaHerb with a very important task after I was appointed as the company's liaison officer for sponsorship. From this day on, I will be devoted only to our partnership."

There's a growing relief among his audience, spurred by this reference to the future. "I'm not going to lie," Kyle lied. "There were long discussions at VitaHerb about our alliance. There were people in California who said that backing The Fletchers was all very well, but who knows your team in Bangkok, Lagos and Kingston, Jamaica?" He's reeling city names off the top of his head, but is pleased with the geographical spread. "They wanted to go for the Premier League. They wanted to offer you peanuts or nothing."

The worried looks are back on the faces of the board members, even just contemplating this scenario. Only yesterday they signed a Danish U21 international, breaking the club record for an outgoing transfer fee. VitaHerb's money was factored into the new player's wages.

"I told them why this was the wrong approach. I said that we had to create headlines of our own, not just latch on to some big name club we share nothing in common with. This town is not only about your magnificent football club and its 150 years of history. It's about upstart industries and underdog businesses thriving and growing. It's about unlocking the potential of both the town and the club." Keep going with the bullshit, he thinks. People are nodding. "Here's how we get the attention of the outside world. We are offering a new five-year sponsorship deal, the likes of which has never been seen at this level of football. We are going to quadruple what we have paid you up until now." There's an incredulous gasp. "No negotiations. No conditions, no snags or hold-ups. VitaHerb loves you, and we want to see you prosper with us hand in hand. VitaHerb is going to be great for your health!"

There is a stunned silence as everyone takes this on board. It occurs to Kyle that no-one is taking him seriously. The offer's so good that it must be a hoax. "Mr Vickie!" Kyle commands, gesturing at the chairman. "Have your people draw up the contract right now. I will sign it before we've finished the champagne.

Draft a press release and let the world know. The Fletchers will no longer be the butt of jokes about scraping the bottom of the barrel!"

Now the joy is unleashed. Kyle has done his research. He knows that the existing deal was already a generous one, which was another reason why VitaHerb had wanted to terminate it. A sum four times that is worth more than the sponsorships of all the other fourth division teams put together. Everyone's shaking his hand, the cheap Sainsbury's prosecco is fizzing down the sides of the plastic flutes and then down the ruddy necks of the board, everyone's talking at once, and Bob Vickie is now very keen to get to know Kyle Moore, and make sure that he doesn't leave the room until his signature's on the line. Figures are briefly discussed, and Kyle tells them to round it up to the next million. Every year. "The company's expanding every day," he says. "It has more cash than it knows what to do with." He scans the press release and approves it. Fighting the urge to laugh, he signs the contract. He quaffs prosecco and talks at length with Gina Hussingham. All the admin staff have been told to knock off work and come to celebrate. What a day!

When the call from Trevor Dunsett comes, Kyle keeps him waiting until he finds the perfect spot for privacy. "Now fire away, Trevor," says Kyle. "I'm standing on the centre spot of the pitch, so no one can hear us."

"Fire away's the right bloody word," yells Trevor. "You're so fired away that the only place you'll get a job is in the circus as a human fucking cannonball."

"You set me a challenge, and I think I dealt with it very well," says Kyle. "Didn't we talk at the job interview about using our initiative to create good vibes and good news?"

There's a pre-explosive lull from the other end of the phone. "Listen ... you ..." blusters Trevor Dunsett. "You can't do this. You have to tell them. I'm coming straight down to the club now."

"I thought you were in California," says Kyle, feigning surprise.

"Anyway, I don't think you should come here in your current mood, Trevor. Imagine the dreadful publicity. VitaHerb rescinds generous sponsorship deal with local football club. Why would you do that?"

Trevor hangs up.

"He needs to take more VitaHerb," mutters Kyle, putting his phone away and taking his time to walk with a straight back towards the dugouts and the players' tunnel, aware that Bob Vickie and board members and maybe Gina Hussingham will be watching him from the hospitality suite.

If he can pull this off, Kyle's on the rise, and so are The Fletchers.

Eventually, one of these promotions may come to pass.

***

Kyle stands up, his heart beating like a Pet Shop Boys 12" re-mix. Everybody is looking at him. Everybody is wondering what the fuck this kid is going to say.

"Thank you," he croaks. "Thank you for welcoming me here today." A rubbish start. He starts to sweat, and he places his hands behind his back because he doesn't want anyone to see how much they're shaking.

"Well, it's like this. Unfortunately, VitaHerb has been forced to revise its strategic objectives for the coming fiscal challenges ... "

"Speak English," says one of the board members.

The interruption throws Kyle off. He stares down at a fork and wishes that he was it. He wishes he was a fork. That's all he can think. What's it like being a piece of metal used to skewer and shovel food? It exists, right? So theoretically, he could have been that fork, and that fork could have been Kyle Moore. Can't we just swap places?

"Do go on," says Bob Vickie. "And please, Geoff, no more interruptions." The man who interrupted Kyle shrugs.

"I'm very sorry," says Kyle, and then he starts to cry. Not sobbing, but he can feel his cheeks taking on water. Jesus, this is embarrassing. "I just can't," he says. "I've only been with the company for a week. They're utter bastards. You don't want them as a sponsor anyway. They're conmen. It's fraud, the whole business is a giant global pyramid scheme. You're better off without them."

"I think he's saying there's no deal on the table," the board member called Geoff says.

"They want to go Premier League," says Kyle.

"And they kept us hanging half the bloody summer." Geoff again. Bob Vickie is no longer telling him to shut up. In fact, he's just staring out of the window, like a new sponsor might arrive by hot air balloon and land in the centre circle.

"He's not wrong about them being bastards," says another board member. Bob Vickie snaps out of his trance and says to Kyle gently, "Sit down, son. It's not your fault."

"I'm a fan," he says. "I've been coming here since I was five years old."

"Shame we'll have to lock the ground up soon," says Geoff.

A long gloomy silence. Bob Vickie brings Kyle a cup of coffee, then tells the waiting staff that they can go home for the day, he'll take care of the food.

"Is there no one else in the wings?" Kyle asks, knowing how hopeless he sounds. Geoff snorts.

"I'm afraid not," says Bob Vickie. "That's our fault. We trusted your company too much."

"I can help you look," says Kyle, prompting another unhappy noise from board member Geoff. "I'll work for free."

"Do you have any contacts?" someone asks.

"I speak fluent Japanese," says Kyle, and for a few seconds that hangs in the air until Geoff gets up and leaves the room. A short time later, everyone watches as he walks out on to the pitch, his jacket slung over his shoulder, then lays down in the centre circle and stares up at the sky.

"We need to start selling next season's shirt, even with nothing on the front," says Ellen Hearst, who will turn out to be Kyle's new boss. She is the club's marketing manager. By Christmas, the Fletchers are just outside of the playoffs, and boast a Japanese hi-tech firm as their shirt sponsor, and Kyle has a salary. He's in love with Ellen, who's married, but he's going out with Gina, who's not. He goes drinking now and then with the board member known as Geoff, and Bob Vickie treats him like a lost son. Kyle wonders if his mum would have a chance if Bob's marriage ever broke up.

On a business trip to Japan, he meets up with Miyuki, but nothing happens. Except that they hold hands again at a jazz club, and that's just fine, because he doesn't want to be unfaithful to Gina and then have to lie about it. While trancing to a long clarinet solo, he thinks: there are so many ways in life to avoid trouble.

The Ropewalk Revival

The multi-billionaire Luca Romano knocked on my front door on what would otherwise have been a forgettable November evening, 40 years after we'd played football together for the last time. Now bald, but still handsome and smiling from lobe to lobe like the eternal winner he was, Luca stood more or less on the very ground where he'd once delivered precise and perfectly weighted crosses on to my virgin forehead. At first we embraced, tentatively, but then we began to jump up and down, showing far more emotion than we ever did while celebrating teenage goals (that would have been uncool). It was fitting that our joyous, unexpected re-union was taking place on the requisitioned stretch of land where the Ropewalk used to be.

Once tucked in between off-limits marshland, the railway line to Grimsby and the back garden of the town butcher, the Ropewalk and its neurotic wooden structures had hosted football in our town long enough for no living person to be sure when the ground had opened. Now it was my home, a flat and vapid residential estate called Wellesley Court where I'd bought a house 27 years ago. As Luca said when we'd settled down to open the bottle of Italian red he'd brought along (just as well, as I no longer kept alcohol at home), they hadn't even been bothered to name it Ropewalk Close. No respect for tradition here, he said. Why did you not protest at the time? And who or what the hell was Wellesley?

I couldn't remember, truth be told. Not long after Luca had left, the football club had accepted an offer from a property developer and merged with the cricket club. The cricket field was big enough to accommodate a football pitch without encroaching on the wicket, and there was enough cash from the sale of the Ropewalk to pay off the club's considerable debts, keep it financially stable for years to come, and to build a functional stand that sheltered Market Rasen Town's two dozen fans from the rain.

"And to hawk its waning soul," said Luca. He hadn't lost his knack for an attention-seeking turn of phrase.

"There's never been the same atmosphere at the new place, right enough. It's fine for cricket, but for football it's way too big a space. At the Ropewalk, you could always hear there was a game on a couple of streets away."

"And how many goals did you score at the cricket ground?"

"A few. But I stopped playing when I was 30. You know, kids and everything. Too much other stuff going on at the weekend."

"What did you do on Saturdays that was so much more exciting?"

I shrugged. "We'd bought this place by then, and when you buy a place there's always stuff that needs doing." I looked at him for a second. "Unless you have staff."

"Family," said Luca, ignoring my last comment. He said this word with a slight Italian intonation, a nod to the way we used to take the piss out of him at school. Even though he'd grown up near Nottingham and didn't have any trace of an Italian accent. The word was left hanging. Did he know that Jessica had left me?

Did he even know that I'd married her in the first place? Jessica was his first girlfriend, and he'd left her behind when his family disappeared overnight. She became my first girlfriend too. I consoled her in his wake, desolate that he'd never said goodbye, and that she was hearing nothing from him, neither a call nor a letter. My first and only girlfriend. My first and only wife. My only ex-wife. Who didn't leave me for another man, in case you're wondering. She left me for a language school in Quito, Ecuador.

"What am I going to do out there?" I'd asked, confident that this was never going to happen. It was such a faraway plan, such a far-out plan, conceived out of nowhere, it seemed to me. A long silence, before she said, "The idea is that you're not really coming along, Alan." The idea. That's an idea? I couldn't speak. Our eldest, Josh, was already off studying in Manchester. Jane was 16, and was apparently very much up for trying something new a long, long way from Market Rasen.

I decided to fill Luca in later on what had happened to my family. There were still too many questions to ask about what a household name software entrepreneur was doing here in Wellesley Close. Presumably just passing through for a nostalgia break, on the way from one international business meeting to another. Not that Market Rasen is on the way to anywhere, international or not.

"I've been meaning to come by for years," he said, then smiled. "Been a bit busy."

"How did you know where to find me?"

"I asked around the pubs. I got lucky in the Aston Arms. They said to tell you that you should show your face more often. Apparently they've not seen you for a while."

"See anyone you recognise?"

"Nobody at all, though I wasn't hanging around searching peoples' features and trying to imagine how they looked 40 years ago. I wouldn't have recognised you either if you'd walked down the street towards me."

"Well, that wouldn't have been a problem for me. Your face is quite well known nowadays. Didn't they recognise you at The Aston?"

Luca laughed again, like he always did, which was why no one disliked him, why most people loved him. When the school wankers would follow him around and shout, Hey, Luca, tell your papa to make us spaghetti, Luca would answer in the same cod-Italian, Sure, signora, you want bolognese or carbonara? and then there was no point taking the piss out of him anymore, he refused to be wound up. And his tormentors were too thick to realise he'd just called them a woman.

"They looked at me like they were looking at someone they might know," Luca said. "But people don't make the connection because it seems too implausible. One of the world's five richest men turning up in the local pub of a tiny town on a Tuesday night in November. It can't possibly be true."

"On the other hand, "I said, "I've dined out plenty of times on the story of how you fed me enough crosses to make us county champions with a goal difference of plus 67, and maximum points."

"I'm sure you have. Still got the cuttings?"

"Of course. Haven't you?"

"Even if I kept any at the time, they got lost in the rush to move. We pretty much packed cases and left. I left behind my Panini albums, all my records, photos, diaries, love letters..."

I had good news for Luca. His stuff was still in a box in our attic. It was Jessica who'd broken into the house they'd been renting on Chapman Street, looking for clues as to why they'd upped and left, or perhaps hoping he was still hiding in the cupboard under the stairs. She never explained why she took his things, forcing me to carry all his LPs in a campers' rucksack that was lying around, while she stuffed his personal effects into her school bag. I just assumed it was her way of holding on to him. I never once looked through the box it all ended up in. Maybe Jessica did, but I never asked.

When I brought the box down, Luca literally danced with delight, hugging me and thanking me as though I had kept a promise we'd made in blood four decades earlier. When I explained it had been all Jessica's doing, he just said, "Ah," apparently distracted by pages filled with stickers of hirsute footballing heroes from the early '80s. Two brown envelopes filled with family photos had him in tears. When he flipped through albums by ABC, The Cure and Haircut 100, he wanted to play them right there and now, but I no longer had a record player. He made a call to have one delivered to the house, that very night, but he was forgetting in what part of the world we were living. When he hung up, he muttered, "Fucking useless, that guy, really fucking useless, time and time again." He suddenly looked out of place, standing in the middle of my living room with his cell phone in his right hand, aggrieved and ready for some kind of action. I suggested that he sit back down and have another glass of wine. He snapped out of his low anger, then smiled at me and said, "Of course. Thank you, Alan."

"So what happened back then?" I asked, once he was settled. "There was a rumour about your dad getting an unwelcome visit from the tax man."

Luca pulled a face and shook his head. "Not really that, though I'm sure a house-call from the Inland Revenue would have caused my father some problems. He owed money to local people. Lots of them. Builders, electricians, plumbers, food wholesalers. All the people that built his restaurant, the only one in town, and he could never quite make enough to pay them back. I'm surprised the true story didn't get out."

"People are funny about that stuff here," I said. "No one wants to admit they got fucked over, especially by a charming, dashing Italian who talks like a film star and looks like one too. How is he?"

"Long since passed." Luca made a dismissive gesture. "It actually took me a lifetime to forgive him for leaving this place."

"Really? I always assumed you never looked back. We all did. Jessica too."

Again, he ignored the reference to my wife. My ex-wife. He asked instead with a look that almost made me want to cry, "Can I see the cuttings?" Like all the gargantuan riches he'd accumulated down the decades could be exchanged for old newspaper reports about how we'd beaten Birchwood eight-nil, and how he'd run their left back ragged, scoring three goals himself and setting up five for me.

I took the scrapbook down off the shelf, next to the family photo albums. It was my mum who'd cut out the match reports from the *Market Rasen Mail* and glued them carefully to the page, then covered each one with a translucent, adhesive layer that had preserved the ink and the paper so well down the years. In truth, I'd had this scrapbook out on my lap far more often than the family albums. Though Jessica had once wondered out loud if there was anyone left in town, or even the world at large, who had yet to be impressed by my connection with Luca Romano.

On the scrapbook's very first page was a team photo taken by my dad, blown up and pasted in. It was from the latter part of our only season, and we were all wearing the faces of high-fliers, cocky and untouchable in our dominance, chests out like the medals were already around our necks. And standing to the right at the end of the back row was Luca's father, Elio, proprietor of Market Rasen's first Italian restaurant. Founder of the Market Rasen Calcio Boys' Club, formed after the school had banned Luca from playing. He'd missed training once too often, and during school matches he never bothered tracking back, according to our PE teacher, Mr. Sandringham, who declared that no one was too good to be dropped. He was visited by Elio at school, and the police were called. Elio wasn't always a master of charm. There were no charges, in the end, and Elio persuaded Market Rasen Town to start a Sunday boys' team with its exotic Italian name. It was the school team, plus Luca. We didn't mind playing twice a weekend, because playing with Luca meant we were guaranteed to win.

"I remember this game well," Luca said, pointing at the match report of a 2-1 win away at Leadenham. "It was the closest we came to dropping a point. They had two lads in central defence that combined to stop you, again and again, you just couldn't get anywhere near my crosses that day. And I was coming back after the flu and couldn't get into my game."

"Your dad was yelling at you to stop dribbling. And then ... "

"I yelled back asking him if he was Mr. fucking Sandringham, and I got a stiff lecture from the ref about my language!"

"Yes!" I cried, and we both collapsed back onto the sofa. "I used to see old Sandy sometimes down the Red Lion before it closed. Years ago, not long after I'd left school. I told him about what you'd said to your dad, and how your dad just lifted his arms and laughed."

"And then I got the ball and was so mad at him that I beat three players out on the right, fired in a shot that hit the post ... "

We looked at the match report and read the line together, "... and there was Alan Nilsson, perfectly placed to poke in the rebound, like a sneak-thief on a crowded train."

That had become a catch-phrase in the changing room, partly because it was funny, and partly because it didn't really make any sense. "Let's go out and win this like sneak-thieves on a crowded train," our captain Lenny Pullard would shout. It was Elio who wrote the reports, and as English was not his first language, the reports were full of strange and wonderful linguistic turns. It was another reason why I had the scrapbook down so often, although by now I could recite most of it off by heart.

Once we'd read all the reports, with added memories, Luca collapsed back onto my weary sofa with a satisfied smile.

"What did he say, Mr. Sandringham?"

"When I told him what you yelled at your dad?"

"Yes."

"He didn't think the story was funny at all. He shook his head and muttered something like, Luca Romano, what a waste of raw talent. Like if he'd been your coach, he'd have turned you into an Italian international."

"Maybe he would," said Luca, "if he hadn't dropped me from the fucking team. I quite liked him, though. I even understood why he dropped me. And I didn't like my dad storming into school to make an idiot of himself on my behalf."

"Would you trade an Italian international cap for everything you've achieved since? Did you even keep on playing?"

"I can't answer your first question. It's kind of beside the point. In many ways," he went on, pointing at the scrapbook, "this one season was enough. I don't know if it would have got any better. We went to America, I played for some youth club, but I could score goals there with my eyes closed and just playing with my left foot, so I quit altogether. I was suddenly fascinated by computers instead. And anyway, it just wasn't the same without your lunking big head in the middle waiting for my crosses."

"Too bad," I said. "Though I suppose it wasn't that different for me. Remember that interest from Lincoln City? That bloke who came to watch us twice and then, after the cup final we won 6-0, asked us for our phone numbers, and said he'd be calling us to come in for a trial?"

"Of course, I remember." Luca said this so quietly, it was like he could hardly get the words out.

"Then you were gone."

"And?"

"He never called."

"You didn't try calling the club?"

"What 16-year-old has the balls to do that? What was I going to say? Oh, some bloke in a black coat came to watch me the other week and said something about a trial, but he hasn't called me. I was wondering what time I should come in to show you my talents."

"You should just have knocked on the door with your boots tied around your neck, demanding to be seen." Luca was suddenly wrought with conviction, like this was just yesterday.

"Sounds like a scene from *Roy of the Rovers*," I said.

We dropped into a long silence, staring at the now empty wine glasses and thinking about what could have been. He was probably right. My story about not getting a trial with Lincoln was threadbare.

"Truth is," I said, "I didn't have the self-belief. I was sure I only looked good thanks to you."

Luca said, "Aww" at this, then we stood and embraced, and I walked him up to his room at the Advocate Arms opposite the market place. I said that I presumed he'd be on his way in the morning, but if he gave me an email address, I'd scan the match reports and send them to him.

He wasn't planning to move on for a few days, he said. "You're going to think I'm insane, but these were the happiest two years of my life. That second year playing with the Calcio Boys' Club was just the finest year. I got on with everybody that year, even my dad. When I played, I felt like I was floating, like I would never lose the ball or make a mistake." Then he asked me if I'd join him at the hotel for breakfast.

"Some of us have to go to work in the mornings."

"What do you do?"

"Branch manager, Endsleigh Insurance. Here in town."

Luca looked me up and down. "You're too tall for insurance. Fancy a change?"

I let out a short laugh at that, unsure how serious the question was. "This is Market Rasen, we don't do change," I said, and we embraced again, briefly this time, and then I walked across the market square, past the almost deserted Aston Arms, and down Waterloo Street and back towards my housing estate and former football ground. My steps were as heavy as my soul. Me and Luca, up front for Lincoln City. Up front for Liverpool. Up front for Inter Milan. Give and go, Nilsson to Romano, Romano past two, plays it back to Nilsson, he never misses from there, what another unbelievably clinical yet beautiful goal from the European champions! In the dark, I swept an imaginary ball into the far corner and turned to face Luca, and then the crowd.

Lights out, curtains drawn. Not a sound.

I hadn't really believed that Luca would still be in town the next day, but there he was, knocking on the window of Endsleigh Insurance (formerly The Electrical Shop, where he'd bought the ABC and Cure albums) with a massive smile, then walking right in and ordering me to meet him for dinner at the Advocate Arms at seven. I had no plans, no excuses, and no reason not to go. After he breezed back out, my secretary Diane just stared at me, and then at the door.

"That wasn't Luca Romano, was it?"

"Don't be daft, Diane. What would Luca Romano be doing in Market Rasen?"

"He used to live here, you told me yourself, about how you played football…"

"Can you call head office and ask them about the next year's first quarter sales targets? They were supposed to be sent last week. And you didn't see Luca Romano, just so we're clear about that." Diane had little control over her tongue, and I couldn't imagine Luca wanted a crowd of curious onlookers gawping at us over dinner.

As it happened, the restaurant was empty but for a party of four retirees celebrating a 70th birthday in the corner, and Luca sitting on his own with a bottle of red wine open on the table.

"I ordered this already, I apologise," was his opening comment as he stood up and embraced me again. "I can order white wine or a beer for you, if you'd prefer."

"This is fine," I said, "if you don't mind sharing." I sat down. He was riffling through paperwork. Very old papers, by the look of it. He held up the pile in his fist and smiled.

"I've been paying off Elio's debts."

"Who to?"

"Tim Freeman."

"He was two years below us at school. How come you owe him money? He lent you five pence for a bag of crisps?"

"Not quite. His father Kevin was our electrician when we were renovating the restaurant. Now Tim has the business. You use him?"

"Of course," I said. "Sound bloke, good worker, and the only electrician in Market Rasen unless you want Tubby Gill to fuck it up for half the price and off the books. How did he greet you?"

"Suspicious at first, then baffled, then with guarded delight when he realised how much I was offering him with added interest and compensation, followed by renewed suspicion that he was being subject to a scam and that the whole thing was being taped by a secret camera crew."

"And ultimately?"

"Bank transfers appear in seconds nowadays." He held up another old bill. "I can't trace Pavel the Plumbers. Do you know what happened to them?"

"Jiri Pavel had a heart attack, only 51. His missus sold up and buggered off back to Czechoslovakia and took the six cats with her. She said even communism was more fun than Market Rasen."

Luca raised an eyebrow at that. "Did she really say that? My memory is that she barely spoke English."

"Popular folklore, passed on in the oral tradition and possibly invented by me."

"I'm guessing you don't have her address," was Luca's response to that. "And Henry Kasper, the builder?"

"Retired, probably still lives in Owmby unless I missed his obituary." Luca showed me the bill, and I couldn't help but whistle. "Jesus Christ, that's a lot of money now, let alone back then."

"I know," said Luca. "I feel terrible. But I'm glad he was able to retire. I'll head out there tomorrow and try to track him down. Is Owmby a big place?"

"To a stunted Chihuahua, maybe." Again, Luca gave me a long look. He was in a different mood tonight, I felt much more like I was dealing with a financially powerful multi-billionaire rather than an old football friend.

"To a stunted Chihuahua," he repeated. "I'm sure that when you were 16 you were much funnier."

"That's what Jessica used to say as well."

"There's another important debt of my father's that I want to settle."

"I'm hoping you're going to say it was my dad, but that hardly seems likely given that he was a driving instructor."

"Too bad, but you're right. Your father wasn't owed a penny. And I never even asked last night if your mum and dad are still alive. I'm sorry about that, Alan." He suddenly sounded less uptight, like business had been dealt with.

"Both gone, both struggled with leaving. It was a long haul with colostomy bags, nursing homes and blank memories."

"I'm sorry to hear that."

"I'm glad they're gone," I said, surprising myself. "Don't get me wrong, I don't mean … "

"I know exactly what you mean," he said, and placed a hand on my lower arm, and it felt like he was radiating this avuncular sense of security. Tears started ebbing at my eyelids. Luca was decent enough to leave a silence before resuming business.

"It's the football club," he went on.

"What is? What do you mean?"

"Elio owed the football club a ton of money. Owes, I should say."

"How?"

"Well, last night we were looking at pictures of us in those fancy kits we had, home and away, with Elio's Restaurant across the front. Those shirts were like silk. Maybe they even were made out of silk. My dad was supposed to pay for those, that was part of the deal when he founded the team and aligned it to the club. But it seems he must have persuaded the club to stump up, no doubt citing temporary cash flow problems. And the ad hoardings for Elio's Restaurant he had constructed and painted, and that ended up just leaning against the old wooden fence? That turned out to be free advertising too. I've got the invoice right here."

I said that I was sure the club had got over the blip in its income by now, especially after having sold the ground all those years ago.

"Maybe that was why they had to sell. My dad's debts."

"Surely not. The club owed the bank a ton by the time they sold the ground."

"And a lot of that debt was the result of Elio not keeping his promises. You could say that it was my dad who killed the Ropewalk." Luca sounded way harsher than he needed to for this historical transgression, long forgotten by everyone else in town.

"A housing development killed the Ropewalk," I said.

"Or Elio enabled the housing development. Whatever it was, I want to compensate the club. Who's in charge there nowadays?"

"No clue. I barely even read the match reports. I honestly don't think you need ..."

"Please find out for me, Alan. Then we can talk."

"About what? With who?"

"With whom," he said. "You and me, Alan, talking about Market Rasen and the Ropewalk. A proposal and a partnership.

Some vision for this place."

"Are you kidding me?"

Luca sighed, like he was now disappointed that he was going to have to explain.

"Listen, I don't need to kid when it comes to money. You know how much of it I have. The whole world knows. I could buy this whole town tomorrow and erase it from the map."

Luca was getting loud, and the pensioners' birthday party in the corner had stopped for a second to stare. The former winger caught himself, smiled at the old folk, and gave them a gentle wave. They resumed eating, but now they were murmuring rather than talking, and casting cautionary looks our way.

"What's your thinking, Luca? If it's a football club you're after, you'd be better off buying Lincoln or Grimsby. I'm sure they'd both be interested."

"That's a facile remark, Alan," he said with a contempt that hit me. "I have no connection with those places. I never even went to Lincoln or Grimsby, except when we played teams there on away trips. I hated them. They wanted to beat us. They were never good enough, but they thought they were. They couldn't understand how Market Rasen with their pretentious Italian name and their high-quality blue and burgundy linen or possibly silk shirts were so much better, and they couldn't even shake our hands after we hammered them. Though in a way that made victory sweeter still."

Bloody hell, I thought. He thinks about those games even more than I do.

"So Market Rasen Town FC it's going to be then. Though I'm sure you've thought of a new name already."

"Il Miracolo Market Rasen," he said, and laughed.

"I don't know what that means."

"You will, though," he said. "Once we've rebuilt the Ropewalk and thousands of people are coming to watch us every week."

"Should I dust off my boots?"

"No, but you should dust off your head, Alan. Before you stagnate. Before the colostomy bag and the nursing home and the memory loss."

I toyed with the menu. I hadn't even looked at what we were going to eat. And I wondered if Luca was insane enough to try and make this happen.

"Where are you planning to build the New Ropewalk?" I asked mildly. Luca looked surprised at the question.

"Come on, Alan, isn't that obvious? Exactly where it was before, of course!"

***

I shouldn't have been surprised to witness how quickly money makes a small town move. When it's on your front door step, though, it still takes you aback. No one in Market Rasen would ever have dreamed of expecting or asking for this kind of attention and investment. Yet it was just as instructive to see how soon we came to adapt and then take massive sums of money for granted.

The press had picked up on Luca's presence the very next day. Maybe it was Diane's liberal tongue, maybe it was the four grey-hairs who'd been disturbed by Luca's brief loudness. By the time the first reporters showed up at the bar, he was already out of the Advocate Arms and had bought The Old Rectory at Linwood, about three miles out of town. The place was staffed and furnished when I rolled up in a taxi just two days later. I thought he was inviting me up to take a look, but in fact it was a three-course dinner for myself and the entire board of the Market Rasen Football & Cricket Club, and their partners too. Everyone but me was dressed up, and I managed to side-track Luca and tell him I wanted to go home, I felt completely out of place in my tatty jeans and a roll-neck pullover — clothes I'd owned since before I was married.

"You don't get to feel out of place in my house," he said, then sent me upstairs to an opulent room full of wardrobes and mirrors where someone who appeared to be his personal tailor fitted me out in a charcoal grey suit, white shirt and burgundy tie that somehow was just right. Luca popped his head around the door and gave a "wow", before adding, "Just so that you know, please don't mention the Ropewalk tonight. Baby steps. First I need to have everyone on board. I don't want to blitz them." I said nothing, I was still too busy looking at a bold new version of myself in the mirror.

"Alan?"

I turned around. "Yes?"

"You got me?"

"I don't get anything anymore," I said. "I'm feel like I'm treading water in a parallel universe."

"Ah, that's more like it. Imagination Alan. Do you remember him?"

"Not really."

"We can get him back," said Luca, coming into the room now, and again the mere touch of his hand on my arm worked like a super-drug. "Nice job, Adrian," Luca said to the tailor. The man barely nodded, as though paying him a compliment was akin to an insult. Of course he'd done a nice job. The tailor then left the room, though I saw no signal giving him that instruction, and Luca sat down on the edge of an antique chair upholstered in a lush red velvet. He indicated that I should do the same.

"Name me a salary, and I will make you the Director of Operations at Market Rasen Football Club."

I felt like my head was swimming. "I can't do that," I began, "I've no experience…"

"Yes, you do. You run an office. This will be similar, but with more people, plus you will have a lot more fun and it will be 50 times more rewarding, and you can go on holiday four times a year.

And even if it all goes up in smoke — which I promise you, it won't — I will write a clause in your contract giving you a massive pay-off so that you need never regret that you no longer work in that shitty little office on King Street."

"Can I think about it?"

"Yes. I will give you up to 10."

"Luca …"

"Jesus, I'm just kidding, Alan. Before I employ you I'm going to take you to fucking Vegas for a weekend or something and we'll re-ignite your lighter side even if we have to rip it out of your bone marrow." I didn't say that I could imagine no greater punishment to my heart and soul than a weekend in Vegas. "Listen," he went on, "it's okay, just sit in tonight, see how they react, and I will tell them that you are very keen to be involved in some capacity. Tonight, we are just investors with vague proposals. We do the takeover by stealth."

We, I thought, as Luca stood up and slapped me on the back, like I was his equal and this was a done deal. Maybe it was. Perhaps he'd talked to all the members of the board individually and made them cash-heavy promises too.

Back downstairs, I watched Luca at work. His seduction was effortless. Elaborate cocktails, lavish canapés and aristocratic levels of service combined with epic flattery, grandiloquent laughter and golden memories of Market Rasen to soften up the seven men and their wives before we'd even sat down at the table. During the first course of carrot and leek soup, Luca humbly offered his hospitality tonight in return for the money that his father owed the club. All those present said they had never known such a debt existed. For a while, Luca let them think that the dinner was the debt, and that they were privileged to be in his company as part of the pay-off. What a story to tell! But there was more to come over the roast pheasants that had been shot in the Rectory's fields and surrounding woodland that very morning. Luca wanted to pay the club back the money owed, with interest accrued over 40 years, plus a hefty lump sum by way of recompense for his father's disgraceful, dishonest behaviour. The money would be enough to keep the club out of financial difficulties for decades, provided that it was spent wisely.

"That's really incredibly generous of you, Mr. Romano," said the club's President, Mike Foley, who'd been club captain when I played in my 20s. Mike was decent — a heating engineer and a father of four. He looked up and down the table, fishing for approval for whatever it was he was going to say next. "I'm sure you'll find that everyone here agrees that this would be a most welcome injection of … means. We're always looking for new sponsors, so if, you know, we can put your company's name … "

"That won't be necessary," said Luca. "At all. You don't need to name anything after me or my company. I'm the one at fault here because of my family's debt. It's the club who is doing me the favour of forgiving me after all this time."

I thought Luca was laying it on a bit thick by now, but they were all lapping it up, and there was a frisson of excited conversation around the table. Perhaps they were imagining a second floor to the club house with an executive suite offering the kind of service they were enjoying tonight. There was, however, a tiny hint of dissent in a question that came from Winston Halliday, a stalwart centre back at Rasen for 20 years (and another ex-team-mate of mine), and now the club secretary. Winston was a social worker and, unusually for Market Rasen, held forth on politics without caring who might be offended.

"Could I respectfully ask, Mr. Romano," said Winston, "what you want in return? Because we all know how vast wealth is created, and it isn't through philanthropy and warm, fuzzy feelings for the football team you played for in your youth. Now, I'm not questioning the sincerity of this very welcome gesture. We are most grateful, every last one of us, I'm sure that we all agree on that. But I just want to check that we are not, so to speak, signing up for anything that we might regret down the line. Plus," he added, turning towards me, "what is Alan Nilsson doing here? He has nothing to do with the club apart from having walked out 20 years ago calling us all unspeakable names and declaring that he would never have anything to do again with such an amateur bunch of incompetent ... I won't say it in polite company, but it's an alliteration."

Everyone looked at me, just as I was blushing, and then they looked at Luca, who burst out laughing. "Alan, you lost your rag? I never thought it was possible."

"I can't really remember it," I lied. "It could be that I'd had one or two too many pints of Guinness. Maybe something to do with me getting subbed out that afternoon after having a shite game." There was polite laughter from some of the Board members, who likely didn't want to jeopardise Luca's payment with an unseemly row.

"No, it wasn't that," said Winston. "You were banging on yet again about how you could have played for Lincoln City, but that there weren't the right players at Market Rasen Town to bring out your undoubted talents and prompt you to score more than your usual 10 to 12 goals per season. And then Rod Durrell, who was manager at the time, said that maybe the kind of player who'd better serve you was in the Reserves. He was only joking, but you lost it."

Dead silence, though Luca still looked like he was delighted by the story.

"Yes," I said. "I remember now." The incident had obviously made an impression on Winston. His recall was dead accurate. "That's pretty much what happened. I apologise now, although it's a bit late, and I can't offer you as much money as Luca."

There was general laughter at this, mainly out of relief that I hadn't squared up to Winston brandishing a pheasant bone. Winston himself gave a conciliatory nod in my direction, and maybe now he'd return my greeting when we passed each other on the main street. Luca took the evening's narrative firmly back in his fist, becoming the raconteur of our glorious year in the U16s, and reiterating the momentous, formative two years of his life that he had spent in our small market town. Alan here, he mentioned more than once or twice, had been such an important part of that. Not only had we boasted a psychic understanding on the football pitch, we'd been best of friends off it as well. When Luca was spirited away by Elio at two in the morning, along with his mother and two younger sisters, his world had collapsed overnight.

Still no mention of Jessica.

"I just want to give something back now," he said. "And if it seems funny that it's taken me 40 years to get here … well, I've been taking care of other business."

More polite laughter. Just how do you deal with a person so wealthy that he could give the order to crush you or your club or your town in half a second? Callum Browning, a Scottish exile who was vice chairman of the club, and still played for one of the cricket teams in his late 40s, tentatively asked if Luca might be interested in a longer-term investment. "Perhaps to not just upgrade the facilities, but to attract a better class of player and maybe take us up to the next sporting level?"

There was a worried silence, presumably at the thought of being just a bit too greedy too soon. Looking for the second cheque before we'd even banked the first. Luca played it well, sounding like he might be mildly offended by the suggestion at first. He hadn't really thought about that, but he would certainly give it some consideration. Now that he had bought a base in the area — he gestured around him — perhaps a firmer commitment would be fitting. After all, he'd partly made his fortune by looking at under-achieving firms and seeing nothing but potential before taking them over and pumping them until they soared. That might also be true of central Lincolnshire.

That was the winner that released the crowd into a barely controlled ecstasy. The drink kicked in and the limits were lifted. Though I didn't hear anyone use the phrase "Premier League football in Market Rasen in 10 years," I did hear talk of Netflix documentaries, a new era of wealth and prosperity, and staging county cricket games at the Rase Lane sports field.

Everyone left between midnight and 2am — the seven couples in four different cars. Someone had tipped off the cops, though, and four of the seven Board members were arrested on Linwood Road on drunk driving charges. No prizes for guessing who got the charges dropped within the hour. What luck that Luca's lawyer had arrived just an hour or two earlier and could be summoned from the guest annex in the back yard to go down to the station and smooth things out.

At 3am, I asked Luca if he could call me a taxi. "Why didn't you drive?" he asked me. "I don't have a car," I replied. "You'll need one," he said. "Unless you're going to cycle out here every time I need to talk to you. Don't worry, I'll take care of it. What do you want?"

"Fiat 500."

"Be serious."

"A limousine with a driver."

"I can have one of those take you home. Or you can stay in one of the spare rooms. You want sex? There are girls here. You could definitely do with getting laid, Alan."

"You have girls here? I mean, *girls?*"

Luca sighed. "Women, if you must. I have everything. Absolutely fucking everything."

"Except for the Ropewalk, because it no longer exists."

"It will."

"I'll take the chauffeur with the limousine, please. I like to be in my own bed at night, thanks. On my own. No girls."

Luca smiled. "Our roles have reversed. Now you're my wing man."

"Not really," I said. "You've done all the hard work, I'm still just waiting around in the six-yard box to reap all the benefits."

"Like you did with Jessica," he said, though he wasn't smiling, just holding his empty glass out and staring at the carpet.

"Yes, I suppose so."

There was an endless silence, and I almost started to drop off. Perhaps I could just kip on the sofa here until one of the maids came in to hoover the next morning. But then Luca spoke again.

"That was the worst part of it all. I was so in love, and yet my father forbade me any kind of contact. No one in Market Rasen was allowed to know where we were. No calls, no letters, and of course once we were in the US, how was I supposed to see her?"

"She felt the same."

"Did you soak up her tears?"

"Of course. I'd been besotted with her since junior school."

"I'm sorry."

"Why?"

"I don't know. You got to marry her, after all."

"Fucked that up, though. I was too boring. You're right about me."

"Nobody's boring if you prod them in the right spot. Same applies to places. We can wake this town up. It won't take much."

"Just a little cash. A little drop for you. But a massive fucking wave of wealth for certain people in Market Rasen. Including me, apparently."

Luca looked at me with the boyish smile he'd used to charm Jessica. "This is not about the money for me, Alan, that's just the cracker on the nutshell. You should sleep on my offer now, then come back here tomorrow with whatever number you want, and then I will say yes, and then we will get this thing in to second and third gear, trending upwards. Il Miracolo Market Rasen!"

I fell asleep, and by some process of butlers, chauffeurs and matrons, woke up at 11 the next day in my own bed, quite alone.

***

A couple of weeks later, something quite unusual happened. Someone who lived on Wellesley Close knocked on my front door. I lived at the bottom end of the close, the first house on the left as you entered from Waterloo Street, so my contact with the neighbours down the years had been limited to waving at them as they walked or drove past me if I was out in the front garden. Which wasn't that often. I mowed the lawn every two weeks in summer, and Jessica kept the weeds down and planted some flowers. Since she'd left, I paid Simple Billy to keep it tidy, though I never really checked if he'd done a good job. There'd been a street party once for some royal thing when the kids were young. They really wanted to go, and Jessica pressed me for days, but in the end she was the one who took them. She did pretty much all that kind of thing. Flesh-cuts, colds, the flu, packed lunches, outings, outfits, birthday presents and parties — my memory of their youth is me looking out of the living room window as Jessica lead them off down Waterloo Street and I turned with relief to the peace and quiet and my newspaper. Years of failed attempts to get the kids to kick a football had worn me down.

I'd talked to Jane by video call the night before. Since moving to Ecuador she'd texted me almost every day, and we talked about once a month. She told me about her life and her boyfriend. She ignored my questions about her mum. She'd long since moved out and moved on. She'd never once come back to England. I'd never been to Ecuador, in 12 years. I'd decided that to take my first ever plane ride if I became a grandfather.

"Was I a crap dad?" I asked. She looked very flustered at that question, and didn't want to discuss it "right now", this wasn't the way to approach an issue like that. And all I'd wanted was for her to say, "You were fine, dad, don't rattle your head about it." With one clumsy question, I had turned it into an issue. I should never have asked. So I called Josh, who was just getting ready to go out and didn't have time to talk. I could hear his husband in the background chivvying him along. So I told him that he shouldn't forget how much I loved him, and there was a stunned silence. "Have you been drinking, dad?" I knew he was joking, because he said it with a kind of laugh. It was no easier for him to hear it than it was for me to say it. "No," I replied. "Now give my very best to Atiq and enjoy your evening." Thanks, Dad, he said, but he didn't say that he loved me too. It had never come up. Now I was pushing for love, like a needy old man.

So anyway, my neighbour Deborah came to the door. Her husband had left years ago, some scandal involving a farmer's wife I can no longer recall, and we hadn't seen him since. She was around 10 years younger than me, and there was something about her that I'd always liked, because she was the only one on the close who ever gave me a smile. She had two teenage sons who still lived with her, Henry and Philip. Henry was about to leave school, liked to drink and fight, looked right through me every time he passed like he'd never seen me in his life. You'd see him hanging about in the market place with his mates sometimes, smoking and trying to look territorial. Philip was a decent lad, always said hello, very shy and polite.

I'd idly given half a thought now and then to Deborah turning up on my doorstep one night with a bottle of wine. It wasn't exactly a longing, as such, more like a vague fantasy with me thinking, "Yeah, that would be alright". But it didn't have to happen. The scenario was always dampened by the thought of having to engage at some future point with the tearaway Henry.

Deborah wasn't smiling with a bottle of wine in her hand. She was waving a piece of paper and looking angry and concerned. "I know you don't like being disturbed, Alan," she began, and I thought, wait a minute, who says I don't like being disturbed. "But did you get one of these?"

The piece of paper bore the heading of the company that I now worked for, Cosmic Rase, though fortunately my name was nowhere to be seen. CEO and President: Luca Romano. We had 25 people working for us already, and had taken over the main room at the Corn Exchange until we could find (or Luca could build or convert) an office big enough for all his plans. Plans which had been kept remarkably secret up until now. If the sole reporter at the *Market Rasen Mail* knew anything, she'd been persuaded to stay silent.

I didn't actually know anything about the letter. My work still only concerned dealings with the Cricket and Football Club, and so far that had entailed me searching the archives of both the club and the Mail so that I could find old photographs of the Ropewalk to help the architect design Luca's vision of the reconstituted ground. So I took the piece of paper from Deborah's hand and read how she was being offered twice the market value for her house.

"Bloody hell," I said, because I was genuinely surprised. "Do you want to come in?" No, she said, she had things to be getting on with. So, I hadn't received a letter like this? I had not, I said, reading on from the first paragraph. Luca was talking about "an exciting, innovative development project the likes of which this town has never seen. Not only am I offering you twice the current market value of your property, but I will grant you a one per cent share in Cosmic Rase, ensuring that you and your family will continue to profit from your sale for decades to come." I almost asked her what she was waiting for, but she didn't seem at all happy, standing there with hands on hips and an impatient glare as I scanned the missive.

"Did everyone else on the Close get one?"

"Yes," she said. "We're having a meeting at the Stevensons' tomorrow night at eight, if you can make it."

"I'll be there," I said. Luca would definitely want me there. "Er, which number are the Stevensons at again?" I didn't even know who they were.

"They're the ones on Lady Frances Drive. The house on the other side of the hedge with its own access road."

Of course, the driveway that used to be the gravelly lane that lead to the Ropewalk. Bound by hedges for 70-odd yards until you came around the corner and there it was, to the left of the rutted car park, a rectangular football pitch with hints of green grass.

"I'm guessing that they're not happy about this either," I said.

"Not happy? He's a fucking Tory, Alan, and he's a businessman. He's got the MP coming along. He's not going to let himself be pushed into this, and neither are we. Why the fuck do they need this bit of land? There are dozens of sites around here that no one's using."

"I'll be there tomorrow," I said.

"Thank you, Alan," she said. "The others said I was wasting my time asking you, but I said you'd be on our side, you've lived here longer than any of us."

"Well … " I started to mumble, but she was already on her way. I went back inside and texted Luca that I needed to see him, could I come out to The Old Rectory. He gave me the thumbs up and wrote, "Any time for you, my friend." I waited for 20 minutes or so, somehow imagining that Deborah was spying on me and texting to the neighbours, "It's just like we thought, he's working for Romano and now he's driven off to HQ in Linwood to tell him everything."

When my paranoia had ebbed, I went into the garage to unplug my new e-car, and eased out on to Wellesley Court and down Waterloo Street, regretting only that the trip was going to be so short. The car's stereo sounded five times better than any sound system I'd ever owned. Infected by Luca's retrospective enthusiasm, I blasted out Gary Numan and the Human League and sang all the way.

Luca was in a hot tub in one of the outhouses, drinking champagne, with a 'girl' on either side of him (they were both well in to their 30s, and in fact admin workers at Cosmic Rase). I'm not kidding, and why should I be, it seemed to be the natural setting for such a meeting. He invited me to join them all, and I even thought about it before I said no, and Luca joked that he wouldn't discuss any business with me until I was sitting in between him and Jennifer. Jennifer said, "Come on Alan, you always looked so damned serious." Jennifer was American. And then I thought, fuck it, and I let the spa attendant, or whatever he was, bring me a towel and swimwear and a bath robe, and then I got changed and joined Luca and Jennifer and Katrina, and then I began to drink champagne and almost forgot why I'd come in the first place.

"I presume you're here because your neighbours received my letter."

"Yes. And I was wondering why I didn't receive one too."

"We'll get to that. How are they feeling about my proposal?"

"Angry enough to have called a meeting tomorrow night with our local MP."

"Sir Edmund."

"Yes, *Sir* Edmund, the grandmaster of grease." Luca laughed, the 'girls' had moved next to each other and were talking about something else.

"He was here today already. You should go to the meeting to show your face, but I already know how it will turn out."

"You paid Sir Edmund off?"

"That would be too crude, wouldn't it? Sir Edmund doesn't get money in a brown paper bag, too many of his ridiculous colleagues have been brought down by that error in the past. There are certain favours that we will grant him over time, and it's all completely legal."

"I'm sure, but I'd rather not know. But please tell me that he wasn't in this hot tub before me."

"Our meeting was out in the woods, where there are fewer ears, and fewer interruptions."

Luca re-filled our glasses, and again I had one of those moments where I wondered what the fuck I was doing here, and how long it was all going to last. And I even thought of saying to him, "I don't believe in all this, Luca. There's something not quite right about it. Your plan is unworkable and absurd. Apart from you, everyone here's working out of their depth." Instead, I accepted the glass and all four of us chinked and cheered, and I felt Katrina's leg brush mine under the water, and then I caught Katrina's eye and she smiled at me, and I thought, is that a part of this too, whereby a man in his 50s gets to sleep with an attractive co-worker in her 30s because he's friends with the billionaire boss? Is it so easy? Is it so banal? Would there be any pleasure at all? And is it healthy for a man to go 12 years without sex? In fact, make that 14, because Jessica refused me any physical contact at all the last two years before she left for Ecuador.

"So why did I receive no letter offering me twice the market value for my house?"

"Well, we've done some measurements with the architecture, and your property is not in fact close to the original pitch, which was further north where your neighbours live, and the Stevenson house on Lady Frances Drive."

"So, I'm spared the future compulsory purchase order? Besides, won't the Market Rasen Town FC megastore be right there at the entrance? Or the executive banqueting suite?"

"Ha, the old cynical Alan," said Luca, turning to his audience of Jennifer and Katrina. "The boy who questioned everything and thought he was going to change the world with devout sarcasm."

"Wait, I thought I was Imagination Alan. Which completely inaccurate image of the earlier me do you want to remember?"

"Either way, it's good that we are getting more and more of you back. To answer your question, I thought you might want to stay there seeing as you've lived there so long. Plus, it would be useful to have you there on-site, so to speak."

"I don't care about the house either way," I replied. "It's just a house. But it's going to go down really well with my neighbours when I tell them that I'm not only exempted, but that I'm working for the company that's planning to wreck their homes and evict them."

Luca nodded, put down his glass, then kissed Jennifer intimately on the mouth. Katrina was looking at me, and to my horror I found myself becoming aroused. I jumped out of the hot tub, spilling my champagne and smashing my glass, and running off to the changing room with my towel covering my lower body.

"Alan, relax!" Luca called out after me. I got changed, and then called out that I had to go, I had to prepare for the meeting tomorrow night.

I hadn't drunk enough to stop me driving the short distance back to Market Rasen. And in any case, there was no local police speed trap to stop me getting home.

***

The Stevensons may have been loaded, but they had no clue how to put on a spread like Luca had at The Old Rectory for the club board. There was a bowl of crisps, a bowl of peanuts, some plain biscuits, one bottle of mineral water, and a pot each of tea and coffee. "My apologies, we don't have decaf," said Miranda Stevenson. And I thought about how I was getting spoilt, noticing things like this, like why was there no smoked salmon with cream cheese and chives in a freshly baked vol-au-vent? I asked if Sir Edmund was here yet, and Miranda said no, they were just getting started, her husband was "firing up the troops", as she put it, in front of a roaring log fire in the living room. Deborah gave me a nice smile, and I smiled back, feeling guilty as hell. Frank Gilbert gave me a terse nod — he was presumably one of the people who'd said I wouldn't give a shit. There were also the Cutlers, the Lovetts and the Manns, couples in their 40s and 50s sitting on the edges of their seats in a house that was four times bigger than theirs across the hedge, all of them looking nervy and awkward. "Nice of you to make it, Alan," said Davie Cutler with a knowing grin, and then he took a look from his wife Alice telling him that the comments they made at home weren't necessarily to be repeated abroad. Then everybody got to their feet, and I was just about to tell them that wasn't necessary when I realised that Sir Edmund and one of his staff had entered the room from behind. Soon he was shaking all of our hands, saying, "So pleased to meet you" again and again. I thought about all the times I'd wanted to tell him to fuck off, and now here we were, face to face, and I said, "Pleased to meet you too, thank you for taking the time to come tonight."

Sir Edmund was a pro. He listened like he cared. He listened like this was the first time he'd heard about the company Cosmic Rase. No, he couldn't possibly imagine what they were planning on this particular site, it certainly didn't seem to make any sense. He would make exhaustive enquiries to get to the bottom of this, and his staff would get back to us at the earliest possible opportunity. However, he should also stress that at this stage, the company was doing nothing illegal, it was well within its rights to make unsolicited offers, just as long as there was no coercion involved.

"Coercion?" said Joyce Lovett.

Sir Edmund laughed nervously. "You know, gangs of thugs turning up and making life unpleasant for you. Not that we'd ever see anything like that in Market Rasen."

Odd that you're putting it out there, though, I wanted to say, but I didn't. There was a short silence before Sir Edmund asked to see one of the letters. He looked like he was digesting its contents carefully. "Very odd," he kept saying. "Quite extraordinary, really.

What can they be up to? Quite a generous offer, mind."

"Just one more thing that's making me very fucking suspicious, if you'll mind my language, Sir Edmund," said Frank Gilbert. Miranda Stevenson winced, but the MP waved the apology away.

"No, no, I completely understand why you're both suspicious and angry. How long have most of you lived on Woodsley Close?"

"Wellesley," corrected Craig Mann. "Almost 20 years, all of us. And I'm planning to die there too, or be carried out in a straitjacket."

Everyone murmured assent at this, and Deborah added, "It's more than just a street, Sir Edmund. We're a community. We walk in and out of each others' houses almost without knocking. We share and borrow every day. We even go on trips and holidays together, it's a very special feeling on our street, we're all involved in each others' lives, we all help each other out when there are problems, babysit each others' kids in an emergency, or even when it's not. You should have seen us last Christmas morning at Alice and Davie's, no one wanted to leave. There were at least two overdone turkeys!"

Sir Edmund granted us one of his most condescending laughs, said that he'd certainly seen and heard enough to understand how passionate we were, and — getting to his well-heeled feet — promised that he would be in touch. Simon Stevenson struggled to exact a promise from him about some concrete action, and Sir Edmund, holding Simon by the arm (very much how Luca did with me), reiterated something about ... none of us could exactly remember afterwards. Channels and procedures. When Sir Edmund had gone, there was a grand silence, as though we were deciding whether to politely thank the Stevensons for hosting such a lovely and informative evening, or we wanted to acknowledge the truth, that Sir Edmund was going to be fuck all use.

"He'll screw us over," I said.

"Please, the language tonight has been appalling," said Simon Stevenson. "And besides, you really don't know Sir Edmund. He's been most helpful to me on several occasions."

"I'm interested to know why Alan thinks that, though," said Frank Gilbert. "Why do you think Sir Edmund will screw us over?" He repeated the word screw with extra relish, and I sensed that he was no keener on the Stevensons than he was on Sir Edmund.

"Mr. Stevenson here just said it. He's been helpful to him on several occasions. Has he ever done anything for you? No, because you don't contribute to his party, and you're probably not a member. But Mr. Stevenson here is, and he's a businessman, and Tories will always look after their own."

"That's cheap rhetoric," said Simon Stevenson, outraged. "And it's not helpful. We need to look for positive solutions here."

"Then forget *Sir* Edmund," I said.

"Wow," said Davie Cutler. "We hear nothing from him for two decades, now we find out Alan's the neighbourhood rebel."

"Be quiet, Dave," said Alice, clearly embarrassed.

"It's fine," I said. "But I'm not the rebel, I'm your enemy. I'm working for the company that wants to buy your properties. Luca Romano and I are old school friends going back 40 years, before any of you came to Market Rasen. We scored goals together on the ground right beneath our very feet." I lightly stamped the floor to illustrate my point. "That's why I didn't get a letter with what Sir Edmund is calling your rather generous offer."

I had everyone's attention now, but apart from Frank Gilbert getting to his feet like I'd challenged him to a fight in a 1930s movie, there were no words. They were digesting all this information.

"You should leave now," said Simon, like the pompous twat he was.

"If you like," I said to him. "Or you can keep me here and I can give you some advice. I'll be a lot more help than Sir Edmund, who's gone way beyond even your price range, Mr. Stevenson. Because you can't compete with Luca Romano."

The room was as still as a Christmas tree.

Finally, Deborah asked in a tone like she didn't want to know the answer, "What do you suggest that we do?"

"Luca Romano is one of the five richest people in the world," I said. "He's made more money in the time we've been sitting here than all of us have made our whole lives long, including Mr. Big here." I pointed at Simon Stevenson, who went red. Suddenly, I loved the fact that I had an audience. Luca was right. I was enjoying this job, just like he'd promised, though perhaps not in the way he'd have wanted. "He's made more money in the last half hour than the collective value of your houses, and more. Way more."

"So?" asked Alice Cutler.

"Obviously, this is just an initial offer. Hold out for more cash."

"But we don't want to move," said Miranda Stevenson. "None of us." Everyone nodded, bar her husband.

"Then just ignore the letters. You're not obliged to respond."

Another silence, with people re-reading the letters, or fidgeting, or going up to the rubbish snack selection.

"What if, though ... " said Frank Gilbert, and I knew what was coming. I may not have known my neighbours very well, but I knew if any of them were going to break it would be Frank. Working class Tory. "What if one of us decides that we'd maybe like to accept an even higher offer than this?"

I was expecting dissent, but none came.

"Then that's the end of your community," I said. "Unless you make it part of the deal that Cosmic Rase dismantles your houses and rebuilds Wellesley Court somewhere else, brick for brick."

"Phtt!" said Craig Mann.

"We're not moving, any of us, right?" said Deborah, and I felt something for her now, really felt something. Or felt with her. And

I thought, poor Deborah, even though everyone's telling you at this moment in time how much they agree with you, their imaginations are wandering. I won't sell, but if I did, theoretically, how far could we push him? Where could I live that would be bigger and better and quieter, while putting a ton to one side for savings or travel or the kind of fucking car that only Simon Stevenson and Sir Edmund can afford? And no longer having to go round to Frank Gilbert's house whenever I need to borrow his drill?

"And what if," Joyce Lovett wanted to know, "there are suddenly dubious people hanging around and making veiled threats?"

"I'm your guarantee that won't happen. Not ever. Trust me."

"You're working for this fucker," said Frank Gilbert. "Why should we trust you?"

"Because I'm your neighbour. Otherwise, you're working with him and *Sir* Edmund." I pointed at Simon Stevenson, who once again spluttered that I should leave, and I stood up and said that was fine by me, plain crisps weren't my thing. Everyone else made to follow. Outside, Deborah caught up with me and we stopped just outside her house.

"Alan, we can trust you, right? You'll do what's best for the street."

"I'm working for everyone now. I know it's an awkward position, but I'll be upfront, I promise, and I'll do my best to get us through this so everyone will be happy."

"Thanks, luv," she said, touching me lightly on the arm, then she looked towards her house and said, "I'd best be getting in."

I walked the short distance home and texted Luca.

"They will hold out for more."

"Was that your suggestion?"

"Of course. They know I'm working for you. I've told them that I'm their best option going forward."

"Best option going forward — listen to you! Anyway, good work. See you tomorrow."

***

"Remember that time we got hauled in front of the deputy head?"

"Of course, I do," I said, taking a first sip of my pint. Sometimes Luca would send his driver for me at around 9pm and I'd be taken to some obscure pub in the Lincolnshire countryside in a village I'd only ever known by name. Tonight we were sitting in a very quiet corner of the Royal Oak Inn at Snitterby. Luca didn't call these late-night rendezvous to talk business, although that sometimes came up, inevitably. Rather, he loved to talk about those old times, those famous two years he still cherished. I always had the scrapbook along, just in case we wanted to check exactly who had scored how many goals in any particular game.

"I was thinking about it today when I was watching you give your presentation to the District Council. How much your back has straightened out in recent weeks. You're walking taller. You're talking like you mean it. You've got a certain … "

"Swagger?" We both laughed, because we both remembered the deputy head's office, the short and stooped Mr. Latham who was known for being humane, unlike the actual headmaster. This was like an ante-chamber where you could be warned off deviant behaviour in time to save you a stern yelling and a cane across your arse from the Victorian-era boss, with a possible suspension thrown in to knacker your career before it had even started.

Latham was seated behind his desk, we were standing before him in expectation. I'd actually thought he'd heard about our goal-scoring exploits on the weekends, and that he was going to appeal to Luca to play for the school team again, perhaps ready to broker a compromise between the dreamboat winger and Mr. Sandringham. Latham mumbled how there was no need for us to worry "unduly", but there was something he needed to address with us. There were no specific charges, he stressed, and no actual school rules that either of us had broken.

"As if," I said, in mock outrage.

"Yes, well, it's that kind of comment people are noticing," said Latham. "Some of your teachers are seeing you two convey a certain arrogance with your attitude, in class and out of it."

We were both biting our lips by this point, desperate not to laugh and prove his point.

"Yes, but what exactly is the problem, sir?" Luca had asked. "What have we done wrong?"

Latham reiterated that we had done nothing wrong, as such. However, we needed to temper our swagger.

"Sir?"

"Don't walk around school like you think that you own the place."

"Sir, we would never dream of doing the headmaster's job for him," said Luca. At this, Latham threw up his hands in frustration, then ordered us to get out of his sight, but to "at least make an attempt to take on board what I'm trying to tell you."

We made it as far as the fifth form common room, and then to the annoyance of everyone else present, broke into probably exaggerated hysterics at our own private joke that we shared with no one. "Temper your swagger" became our catch-phrase for the coming months.

An elderly couple who looked like they were in their 80s entered The Royal Oak and tottered up to the bar. "Look at that," said Luca. "I'd like to be doing that when I'm their age. Still coming out for a drink at 10 o'clock." We watched them order and sit down. Both of them were drinking half pints of bitter.

"Night cap," I said. Then, I added, "but let me know if I need to temper my swagger. I don't want to get above my station."

Luca smiled. "You're doing a great job. The locals trust you, and your co-workers say you're fantastic to work with because you tell them exactly what you want and when you want it. Communication's like football. It's simple, but hardly anyone can do it right. So keep up the swagger."

"It's not put on," I said. "As you predicted, I genuinely love this job."

"Excellent," said Luca with relish, "because I'm giving you a second job title — Head of Community Liaison. Just keep doing what you're doing, though. Plus, I've doubled your salary."

"There's no need…"

"Stop! No further observations necessary, my friend."

"Thank you," was all I could think to say.

"Thank you for still being here when I came back. I was surprised, though. How come you never went off to college?"

"Because I wanted to earn money so that I could buy a car and impress Jessica."

Luca stared at me, and then said, "Really?"

"Yes, it was that simple. I only wanted to impress her and marry her. At 16, I knew. Instead of doing A levels and getting off my head and playing football, I was focused on becoming deputy branch manager, and doing a car maintenance course. I got so into that, I almost became a mechanic. Until Jessica complained about the oil and grease on my hands."

"And Jessica? She was super smart."

"Did her A levels, then stayed in town because her mum was really ill at the time, and she stayed really ill for about four years. By the time her mum died, Jess was running an old peoples' home and we were married."

"Had she fallen in love with you?"

That question shook me, and for a long time it hung above our table in the corner of the tranquil pub. The old couple were playing dominos, and you could hear every click of the tiles. I wondered if I could just let the question evaporate up the chimney. But Luca wouldn't take his eyes off me.

"I've asked myself that question many times," I said eventually. I shifted in my seat and took another sip, and then I felt a huge weight ascend from my body. "The truth is, we got married because she wanted her mum to be at her wedding before she died. I was the least objectionable candidate."

"There were others?"

"Oh, yes. She was forever dumping me, going out with other men, then she'd come back."

"And you always took her."

"Every time."

"Katrina says that you are nurturing a shattered heart. She says she can see it in every movement of your body. Or at least she could until you got your swagger back. Now she reckons there's a man inside you waiting to explode."

"I hope not. That could get messy."

"I think that's what she's hoping for," said Luca, then let out a leery laugh.

"Come on," I said. "We were always against that laddish thing."

"We didn't need it," he said, nodding. "We just swaggered instead."

"Plus, you had Jessica on your arm."

I stood and went to the bar for another round. When I came back with two more pints, Luca asked me, "Did you hate me for that? Or resent me?"

"Not one bit. It was the natural order. She was the most gorgeous girl in our year, and you perfectly matched her with your long, dark curls and annoyingly blue eyes and cheeky fucking smile. I knew that nothing would separate you. At least, nothing apart from your family kidnapping you off to America in the middle of the night. But you left us both, with no warning, and because we were both so involved with you in our different ways, we found each other instead. But it never quite worked."

"Why not?"

"Because, as you supposed, she didn't really love me. And that came across almost every day in the way she talked to me, and the way that she always seemed irritated when I tried to touch her. And every day, I tried to rectify that by looking for ways to please her that simply didn't exist."

Luca was sombre now. "That's too bad," he said.

"And you? I can't believe a new guy with your looks didn't immediately mix it up at an American High School."

"I was swamped," he confessed. "I decided to shut out Jessica almost as soon as the term started. I forgot Market Rasen and you and the football team. I had to. It was the only way to deal with it."

"And now?"

"I'd be curious to see Jessica again."

"She's been re-married for six years. An Ecuadorian fellow who, according to my daughter, is a dream partner. But with your resources, I'm sure you could win her back."

"I'm not that kind of multi-billionaire. Why does your daughter tell you such things?"

"Because she hopes I can pick up living again."

"And?"

"Now, maybe I have."

***

After our night out in Snitterby, Luca left town without a word and disappeared off the radar. There was a skeleton staff only at The Old Rectory, and my text messages to him remained unread. There was another residents' meeting, and this time we crammed into Frank Gilbert's front room. There was no catering, not even a desultory glass of water. The Stevensons weren't there, and word was that they had already agreed to sell, though I couldn't confirm or deny as the property deals were not my direct responsibility. Cosmic Rase was now offering all the residents of Wellesley Close five times the market value of their properties. Frank held up the latest letter and wanted to know what we all thought. Davie Cutler said that he wasn't comfortable expressing an opinion as long as I was in the room. He'd been thinking about my double agency, as he put it, and was no longer so sure that I could be trusted any more than a character in a John Le Carré novel.

"Fair enough," said Frank Gilbert, who'd appointed himself chairman. "Alan, perhaps you could leave."

"Why?" I said. "I already know what he's offering, and I can tell you that he will keep on pushing that up."

"But come on," said Joyce Lovett. "He must have a limit."

"He wants to reach a settlement as soon as possible," I said. "Have any of you responded to the letters?" There was a general shaking of heads. "Well, if you're all now interested in selling, why don't you ask him how high he's prepared to go?"

"I thought we weren't interested in selling," Deborah said, but she no longer sounded emphatic, and no one even bothered to agree with her.

"I know that's what we said a few months back," said Davie Cutler, stroking his beard and looking down at Frank's old brown rug, which had settled for a life without a vacuum cleaner. "But you have to admit, this is a bit of a, you know ... a game-changer, so to speak."

No one wanted to agree or disagree with that, so after a few moments I said, "If you're moving in that direction, then respond to the letter and say you'll settle for 10 times the market value."

"That'd be over two million quid for this place," said Frank, gesturing at his modest living room. "Surely he's not that keen."

"He has a vision, he has a soft heart for a deceased football ground, and he has unlimited cash," I said, although for the first time I wondered too. Luca had never given me any specific advice on how to persuade the residents of Wellesley Close to sell. He'd merely told me to get the job done.

"Is he insane as well?" Craig Mann wanted to know. "I don't mean, like, certifiable. I just mean that he's living on a different planet kind of insane. This whole thing is somehow not right, you know? It's like it's too good to be true, and could end up being a nightmare."

"He's not insane at all," I replied. "But when you have that much wealth, you do indeed inhabit a different planet. He doesn't think about numbers, he just wants results."

"Will you get paid more if we sell?" Frank, of course.

"Not that I'm aware of."

"But Alan," said Deborah, "what do you think we should do?"

"Don't trust his opinion," said Davie Cutler. "We don't know what he's thinking and what he's telling Luca Romano. They're old pals, remember."

"He's not wrong," said Craig Mann. "I mean, you live here too, Alan, even though you always turned your nose up at us. But what do you want? Do you really reckon this football ground is a good idea? Do you want to strut around it as much as Luca, just so you two can talk about the time you once scored a hat-trick against Dingly Dell Village Reserves?"

Frank let out a guffaw at that one, the rest looked too pre-occupied to find anything funny. Or they were contemplating what it would be like to be a millionaire in Market Rasen.

"Like I told you before," I said. "I really don't care either way."

And for the first time, I believed that. Up until now, I'd jumped on board with Luca's romance. But as soon as you let yourself look over the side of the luxury yacht, you suddenly caught a glimpse of dark, deep water.

"Yeah, well, you've already made your money, I suppose," Frank retorted, but Deborah said he wasn't being helpful, and that we should still all try and stick together. I felt guilty that she was taking my side, and said that Frank's point was valid, I was getting very well paid and that they should bear that in mind when making their next move. Now it was time for me to leave so they could talk about what they wanted to do next.

"But remember," I said. "He's definitely not crazy, although his patience may have its limits."

"So you're saying we should settle soon," said Joyce Lovett.

"I'm not offering any more advice. There's a perception of bias."

"Because if you don't get us to sell, you've failed at your job," said Craig.

"I think it's definitely time for me to go," I said. "Good night, all."

Around three hours later, not long after 11 o'clock and just as I was about to go to bed, Deborah knocked in the door, and apologised for disturbing me so late. Could she come in? Of course, I said, glancing across at her house. The lights were out.

"They're not there, they're at their dad's," said Deborah, reading my thoughts as she came inside, then stopped in the hallway, uncertain which way to go. I gestured her into the kitchen. It seemed the right place for a late-night chat. I offered to make her a hot chocolate, as an ironic nod to the hour, and was surprised when she said she'd love that. I had some in the cupboard, though God knows how many years it had been there. Since Jessica's time? As I boiled the kettle, wondering if the powder would still dissolve, she apologised for a party that Henry had hosted at the weekend while she was in Doncaster visiting her sister. Apparently, it had got quite out of hand until Frank went round and threatened to call the police.

"I didn't even notice," I said. "In fact, I was at work on Saturday night. With Luca, you only work long hours."

"No wonder, at those salaries."

"You know my salary?" I asked, bemused. I didn't even know it myself. Luca was constantly putting it up.

"Not yours," she said hurriedly. "But I know Ali Tibson, and she couldn't help but bragging about how much she's on." Ali was one of my secretaries. She had access to my pay slips as well. There was a silence then for a few seconds, until I changed the subject.

"How often do the boys go and stay with their dad?"

"About once a month," she said. "He really has to push them, though. He's got that farm out there now with his farming tart, near Ludborough. Bugger all for them to do, all their mates are here in town. And he makes them work, shifting pig shit and the like."

"Do they get on with their ..." I wasn't sure what word to use.

"Their step-mum? They don't really mention her. I suppose they're worried I'll cry or have a fit or something."

"Will you?"

"Not any more. You've got to stop at some point. I honestly don't think about it much any more. It's hard to miss someone when they've hurt you that bad. You wonder what you liked about them in the first place."

I placed her hot chocolate on the table. I had a tin of shortbread too, left over from work. At Cosmic Rase, staff were catered for, all day and every day. Deborah fell on it like she'd just got out of prison.

"Oh, this is so nice Alan, thank you. I never buy stuff like this, it doesn't last a minute with the boys around."

We sipped our drinks for a while, and she nibbled on her third piece of shortbread, looking thoughtful. Finally, she answered my question.

"If we had the money from selling the house, I could get the boys a car so they wouldn't be stuck out there at their dad's. I mean, they could visit him, but get away. And we could actually go on holiday, we haven't been away for years. Their dad can't afford it either, and he always tells them it's because I'm draining him for maintenance."

"Do they believe that?"

"They're not that stupid. They know what choice he made. The whole split didn't really make sense for anyone. Her ex is in a bedsit in Skegness, on the dole. Got a settlement because because the farm's in her family, then gambled it away in a few weeks."

She went quiet, but then looked up and smiled when I ventured, "How did the rest of the meeting go?"

"I'm not supposed to tell you, remember? But it didn't really go anywhere, just talking round in circles. At least no one got angry. I just don't know what to do. I suppose that's why I've come round, to find out what you really think."

"I'm not even sure myself anymore what I think. Sell, and you make shedloads of money. Refuse to sell, and you retain your community. I didn't realise until that night at the Stevensons how close you all were."

"Well, that was all a bit exaggerated for the benefit of Sir Edmund, if we're going to be truthful. We don't really just walk in and out of each others' houses, and Christmas Day wasn't that great either — Craig Mann's a real bore once he's had a couple of drinks.

"It is what it is." That was something Luca said a lot.

"What does that mean?"

"I've no idea. It's one of those phrases I've learnt to say in my new job when I don't know what to say. It doesn't mean anything."

"You're a great help," she said, but she was smiling. I smiled back, and then after a few moments of smiling at each other, we started to laugh too.

"Jesus," she said a few minutes later. "That hot chocolate is good stuff. It's the first time in my life I've snogged a new bloke without being drunk."

"Then I think you should take another sip."

"Just tonight, Alan," she said, suddenly concerned. "You should know that. When the boys are home ... I can't. It's just impossible. Plus, Frank seems to think him and I have a thing going, even though I've never as much pecked him on the cheek."

To be touched again, after so long. To be touched for the first time by someone who seemed to mean it, at my age. Move on to the next paragraph if you'd rather: it was like swimming in a placid, crystal lake surrounded by green trees bursting with birds of heavenly song.

***

After six weeks of silence, I was suddenly summoned to The Old Rectory. "You have to see this!" Luca texted. When I drove up, he was waiting for me at the gate, like we were on a play date. Big hugs, great smiles, nothing about his unexplained absence. He lead me into a dark outhouse I'd never seen before and introduced me to "our architect, Paddy van Veen", a tall and serious man in his 40s. "Paddy designed the new opera house in Tirana," Luca said, like that was something I'd know about. "He's won all kinds of awards. And now, look here ... " The lights came on, revealing a table with a scale model of The Ropewalk. Which, at first sight, was impressive. At second sight, it was more than amazing. In the space of five seconds, I was fully back on board. Luca was laughing and opening champagne, Jennifer and Katrina had joined us, and Paddy gave me a guided tour, with reference to a digital presentation that was now being screened on the walls of the former cattle-shed.

The stadium was made mainly out of wood. It was compact — a realistic size for a team playing so low, but with scope for expansion. And it also incorporated many features of the old ground, including modernised versions of the snack cabin stand, the walkway, and the changing rooms. There were green zones and solar panels everywhere, rendering the stadium 'climate positive'. The main stand, populated with miniature wooden fans, included a glass back wall so that you could still see the passing trains, and anyone in a passing train could catch a glimpse of the game. There was a plan to bring the rail companies on board so that trains would stop and 'interactively' watch the games for a few minutes. "That will bring us great publicity," Luca intervened. "You'll get nutters, nerds and journalists coming from around the world to write about this place."

"It looks magnificent," I said. Everyone except Paddy was smiling, clinking glasses.

"It's a fucking dream," said Luca. "Every last detail. Paddy here is a genius. I want it built tomorrow." He laughed. "How are we doing with the residents?"

"They're still holding out. But they're talking about not."

"Great," said Luca. "The higher we go, the more likely they'll sell all at once. It'll be a relief for everyone. Maybe it's time for me to meet them. Bring them out here for An Evening with Luca Romano. Offer them the world and more. Show them I understand what they're giving up, because I too once gave up something I love." He was even more effusive than usual. It seemed like he'd already been drinking for a while.

"Did you already come to a deal with the Stevensons?"

"Of course. You offer someone like that a huge amount of cash and it's just a matter of whether he bites your hand off or your whole arm."

"Which part of your body did he take?"

"I got away with the hand. Apparently he needs the cash right now due to some problems with his company."

"I'm so sorry to hear that," I said, and Luca told me that anti-capitalistic Schadenfreude was not really his thing. Who knew what the future was for his own enterprises? "So," he said, pointing at his toy stadium, "better to spend as much as possible now while the going's good.

He walked around the table with me as I discovered more details in the immaculate model. My own house, converted into the club's shop and administrative headquarters. A children's playground and adventure centre. The Healthy Menu catering court, in addition to the traditional snack cabin at the side of the pitch. The only thing missing was the mud and the adjacent marshland, but I didn't mention either. I didn't want Luca ordering a re-design so that we had an artificial swamp and the old paddle-boat and pensioner with a fishing net who used to retrieve wayward footballs.

"We'll also have a media centre and a club museum," Luca went on. "But maybe that will be in the town centre. I've got researchers working on old match reports so that we can digitally re-create videos of the club's greatest moments."

"Is that possible?"

"I thought you might ask that, you old Lincolnshire Luddite," he said, and then pressed a button on his remote control. All of a sudden, an artificial version of 16-year-old Luca Romano was tearing down the right wing of the old Ropewalk, and placing a cross on to my teenage head before we both jumped into a celebratory hug. In the real world, Luca roared "Gooooal!" and also jumped into my arms, spilling champagne on to the cattle-shed floor. I roared back at him, getting into the spirit. Paddy had disappeared. Katrina and Jennifer indulged us with smiles, like they'd been our wives for the past three decades.

"You'll stay for the Jacuzzi to celebrate this special night?" Luca's question was rhetorical.

"I would love to, but I absolutely can't. I've got a video call with Jane at 10. Something really urgent has come up in Ecuador, but she won't tell me what by text message. I'm sorry."

Luca pulled a face. "You're no fun, Alan." If he knew I was lying, he decided not to make a big thing out of it.

"Family," I said, and he patted me on the back.

"The main thing is, we need to really get this moving. Starting tomorrow. Be back out here by eight, earlier if you can. We'll have breakfast. We need to discuss strategy in more detail. We've bought the club, we've bought the MP, and the town council is absolutely on board and on message. Now Wellesley Close needs closure."

"Of course," I said. I put my champagne glass down, having spilt more than I'd drunk. I bid Katrina and Jennifer a swift good night and drove the three miles home at a law-breaking lick. The boys next door were back at their dad's again, but due home tomorrow.

***

When Jane walked through the arrivals gate at East Midlands Airport two weeks later, for one shocking particle of a second I thought it was Jessica. Of course, I'd seen my daughter on video calls. I knew that she looked like her mother, I knew that she was an attractive young woman. But I hadn't seen her walk since she was 16, when she'd been a slightly overweight adolescent who veered between sarcastic good humour and a borderline suicidal resentment at her own existence. She had more or less dragged herself around, as though moving was a chore demanded of her by unreasonable elders. Now she sashayed towards me, tanned and confident and correct in her rhythm, laughing at me already, just like she always had for being the archetypal awkward dad who hadn't known how to deal with his children and their particular needs. And my heart dropped through my hips and crashed at my ankles, because I thought there had been a mistake, that Jessica had taken the money I'd sent for Jane's air fare and decided to come instead. For reasons that were not yet clear. And then I realised it was my daughter, of course it was. And not the woman I'd wasted my hopeless love on for 40 odd years.

We both cried, which I thought was a good start, even though it wasn't something I did on a regular basis. At least, not in public. Jane blurted out that she had vowed never to come back to England, but she was already glad that she had. "I needed to jump over my own fears and inhibitions," she said. "Did you get that out of a self-help manual?" I asked, and immediately worried that maybe she was now into self-help manuals, even though it was the kind of thing we'd always laughed at. "Ah, same old dad, always negative about anything positive," she countered, but she was smiling.

"Your mum used to say something similar."

"And yet you refused to take any notice. Bloody hell, the weather." We were crossing from the terminal to the car park. It was April now, but it was windy and fresh.

"Your winter coat is still in the hallway cupboard at home."

"Oh great, I'm sure my teenage tastes will have aged wonderfully. Did you get me Wotsits and Mars Bars in as well?"

"Maybe." I had, of course. I really was clueless.

"Brilliant!" she said. "I'm actually looking forward to that part of coming back."

"Are you planning to catch up with old friends?"

"Dad, no one I knew at school is anywhere near there now. Some of them are closer to Ecuador than they are to Market fucking Rasen."

"You kept in touch?"

"Ah, you know. We follow each other online, present our own versions of a wonderful life. Oh my God, you've got an electric car. Did Endsleigh make you district regional manager at last?"

I didn't answer the last question, which had been a running gag about a decade and a half ago. She wasn't expecting an answer in any case. On the drive home, I let her talk while I listened, wanting to stop the car to tell her that I was sorry that I'd driven them away with my feckless lack of ambition and curiosity. Then I thought, if it hadn't been for my feckless lack of ambition and curiosity, this incredible force of human nature probably wouldn't be sitting next to me, at least not the way she was now.

An hour later, I knew everything about her boyfriend (structural engineer, environmentalist, hates football), her studies and work (writing a doctoral thesis on something to do with colonialism and economics in South America; lecturing on same); their flat (too small, but central); her dogs and cats (I forget the names and breeds, but there are lots of them); and the nation of Ecuador (beautiful, incredible, chaotic). Though barely a word about Jessica, except in passing. Maybe it didn't matter anymore.

We drove into Market Rasen and Jane proclaimed, "Oh my God, it's exactly the same," which was a phrase I heard a lot over the next few days. As we pulled into Wellesley Close, there was Henry sitting on their garden wall, like some kind of ironic welcoming party, staring at us as we pulled up and into the driveway.

"Bloody hell, is that John and Deborah's kid? He used to sit on that wall 12 years ago when he was still shitting into his shorts. What is he now, 17? Has he moved since I left?"

"Not much," I said. "That's Henry. His dad's been gone for years, though. Found himself a farmer's wife."

"So Lincolnshire," was all she could say to that. "Wasn't there another one?"

"Yes, a couple of years younger. Phil. The one who doesn't look like he wants to kill you for ... " the phrase that came to mind was "sleeping with his mum".

"For what?" Jane wanted to know.

"For pulling into your garage and living next door to him."

I didn't tell her that Henry, having sensed that something was going on (he'd started glaring at me instead of ignoring me) had grabbed Deborah's phone off her when she'd been texting me, and read as many messages as he could until she managed to force him to hand it back. He'd then accused her of seeing me "behind my back", and demanded to know why she'd been keeping it secret. Instead of telling him to mind his own business, Deborah had become defensive, which Henry had exploited by telling her that he didn't want to find me round at their house, ever. To my annoyance, she presented this as a done thing. Not that I'd have felt comfortable even talking to his mum knowing that he was in the next room, smouldering with whatever problem it was that he had.

Deborah would text me that she really, really missed me, but as long as the boys were at home, she wouldn't come round to the house. Henry was also refusing now to go and stay with their dad, saying he had to 'protect' his mum. And Frank Gilbert also gave me the hard look whenever our paths crossed (thankfully, not often), as though he had some kind of possession rights over Deborah, or maybe it was just general ill feeling at the whole Ropewalk situation. I missed her, though, and sought out any chance just to catch a glimpse of her through the kitchen window. We'd grant each other a shy wave if we thought no one was looking. Middle-aged adults behaving like lovelorn teens being kept at bay by parents on separate sides of a chronic religious divide. But I didn't want to make life any harder for her, so I just threw myself into my work instead.

Jane tried on her ankle-length purple puffah jacket, giggling like a teen, and ate a handful of Wotsits before putting the packet back in the cupboard. "Never as good as you remember," she said. "I think I need to clean my teeth now." It was late afternoon, and she wanted to walk around town. She decided on her mum's old brown anorak instead of the puffah jacket. She couldn't believe I hadn't given it away, that it was still hanging there on exactly the same peg in the hallway as 12 years ago. We walked outside and Jane called out, "Hi, Henry!" Like she saw him every day. He frowned at her, like she was taking the piss. And then who should walk around the corner and into the close but Frank Gilbert, carrying a bag of shopping and also glaring, until he caught sight of Jane and stopped in his tracks and spat out, "Jessica?"

"Not quite," said Jane. "The daughter, remember?"

Frank went red. "Ah, Jane, of course. How are you now?"

"Older," she said. "How about you?"

"I'm older too." He let out a grunt of a laugh. He hadn't even acknowledged me, standing right there. "You should come round for a cuppa and a chat."

"Of course," said Jane. They both agreed that it was lovely to see each other again, and we continued on our ways, though Frank did take a second to give me a token evil look. I wondered if he'd raised his hopes that Jessica had come back to me, allowing him to continue his non-existent courtship of Deborah.

"I take it that Frank still has no girlfriend."

"He remains Market Rasen's most untouched bachelor."

"He used to make passes at mum, she told me."

"He used to make passes at everyone. He fancies that he's together with Deborah, but he's not."

"Is that why he didn't talk to you? Because you're a rival?" And I wondered how she knew, but she didn't, it was just a passing joke that had accidentally hit the spot. She didn't notice that I had gone red in the face because she was looking ahead, and was soon distracted by the fact that Garnett's sweet shop and Lancaster the butcher's were both still in the same place, both still operational, both still owned by the same families. We walked past her old schools. At one point she took my arm, and I was full of so many feelings, for her and for her mother, and for Deborah too, and even on some much less positive level for her teenage protector and Frank Gilbert as well. Plus, there was Luca Romano and his insane project. It was too much at one go. I dragged Jane into the Aston Arms. I ordered a pint of bitter, Jane had a blackcurrant cordial with lime juice.

"You're fit and healthy?"

"I work out three times a week, and walk the dogs three times a day. I'm on the university volleyball team."

"Weren't you on the netball team at school here?"

"I tried. Though not very hard. No co-ordination back then, and not much enthusiasm either. Mrs. Goodison didn't like me, and I can't say I blame her. Ali Neimann was the captain, and she promised to get me on the team, but only if I let her snog me in the shower."

"She did what?"

"She said that to everyone, and then she never stuck to her promise."

"That's terrible! Why on earth did no one report it?"

"Why? We thought it was hilarious. It was daily teenage life, dad. Much better that the parents don't know. And the teachers. You'd only have gone making things much, much worse."

"Bloody hell," I said, and she patted me on the arm.

"Maybe in another 10 years I'll tell you some other stuff. You're probably not ready for it yet."

At that moment, Luca called me and asked me to come out to Linwood. I said that I had visitors. He told me to bring them along and hung up.

"Drink up, we need to go," I said to Jane. I'd yet to tell her what my new job actually entailed. I was secretly excited. She had to be impressed that I was no longer on the high street selling insurance at the same company I'd been with for over 30 years.

"Do we have to? Right now?" she said. "A Tuesday afternoon in Market Rasen is probably the best time and place to get over jet lag."

"My boss just called," I said.

"Your boss? I thought you were the boss here."

"My new boss."

I was standing up now. Jane stood up too and put on the brown anorak of memory. "What the hell are you talking about, dad?"

"My new boss is Luca Romano. I work for his company, Cosmic Rase. As in, the river Rase."

"Yeah, right."

"Why do you think you flew over here on business class?'

"You told me that you'd inherited cash from great uncle Charlie?"

"Great uncle Charlie didn't leave a penny. I had to pay for half of the bloody funeral. Don't you remember me going on about the goals I used to score for Market Rasen U16s with Luca Romano?"

"Honestly? No, I don't. Not one bit." We were walking down Waterloo Street now.

"Okay," I said. "Then I've got 15 minutes to fill you in."

***

When we walked into the kitchen at The Old Rectory, Luca inevitably was struck by the same error as myself and Frank Gilbert. His usual welcoming smile was conquered by surprise and mutated into a round mouth of astonishment, for once emitting no words. Before he could say the word "Jessica!" I helpfully intervened and introduced Jane as my daughter, over on a trip from Ecuador. Jennifer and Christina, who were both sitting at the table on their laptops, stood and embraced her like they were old family friends, or as if Jane was our South American ambassador. Jane was starstruck and overwhelmed and could barely make a sound. Luca recovered himself and launched back into charm mode, peppering her with questions about her journey, what she was doing here, and Ecuador. He delivered grandiose eulogies in my direction, "my oldest, dearest friend", and all that we were working on here.

"It all sounds like quite the project," Jane said, like she was Luca's grandmother who was sure that it was all very interesting, dear. "Dad was telling me about it on the way here." She had not been at all impressed, and I was still hurting at that. "Why a football stadium?" she'd wanted to know. "Why not something more useful for the community? A leisure centre? A proper theatre company or concert venue? An art gallery-cum-college that fosters and encourages and exhibits local talent?" I offered the bland and untruthful observation that those were the kind of projects we'd be considering further down the line.

"It is more than quite the project," Luca gushed. "This is going to set the standard for all future sports stadia. In 10 years, people will be wondering why we didn't start building sustainable football grounds decades ago. Like, back in the days when this one was razed to the ground. That's when we should have started thinking about this kind of thing! Come on, come on, you have to come out and see the model. You will love it, I promise, absolutely love it." He was either oblivious to Jane's indifference, or thought that he could bring her around, like he did with everyone in the end. That was, after all, his special persuasive talent, backed by interminable sums of cash.

Once we were out there, Jane tried out of courtesy to look like she was interested. The re-created goals played on the wall-screens of my simulated 16-year-old self scoring at the old Ropewalk seemed to bemuse her. Luca noticed that her response was not as wildly enthused as he was hoping, and so he laid it on thicker still. How I had driven the project and was now the face and the originator of change in the town. How everybody in the region would be tapping into their potential, just like her dad now was, and all in the name of progress. And once sustainable stadium architecture was established, who knew what the limits were? Why, perhaps he would look into Quito as the very next location, but on a far grander scale. The company name Cosmic Rase International had already been registered.

This was all news to me. Up until this moment, we had only ever talked about the Ropewalk, which in itself seemed a massive enough scheme to my shortened horizons. And one which would not even be realised until Deborah, Frank and the likes of Joyce Lovett had given us the pretty green light. Was this cross-continental expansion what he'd called me out to discuss this afternoon? Or was Jane's appearance the trigger for Luca to try and impress her on a gargantuan scale, realised right there on the spur of the moment? At one point, I whispered to Jennifer, "Did he really register Cosmic Rase International", and she whispered back, "First I've heard of it."

We had to stay for dinner, of course. What did Jane want to eat? She said that she'd been looking forward to Lincolnshire sausages from Lancasters. I didn't mention that I'd already bought some in, and had been planning to make them for breakfast. They were immediately ordered by phone, and delivered within 15 minutes. We took a tour of the house and the grounds, the wind having dropped in favour of a milder front. We walked around to the adjacent church, Luca talking all the time at Jane, occasionally acknowledging my presence with a reference. I chimed in, when required, combatting a paternal instinct to order Jane back into the car and to drive her as far away from here as possible.

At Jane's request — citing jetlag — dinner was early (Lincolnshire sausages in a burgundy red wine sauce ...), and we managed to get out of there by eight. Luca did not let Jane out of his conversational sights for a single minute, except when she'd gone to the toilet. During that time, he sung her praises and told me how proud I must be to have "produced" such a strong and intelligent young woman. I said that I had not really had any influence on her at all, she'd only turned out so well because she'd disappeared to the other side of the globe. Luca poo-pooed that, of course. And I wondered how long we'd have had to stay — and how many bottles of red wine it would take — for him to try and put her on the payroll with a bloated job title at another unrealistic salary.

"Exhausting," said Jane on the car ride home.

"The journey, or my boss?"

"What do you think?" she said, and I said nothing. I already knew the answer. After a while, I asked the question back, "What do you think? Of the whole plan?"

"I'm out of words, dad," she said quietly. "Let's talk about it tomorrow. I need a massive sleep."

The next morning, though, Jane was still asleep at nine when I left for work. Cosmic Rase (the company name was all of a sudden starting to annoy me — perhaps due to Jane's non-plussed reaction when I'd first mentioned it) was now housed in a container park of offices on the sparse industrial estate just off the town bypass, and here we'd assembled a team that was formed to ensure that all planning permissions would be granted as soon as possible, and that any environmental surveys that the county intended to carry out were — by whatever means — rushed to the top of their priority list. Sir Edmund was very much instrumental in this, blustering in the media about the prospects for growth, and the need to brush aside any kind of 'red tape' that might prevent "this unprecedented and generous investment" (like it was a charitable donation). I had a whole sub-team of employees in touch with Sir Edmund's staff to make sure that he, and the media he talked to, stayed 'on message'. It was depressingly easy. The MP had latched on to the New Ropewalk to present himself both as a friend of entrepreneurial innovation and an environmental cheerleader. Fortunately, I had not been required to meet him face to face since the night at the Stevensons' house when he'd half-promised to look out for the interests of the residents.

Luca was soon bombarding me with text messages, proposing dinners at various desirable restaurants around the county over the following days. I ignored them for as long as I could, until he called me and enquired about "our plans" tonight. I said I'd not had the chance to talk to Jane yet, she'd been sleeping off her flight when I'd left that morning. Well, now was the time to call her, he jovially ordered, it was nearly midday. I ventured that we'd been planning some father-daughter time, and that in a couple of days she was going off to see her brother. Luca ignored me. He had been thinking some more about Ecuador and Quito, he said. He'd had some people do research already, the place would be perfect for a larger-scale Ropewalk. That could be my next posting, and there would surely be a place for Jane in the set-up too, what with her fluent Spanish and local knowledge. I said that we were maybe getting ahead of ourselves, and for the first time since he'd shown up on my doorstep a few months back, Luca betrayed irritation with me.

"Getting ahead of ourselves. It's the old Alan of Market Rasen attitude again." He parodied my morose voice, with an unkind edge. "Can't do this, won't do that, how's that going to work? We have to think fast, Alan, we have to think future. We have to think positive, and we have to be constantly forging ahead. That's what I'm paying you for. What I don't pay you for is to dally, to hang around, to express dragging doubts. That way lies fatal destitution. By the way, send out new letters to the residents of Wellesley Close. Double the offer, and increase each individual's share of the company to two per cent. But this time, name a deadline."

"How long?"

"End of May. No, wait. Bollocks to that. End of April."

"That's ten days."

"I know, way too long." He laughed, but without humour. "But I'm flexible. Have the letters typed up today and delivered by courier this afternoon."

"No problem. What if they still don't respond?"

"Negative thinking again, Alan. Make sure they do. Let them know this is our final offer."

"And if they say no?"

"Make sure they don't say no. I'm being very, very fucking generous here, and I'm also losing patience."

"I'll do my best."

"You surely will. You do your best, you do your job. And dinner?'

I hesitated. "Sorry, Luca. It's just going to be me and Jane tonight," I said. "Maybe tomorrow." Resisting Luca overcame the thought of seeing my daughter's reproachful face if I told her we were spending a second consecutive evening in the mogul's company.

"Fine," he snapped, and hung up.

***

Jane and I decided that we'd spend the late afternoon and evening in Lincoln. We had a brief discussion about whether to go by car or train. I was happy for us to jump into the car, but for old time's sake she favoured the rackety shuttle that went from Market Rasen to Lincoln Central. It was just as quick, you didn't have to look for parking, and in any case, wasn't I working for a company that was all about sustainability?

I had no counter-arguments, as always. I'd submitted to her will pretty much from the first time she opened her mouth right up until her departure for Ecuador.

I hadn't taken the train to Lincoln for decades. We sat on the grimy chugger, surrounded by at least a week's litter, and she told me how she and Wendy Callaghan used to bunk off school on Wednesday afternoons in their fifth form with fake doctors' notes exempting them from sport. Then they'd take the train to Lincoln to meet two young men who were already at the university.

"Something else you didn't tell me about."

"I wonder why."

"What did you do?"

"Dad. Come on."

It took me a few seconds to interpret the look on her face. "Oh," I said. "Blimey. You were only 16."

"Mum knew. She put me on the pill."

I stared out of the window for a few moments at the dull, featureless vistas of West Lindsey.

"I thought you were going to wait another 10 years before you told me this kind of stuff," I said.

Jane laughed. She was more like her old self again now that we weren't around Luca. "It seems like I should have, dad. You were the same with Josh. Everyone in the school knew he was gay before you seemed to cotton on, or come to terms with it."

"I was fine with it!"

"But it wasn't about you, dad. It was about Josh. And when you finally realised, you made it about you." She leaned forward and touched me gently on the knee. I looked back out of the window, deciding whether or not to go in a huff, or just admit that she was right again.

"What should I have done?" I murmured.

"You didn't need to do anything really. Just accept him for what he was. Is."

"But I do."

"Do you? How often do you call him? Go and visit him?"

"I don't feel like he wants me to. Really. It's too odd."

Jane flopped back into her seat and sighed. "Oh, dear," was all she said.

"I did call him a while back to say that I loved him. But it didn't seem to go down very well."

"Yes, he told me about that. Seemed to think you'd been on the beer." She leaned forward again and took my hands. "Show, don't tell. You don't have to make declarations. You're over-thinking it. Just go over there for a weekend and hang out. Be interested in his life. Questions are allowed from the audience. Don't make it difficult for yourself, or for Josh either."

I nodded. She made it sound so easy. The train puttered into Lincoln and we spent an hour walking up the High Street towards the Castle and the Cathedral.

"What did your university boyfriend say when you told him you were moving to Ecuador?" We'd found a Thai restaurant at the top of Steep Hill.

"Oh, he wasn't really a boyfriend. He was probably relieved. I should look him up online. Matthew something or other. Randall? Ravensdale?"

"I wouldn't know."

"He was no better at shagging than I was."

"Jane, please."

"You have to get the experience in before you settle down. Mum says that was your problem. Well, her problem too. Stuck in one small town in one small relationship. Josh and I are glad you did, though, for a while. Otherwise, obviously, we wouldn't be sitting here right now."

"I'm glad you and ... " I struggled to say the word 'mum'. "I'm glad you both analysed it. Presumably on the flight out to Quito with a bottle of champagne."

We set to on a starter of spring rolls and chicken skewers with a peanut sauce.

"No, it took a couple of years before we talked about it. When I finished school and before I went to university. To be sure, we were congratulating ourselves a little bit on how things had worked out. We couldn't really see any downside to it, apart from the fact that Mum had left you behind and broke your heart."

"Good to know that I was in the conversation."

"I told her she should write to you, but she didn't know where to start, or where that would take her. She said it was better just to cut things clean off. That it was easier that way for you too."

I said nothing, just ate. Jane looked at me, worried.

"I'm sorry, dad," she said. "She could have been a bit less brutal. I suppose she thought she was doing the right thing. Or the best thing."

"Yeah," I said. "But really, she just didn't give a fuck."

Jane looked at me, she'd barely touched her food. "Well, you know, that's maybe right. Because for years she felt that you didn't give a fuck either." She shrugged, then focused on a spring roll. It was my turn to sit back.

"If she'd just once ... " I began. I wanted to say, if she'd just now and then seemed like she wanted to be with me. To say that it was me who didn't give a fuck was so unfair, I didn't know where to start. And yet, maybe they were all right — Jessica, Jane and Josh. The three Js against the clueless A. Chugging along like the shuttle from Market Rasen to Lincoln Central. Low level, no drama, no crises, avoiding conflict in case it killed me. Until, one day, the family was gone. Only then did I start to miss them. Only now was I wondering why.

"Still," Jane said brightly. "Now you've got something new and adventurous to dig into at last."

"But that's not what you really think."

She dipped the last of the chicken into the peanut sauce, chewed, swallowed, took a sip of white wine, and then said, "Do you really want my opinion? I mean, this is your big thing now. I don't want to come in and piss all over it."

"Go on," I said. "Squat and release."

"Bloody hell, dad, you're an odd bugger sometimes." She was laughing, though.

"It's not like I don't have my own doubts," I said. "It's just that I've been swept up and along by Luca's momentum."

"Yes, I can imagine that. But it's better than working at Endsleigh, right?"

"About a hundred times better," I said. "But I still can't shake this feeling that something's not quite right."

"Something," she repeated. "Might that something be razing an entire neighbourhood to make way for a vanity project?"

"Yes," I said, and I told her about the letters we'd sent out that afternoon, and how one of the reasons I wanted to come into Lincoln was to avoid the immediate aftermath of someone coming to knock on my door to talk about it.

"You can see why they'd be tempted by the offer, though," said Jane.

"They are, even Deborah next door, who's been the biggest holdout. I advised them to push for the best deal they can get.

I haven't been trying to pull one over on them. It's just … well, that has been the least pleasant part of the job. On the other hand, the last few months have passed in a flash. It's never been anything less than interesting."

Jane fingered her wine glass. "In that case, it's probably better if I don't tell you what I think."

"I'd like to know."

"It's just one opinion. Coming from outside. From someone who lives on the other side of the world and wouldn't even be aware of this story if I hadn't by chance been born here."

"I'd like to know."

She hesitated, took another sip of wine. "I don't know," she said. "I mean, you're selling it to the public as change and progress. But it's not really, is it? I mean, it's not really change. It's regression. Because who is this for, exactly? The community and the region? Or is it for you and Luca, because 40 years ago you used to score goals together? And now Luca is so ridiculously over-loaded and under-taxed that he can sit back and manipulate people's lives just to satisfy this little child inside that wants to re-create his stadium, first as a toy and then as a white elephant when he gets bored of the whole thing. Because people get tired of Market Rasen, dad. Maybe not you. Some are suited to stay, and that's fine, no one has a problem with that at all. But Luca? What happens if Market Rasen Town FC don't go in the direction he thinks that money will take them? What if his wooden stadium is empty every weekend? What if he suddenly decides to tear it down and rebuild Wellesley Close exactly as it was before?"

"With Henry on the garden wall."

"Jesus, I hope for his sake he gets out of there. Out of the close and out of town. Though maybe he's the kind that likes to stay. He has that expression." She pulled a face, and it wasn't a kind one.

"You're being a snob, Jane."

"Ooh, a reproach! Watch out, Dad, you wouldn't want to get in a fight. Yeah, you're right, though. Sorry about that." She was almost laughing.

"Anyway, thank you for your take."

"Are you pissed off at me?"

"I'm pissed on, not off, remember?"

"Seriously, dad. I'm just waltzing in here after 12 years and sounding off. But what kind of crowds do the football team get?"

"A few dozen. But there are more coming now that we've started to do well. Maybe 150 or so." Luca was paying two full-time coaches, and several players above our level had been lured to the club and were getting paid handsomely in cash. Everyone knew it was going on. Opposing teams just wanted us up and out of the league. The Lincolnshire FA was not going to try and mess with Luca Romano. Wherever you found his name, you found people prepared to tolerate or foster his presence in the hope of a gold rush.

"How many people are supposed to fit in this new stadium? I seem to remember the figure of 3,000 from last night's exciting tour of the wooden model."

"That's right, with further expansion down the line."

"That's more people than live in the town."

"The thinking is that the town will expand. And that people come in from the surrounding area."

"What? East Barkwith? West Torrington? Legsby?"

"You're deliberately naming very small villages. Luca would also say you're being negative, and that's a dampener on growth and creativity."

"I'm being realistic. What if his business collapses? What if he dies? What if he decides to buy Manchester United instead? It's not like you have his ear, is it? Does he even take advice from you? If the stadium was half built and he looked like backing out, would you have the conviction and the weight to persuade him to stay?"

"In Germany," I said, "a software mogul took his boyhood team to the first division. That town's population is the same as Market Rasen."

"And? Where are they today?"

"Still there, almost 20 years later. Stadium holds 30,000 people, albeit built in a bigger town nearby. They've played in the Champions League."

"Oh," she said. "Well then, put some heavy masking tape around the mouths of the naysayers. Like I said, just one opinion."

I moved forward again, took her hand and looked her in the eyes. "I am very glad that I heard what you have to say. Thank you."

"Wow, dad," she said. "Top liaison professional. You held my gaze and almost looked sincere. And I bet they didn't even send you on a course."

Then we ordered more wine as I ignored the vibrating phone in my trouser pocket. We dropped the topic of when Market Rasen might be playing Champions League football, and Jane started telling me 12 years of stories from her life, and Jessica's too.

We went to the Wig & Mitre for a couple more drinks and then took the last train back to Market Rasen, the sole travellers in a weaving, wheezing carriage that seemed to be begging for its final shift. Jane nodded off, still coming around to the time change, while I stared out into the darkness and continued to spurn my demanding phone. I was beset with fresh doubts about the wisdom of The New Ropewalk and the project to place a backwater town on the map. Was this really what Market Rasen wanted? Hadn't it been just fine stuck out here the past few centuries, troubled only by the transient crowds on race day?

"Oh yeah, Market Rasen, you've got a racecourse," is what people say when you tell them where you're from. I'd been once in just over half a century, back when I was a kid. Come to think of it,

Luca and I had gone together. I'd lost 50 pence on a horse called Great Expectations. He'd placed a series of bets across several races and came out seven pounds to the good. He seemed keener to explain how he'd done it than he did to gloat about this minor fortune. It all seemed highly specific, and I couldn't get my head around the odds and how they were spread out. I'd not gambled a single penny since.

Jane and I walked in silence through the midweek streets, all lights dead for the night. I was half expecting to find Luca waiting for us in front of the house, demanding to know where we'd been and why I hadn't taken his calls. Wellesley Close, though, had a different kind of surprise. My electric car, which I hadn't bothered parking in the garage because it had been fully re-charged the night before, was garnered with a single ticker of blue and yellow police tape. The car itself had been properly vandalised. All the windows and all its lights were smashed in, and the panelling had been buckled and battered.

"Fucking hell, dad. What's happened?"

"Angry neighbours, I'm guessing."

I finally took my phone out of my pocket. It wasn't just Luca (17 missed calls) who had been trying to reach me. There was also an unidentified number (two calls) and Deborah (38 calls). I pressed her number and she picked up immediately.

"Alan, at last. Bloody hell, I've been trying to reach you all night."

"Are you at home?"

"No, I'm in Lincoln, at the police station. Listen, your car ... "

"I know. I'm standing right in front of it."

"I'm so sorry, Alan. It was Henry. Egged on by Frank, but Frank's nowhere to be seen. Made himself very scarce. I tried to stop him, but he was drunk or high on something. I'm so sorry, Alan, I really ... "

"It's okay, Deborah. Calm down." Jane and I had now entered the house and I was sitting in the kitchen while she put the kettle on. "It's only a car. Are you okay?"

"I don't know what to do, Alan. I just don't know what to do anymore."

"Where are the boys now?"

"Henry's here, in custody. Philip's trying to keep me sane."

"Are they keeping him in overnight?"

"I'll say. I'm trying to get the police to let him come home."

I wasn't sure if I was happy about that idea. I remained silent. Deborah let out a huge sigh. I was finding it really hard to think of us together with this wrecker in the background.

"I'm going to sell, Alan," she said suddenly. "I don't care anymore. I'll sign whatever you give me. But please come out here and tell them to let Henry go. Could you vouch for him, just this once? Maybe that'll change the way he sees you." She was speaking in low tones now. "I don't care what you say, just ... I don't know. Say we're good neighbours and that this was a misunderstanding over a dispute or something."

"Maybe you need Frank for that, not me."

"Alan. Please."

"I can't come out now. I don't have a car. And we just came from Lincoln on the last train."

"Can't you knock up the Manns? Or the Cutlers?"

"They don't like me, remember? Why don't you call them?"

There was a silence at that, and I realised in that moment the wrong path I was treading.

"Because I wanted you to come out here, Alan," said Deborah, but in a brittle voice now. And then she hung up and wouldn't pick up again. About 10 minutes later, standing with a cup of tea in the front room, I saw Davie Cutler driving out of the close. In that time, I'd told Jane everything about my neighbourly affair.

"Second chance, and you fucked it up," was her verdict. I couldn't see any way to argue with that, but I gave it a try.

"Don't you think it's a bit much? Her idiot kid wrecks my car, and then she wants me to come in the middle of the night to talk him out of jail?"

"That's a fair point. It's not about your poxy car, though. It's insured, right?"

I nodded.

"Good, then it's just a material problem. Bloody hell, I can't believe I have to explain this to someone almost 30 years my superior. She just wanted ... "

"It's okay," I said. "I get it."

"I'm glad to hear it," she said. "Now I can go to bed. Oh, and by the way, I'm heading to Josh's tomorrow."

"Wait, I thought you weren't going until Friday."

Jane held up her phone. "Your boss has tried to call me two dozen times tonight. That's fucking creepy, and it's especially creepy because I don't know how he's managed to find a private Ecuadorian mobile number, and before you say anything ... " (my mouth was already open) " ... I know he's one of the world's richest men blah blah, but I don't like him and I don't want to be anywhere near him. I've met men like him before, powerful men, big dicks in Ecuador who think their wealth and position means they can pull the knickers off anything that moves. Never, not with me, I don't give a fuck if he pisses pure gold and shits big cracks of cash. I love someone else, it's as simple as that, and even if I didn't, I would not be open to this kind of hectoring courtship." She held her phone up again. "So, I've blocked his number and I'm leaving early tomorrow, and I think you should come with me. If not, then the next day. Come and spend the weekend with your son and daughter."

"I have to work," I said lamely.

"No, you don't," she said. "Is the New fucking Ropewalk being opened tomorrow? Is it breaking ground day? Is there a crucial meeting of the planning commission or the county council?"

"No," I said. "None of that."

"Are you planning to fix things with Deborah?"

I hesitated. "Probably not. Not right now."

"I thought not. Anyway, sleep on it, and then make the right decision."

She came over and kissed me on each cheek and wished me a good sleep. I turned off the light, closed the curtains and sat down with my now lukewarm tea. I'd left a small gap so that I could see the close outside. Around one hour later, Davie Cutler returned with Deborah and the boys. Davie parked in his driveway and the three of them emerged from his car. Deborah looked like she was thanking him profusely. Henry and Philip shuffled into the house, heads down and focused on the floor, almost like they knew I was watching. Deborah soon trotted after them, and didn't look my way either.

Once they were out of sight, I opened the curtains a little wider and stared at the bruised and broken vehicle. Made by a company 51% owned by Luca Romano. I'd pretty much got the thing for free. As though he could read my thoughts, Luca rang again. It was quarter to one in the morning by now, an unprecedented hour to be awake in this town. I turned the phone off completely and went to bed.

***

When I returned from Manchester four days later, having spent more quality time with my children over a long weekend than I had in the previous three decades, the presence of its multi-billionaire had been erased. Il miracolo. When I'd finally checked my phone on the train home, I'd seen that Luca's last call to me had been early on Saturday morning. It was now Monday evening, and a quick scan of the internet showed me that The Old Rectory was back on the market, and for much less money than we'd been offering for the houses on Wellesley Close. I took a walk up to the industrial estate, and the improvised offices were shut and looking like they were ready to be loaded on to trucks. I called Ali Tibson to ask her what the hell was going on. She'd been trying to reach me all day, but I'd assumed she'd just been wondering why I hadn't shown up for work.

"We were hoping you'd be able to answer that question," she said, sounding less than cordial. "We all turned up for work this morning and the crates were locked, and all our personal items were sitting outside in boxes. What the hell's going on?"

"Are you at the pub?" There was a lot of noise in the background.

"Yes, we've been in The Aston all day drowning our sorrows. But the atmosphere's improved since Shelley checked her bank account and saw that she'd had a year's salary paid in."

"I'm pleased to hear that," I said. "I've been in Manchester all weekend. I've no idea what happened." Which was technically true.

"Fancy a pint?" was Ali's response to that. "Though you'll have some catching up to do." And probably a lot of questions to answer as well. I said I needed to take care of some personal matters. When I walked home, I could hear the noise from the pub from the bottom of the street by the old mill, and was even tempted just to go up and join them. But the Aston was no longer my scene, and I was still floating on the warm vibes of a wonderful weekend with Jane and Josh and Atiq. I felt no need whatsoever to get drunk.

At home, there was a courier-delivered envelope lying on my front doormat. I opened it up on the spot to find a letter on Cosmic Rase-headed note-paper informing me that my employment had been terminated "due to the imminent liquidation of the company", and that a year's salary had been transferred to my bank account. When I checked my account on my phone, the amount was far, far more than just a year's salary. I looked across the close to Deborah's. There weren't going to be any more letters offering her a fantastical sum for her house. The curtain twitched, and there was Henry staring out at me. The rage he'd taken out on my Tesla didn't seem to have dissipated. I briefly considered how long he could be sent down for criminal damage, and then I thought about how I needed to let go of thoughts like that.

And then all of a sudden I was hit by a tsunami of varying sensations. I was completely free, I had no job, and a ton of money. And just as that delicious thought rushed through one part of my head, it collided with a comet of fear, guilt and insecurity bolting in from the opposite direction. Explosion. Who am I? What the fuck am I going to do now?

My eyes swam around my head and I had to sit down on the garden wall, still holding the dismissal letter.

Frank Gilbert came out of his house and started walking towards me, with a purpose. I thought about ducking inside and locking the door, but I had nothing to be scared of. Maybe he'd summon Henry and they'd give me the same kind of treatment they'd given my car, but at least it would be done then. Stay away from Deborah, move away from our houses.

He stood in front of me, legs slightly apart.

"Now then, Frank," I said.

"Is it true? Romano's left town."

"Just like his father," I said.

"You what?"

"Yes, he's gone."

Frank snorted. "Great. Just fucking great. All that bollocks he's put us through, and now we end up with nothing."

"Tell me about it."

"Really? I bet he's seen you alright." Frank pointed at the letter in my hand, like he somehow already knew its contents.

"True enough, he has," I answered. Partly because it's wrong to lie, we all know that. And partly because, at that particular moment, I was happy to have come out of this better than Frank Gilbert.

"Well, bully for you."

"What is this? The school playground?"

"Fuck off, Alan."

"Have a nice evening yourself, Frank. Mind you don't beat up any cars on your way home."

Frank turned around at this and walked up the drive to Deborah's house. But when he knocked on her door, she opened the upstairs window and called down to him, "Just go away, Frank. Stay away from my house and my sons. Why do I have to keep telling you?"

I watched Frank, purple as a bruised plum, walk back towards his place. He didn't look back in my direction, but he knew I was watching him every step of the way.

***

I went walking across Derbyshire and South Yorkshire for a few weeks. In the evenings, I would sit in the corner of a pub with a pint and write postcards to Josh and to Jane, now back home in Ecuador. I also made several attempts to write a letter to Deborah, but they ended up discarded and destroyed in the ashtray. Finally, I managed to write to her that I was missing her, that I wished she was walking with me on the trails, and that I was sorry for what had happened on the night of the 'car incident'. I said that I was willing to try again. I told her to call me at any time, if she wanted. I even wrote to her all the pubs, hotels and B&Bs where I was staying over the last two weeks of my hike, hoping that she might just turn up. I posted the letter, and waited for a call or an appearance, although in reality I knew that I was deluding myself to help pass the time.

When I got home, it had been posted back through my letterbox, although it had been opened and read. She had written on the outside: No. D.

I asked the town's estate agent Vera Cree to drive me out to The Old Rectory. We walked around the empty house, gutted of every last fitting and piece of furniture. Vera seemed impatient, like she knew I wasn't really interested in buying the house, and we moved quickly from room to room. I asked her if there had been many viewers, and she gave a non-committal response, like it was none of my business. In the outhouses, the Jacuzzi had been left in place. In the room next door, the model of the Ropewalk also remained untouched. Vera stood at the door, her hand on the light switch as though this was worth no more than a two-second glimpse, but I pushed past her and stood looking over Paddy van Veen's mini-realisation of Luca's grandiloquent vision.

"So this is what you came for," said Vera. "Could have saved me the time."

"Does it come with the house?"

"No idea. Might be better off making it a permanent exhibit it in the market place. So that next time we're better warned."

I looked at her. Mid-30s, smart, sassy, and not the kind of friendly you expect from someone who was supposed to be trying to sell you something.

"Why are you so pissed off about it?"

"Isn't the whole town?"

"I don't know," I said. "I haven't spoken to the whole town."

"I bet," she said. "Given what they're saying about you."

"Damned by association," I muttered, and Vera responded, "But wealthy enough now to buy this place, I expect."

"Is that any of your business?"

"Maybe. It's my town that got fucked over. A boom to raise our hopes, then bust overnight. Nice and easy plaything for Luca

Romano. And you too. Shit for the rest of us. And especially for the football club." Vera's husband was still an active player.

"He saw everyone alright, I believe." I had stopped looking at her impatient, judgmental face, and was leaning down to inspect the detail of the substitutes' bench, with six players apparently shouting at the linesman standing directly in front of them.

"Can we go?" was her response to that comment.

"Can you give me five minutes?"

"No," she said, scrolling on her touchpad. "But I've checked — this toy of your former boss is not listed anywhere in the inventory. If you give me a grand in cash first thing tomorrow morning, I'll leave this room unlocked for 48 hours from 1pm."

"But it still belongs to Mr. Romano, as long as the house does."

"In theory. In the unlikely event of anyone finding out, you can always say that you were just looking after it for a friend."

***

I called Mark Skelly to come and tow the e-car. I left it there for a long time to remind Frank Gilbert that he was an accessory to thug violence every time he walked past it. Frank, though, had started to take Henry down the pub with him, and every time they walked past it they stopped to laugh. Then on their way home they would smash it up even more until Deborah came out and yelled at them. Frank had also found a job for Henry at the garage where he worked, as a trainee mechanic. I wondered if this was helping him make any in-roads with Deborah. But Frank didn't actually call at the house any more, just waited on the pavement until Henry came out and joined him to go up to The Aston.

As soon as they walked around the corner, I was possessed by the thought of Deborah at home alone, as Philip had taken to going on long cycle rides with a mate. The two of them would set out on summer evenings in lycra gear, and be gone until it started to get dark.

On the night I'd finally worked up the courage to go around and knock on her door, I saw her driving off somewhere. After that, she was out every night. She didn't stay out late, she was usually back by 10.30. And yes, I was keeping an eye out. Thanks to reports in the *Rasen Mail*, her scandalous secret life was soon revealed. She was involved with the local WI and the Amateur Dramatics Society.

I would unlock the door to what had once been Josh's room, and sit and contemplate the New Ropewalk. I'd copied the old match reports and had them framed and hung them all around the room. I mooched around, reading them over and again. I was missing the job. I'd been invigorated in my time as a big shot, even if now I felt only embarrassment when I thought about me grandstanding at council meetings, and the way I'd talked down to my neighbours when they'd been desperately seeking my guidance and advice. There they were, caught between their previously stable community and a rapacious billionaire intent on tilting their lives on the back of his own capricious whim. Just because he could afford it. And now they were left the nursing the thought of what they might have had and where they might be now if they'd taken his offer, like the Stevensons had. The Stevensons — it's always the same ones who come out on top.

I've had journalists calling and asking for my inside knowledge. It's nice to think of all the things I'm not going to tell them, and the room they'd surely love to see if they knew it even existed. I'm tempted, it's true, to shop *Sir* Edmund, but then I don't have any actual proof that Luca bribed him. I can only raise certain questions. But there's been enough upheaval, more than a town like this really wants to handle. And in truth, I don't want a second's more attention.

This Christmas, I'm invited to Manchester for the first time. In January, I'm starting evening classes in Spanish, four nights a week in Lincoln. I've booked a trekking tour in Ecuador next spring.

I've also put the house on the market. Craig Mann stopped the car the other day when I was out in the garden, trying to make it look presentable for potential buyers. The 'For Sale' sign had just gone up the day before. He wound down the window and shouted, "Hey, Alan, make sure you hold out for the highest offer. Ours was worth two million last year." Then he drove off without waiting for a response.

I've put the New Ropewalk into storage, along with all the framed cuttings. It would be too odd having strangers coming round and wondering what the hell it was. It was time to put it away. Time to get away. Time to stop going back.